Garth bowed. "I beg your pardon, madam.
I did not see you."

He glanced at Lady Keswick for a moment before she waved an indolent

Married. Garth did disappointment.

"My dear, meet the ___ ___ ___ ___ ___ lady continued. "Mrs. Tr___ ___ companion."

A widow, then. He cheered instantly. Illogically.

He inclined his head. "A pleasure to meet you, Mrs. Travenor."

A shaft of sunlight released by a passing cloud gilded the young woman's warm-colored skin, illuminating the quiet purity of her expression. A virginal widow? Hardly likely. But a woman best avoided.

She was the kind of woman who expected the parson's mousetrap at the end of the day. He had walked that path once already. He didn't want a wife. The thought made him shudder.

"Enough, Stanford."

Garth realized he was still staring at the widow and dragged his gaze back to Lady Keswick.

The elderly woman smiled at her companion fondly. "Rose doesn't deserve your kind of trouble."

* * *

Lady Rosabella's Ruse
Harlequin® Historical #1078—February 2012

Author Note

When I first met Garth in *The Rake's Inherited Courtesan* I just knew I needed to write his story. He popped up again in *The Rake's Intimate Encounter* (a Harlequin Historical® Undone! ebook) to remind me of my promise. As all bad boys do, he finally got his way. I do hope you enjoy learning more about him and Rose as much as I did.

If you would like to know more about me and my books you can find me at my website, www.annlethbridge.com. Drop me a note, I love to hear from readers. If you would like to join me as I explore Regency England on my blog you can find me at www.regencyramble.blogspot.com.

Lady Rosabella's Ruse

ANN LETHBRIDGE

Harlequin®

TORONTO NEW YORK LONDON
AMSTERDAM PARIS SYDNEY HAMBURG
STOCKHOLM ATHENS TOKYO MILAN MADRID
PRAGUE WARSAW BUDAPEST AUCKLAND

Recycling programs
for this product may
not exist in your area.

ISBN-13: 978-0-373-29678-1

LADY ROSABELLA'S RUSE

Copyright © 2011 by Michèle Ann Young

First North American Publication 2012

www.Harlequin.com

Printed in U.S.A.

Available from Harlequin® Historical
and ANN LETHBRIDGE in ebook format:

The Rake's Inherited Courtesan #1041
Wicked Rake, Defiant Mistress #1092

*The Gamekeeper's Lady #1041
*More Than a Mistress #1045
Captured for the Captain's Pleasure #1073
Lady Rosabella's Ruse #1078

*Rakes in Disgrace

and in Harlequin® Historical Undone! ebooks
The Rake's Intimate Encounter
The Laird and the Wanton Widow
One Night as a Courtesan
Unmasking Lady Innocent
Deliciously Debauched by the Rake

and in Harlequin® Historical ebooks
**Princess Charlotte's Choice

**Royal Weddings

I would like to dedicate this book to the bad boy
in my life, my husband Keith, who knows
beyond any shadow of doubt he is the model
for all of my heroes.

I would like to thank Joanne Grant, my editor, and all the
wonderful staff at Harlequin Mills & Boon for their help
and support, for without them there would be no book.

And finally a big thank you
to the readers who keep reading.

Chapter One

The weight of tedium hung heavy in the air. After only one hour at Lady Keswick's Sussex mansion, Garth Evernden, eighth Baron Stanford, was bored. Summer house parties were all the same, deadly dull or wildly hedonistic and utterly predictable.

As he prowled in the wake of his hostess's butler along a corridor lined with every Greek god known to man, he wondered why he hadn't gone to Brighton. A fleeting thought of Prinny and his cronies produced a yawn.

Why had he accepted Lady Keswick's invitation? Ah, yes, now he remembered his purpose. Having delivered Clarissa her *congé* last month, he needed an occupant for his discreet town house in Blackheath. A woman who would entertain his nights and stay out of his days. This gathering of philanderers and fast widows might provide such a woman, but now he was here, hope seemed elusive.

The butler threw back a pair of French doors. 'The terrace, my lord, where you will find everyone gathered.'

'No need to announce me.'

The butler grinned. 'Hadn't planned to, my lord. No standing on ceremony at The Grange.'

He'd forgotten Lady Keswick's refreshing informality. Perhaps his stay wouldn't be so bad.

A group of five or six men in dark coats and women in pastels hung over the terrace's grey-stone parapet gazing at the lawn.

'Look at Fitz go!' one of the men hooted. Hapton. A slender brown-haired dandy of about forty summers, with a penchant for fast women and outrageous wagers. 'I'll wager a pony on him.'

The woman in yellow at his right turned her back on the view and laughed up at Hapton. Mrs Mallow made an enchanting picture with her lovely, if somewhat hard, face framed by luxurious chestnut curls and a lavender parasol. 'My money is on the gardeners. Fitz is all go at the start, but in my experience, he has no stamina.'

General laughter along the rail met the sally.

Seeing Garth, Mrs Mallow waved. Hapton turned to look, grimaced, then swung back to whatever had their attention on the lawn. Taller than most, Garth peered over Hapton's shoulder. It was a human wheelbarrow race. Two gentlemen against two brawny young men in homespun. Garth sighed. God, they were childish. He hoped this wasn't the pinnacle of the entertainment to come.

Having not yet greeted his hostess, he turned away from the view and spotted her seated in a chair on wheels in the shade of a cluster of potted yews. A monstrous red wig battled with the purple of a sarcenet gown cut low enough to reveal an expanse of enormous breasts. Struggling to keep his gaze on her face and not the jiggling mass of flesh, he made his bow. 'Lady Keswick, your servant.'

'Lord Stanford. Welcome.' She offered him a lazy smile, her puffy cheeks swelling to melon-sized proportions and practically obliterating her twinkling faded blue eyes. 'I hope my staff took proper care of you?'

One hand to his heart, he offered his most charming smile. 'The accommodations are excellent. I congratulate you on your new home.'

'Good. Very good.' She eyed him a little askance. 'I expected you yesterday.'

'I had trouble tearing myself away from a prior engagement.'

'I never heard you had trouble bidding a woman farewell. Who was it this time?'

He raised a brow, let the mockery show on his face. 'I don't remember.'

A rich chuckle set her bosom trembling like a blancmange carried by a nervous footman. 'Cheeky rogue. Now I recall why I invited you. You make me laugh.'

She made him laugh, too. Most of the time. He grinned at her. 'Is everyone here?'

'All that's condescended to come.'

He eyed the women speculatively. From this angle, their pink, yellow and blue-clad bottoms were presented in a row like choice desserts on a plate—they looked delicious. Choosing was always interesting.

Tasting could be a disappointment.

A dog, an overweight pug, waddled from beneath the elderly lady's skirts and growled at his reflection in Garth's boots.

'Hello, old chap.' Garth bent down and scratched behind the dog's ears. 'Who are you?' The dog stared up at him with bulbous eyes.

'Digger,' Lady Keswick said. 'Come, sir. Lie down.'

The dog swaggered back into hiding.

A movement deeper in the shadows of the potted trees

brought Garth to his feet. Another woman was seated behind his hostess, her black attire making her almost invisible.

He disguised a sharp intake of breath as he took in the woman's face. Pale olive skin and dark, almond-shaped eyes gave her perfectly oval face an exotic mysterious look. The raven-black hair swept back and tightly constrained at her nape only added to the impression of reserve. His fingers tingled with the urge to see it fall in luxurious lengths to her shoulders. Her mouth tightened as he continued his perusal and he let his gaze linger on her lips. Set in her Madonna-like face, that mouth was a wonder. Full and lush, it spoke of carnal delights while it pretended disapproval.

A woman garbed like a nun with the face of a temptress.

He bowed. 'I beg your pardon, madam. I did not see you.'

He glanced at Lady Keswick for an introduction and was surprised to see an odd expression flicker across the normally placid face. Concern? The look disappeared too fast for him to be sure. She waved an indolent pudgy hand. 'Mrs Travenor.'

Married. Garth didn't quite believe his instant flash of disappointment.

'My dear, meet the worst scapegrace in London,' the old lady continued. 'Mrs Travenor is my companion.'

A widow, then. He cheered instantly. Illogically.

Mrs Travenor rose to greet him. Taller than he'd guessed, her eyes were on a level with his chin. Tall and willowy. She made a stiff curtsy, her head dipping briefly. Jasmine wafted up from her skin. A sensual fragrance for a woman who dressed like a crow. A pair of velvety brown eyes dusted with gold at their centres steadily returned his gaze. 'My lord.' The soft husky voice raised the hairs on his arms. The jolt of unwanted lust annoyed him. There was nothing about this woman to suggest she would welcome a discreet liason. Then why was he interested?

He inclined his head. 'A pleasure to meet you, Mrs Travenor.'

A shaft of sunlight released by a passing cloud gilded the young woman's warm-coloured skin, illuminating the quiet purity of her expression. A virginal widow? Hardly likely. But a woman best avoided.

She was the kind of female who expected the parson's mousetrap at the end of the day. Had walked that path once already. He didn't want a wife. The thought made him shudder. He had an heir. His brother. A man who deserved the title of Stanford, and Garth would make sure he got it.

'Enough, Stanford.'

Garth realised he was still staring at the widow and dragged his gaze back to Lady Keswick. The elderly woman smiled at her companion fondly. 'Rose doesn't deserve your kind of trouble.'

Rose. The name seemed too trite for such exotic loveliness.

Lady Keswick waved a beringed hand. 'Go join your fellow reprobates.'

Summarily dismissed, he joined the party watching the sport on the grass. He didn't mind being warned off. Indeed, this was where he would find his next source of amusement, not with a woman who eyed him with disapproval even if he had seen a flicker of interest in those extraordinary brown eyes.

'Stanford,' Hapton said. 'I thought you'd gone elsewhere?' The man sounded less than pleased. He must have his eye on a morsel he feared Garth would steal. Well, that might make things a bit more interesting.

Garth greeted the languid dandy with a handshake and a raised eyebrow. 'Tracking my movements, old boy?'

'Hardly,' the other man said with a glower.

Further along the wall, a woman's head turned swiftly, her jaw dropping in dismay.

Penelope? His best friend's wife? His stomach fell away. Disappointment, disgust, anger, followed each other in swift succession. He closed the distance between them with one long stride. 'Lady Smythe. What are you doing here?'

Her green gaze beseeched him. 'I—'

Mrs Mallow, her dark eyes gleaming with malicious delight, looped an arm through Penelope's. 'She came with me.'

And that was supposed to make it better? Maria Mallow was the female equivalent of a rake and not above leading a new bride astray. Anger curled tight fingers in his gut, despite his calm expression, as he bowed to the ladies.

Mark would be devastated when he learned of her treachery. And to think, he'd actually felt a twinge of envy for his friend's obvious happiness when he'd attended their wedding a scant two months before.

Or did he have this all wrong? 'Is Mark with you?'

Auburn-haired and freckle-faced, her flush was painful to watch. 'My husband is away on business.' Anger coloured her tone. It sounded like jealousy to his practised ear.

He frowned. 'Does he know where you are?'

She stiffened and something like pain darkened her gaze. 'Mark doesn't care what I do.'

Had the blush of happiness faded so quickly? He found it hard to believe. Yet here she was, at a house renowned for high jinks among the guests.

Mrs Mallow patted Penelope's hand. 'What is sauce for the gander...' She raised a brow. 'Surely that is your motto, Forever?'

Forever was a nickname he'd earned years before. He ground his teeth. It was not his motto, though others here would claim it. Hapton, for example. Or Bannerby.

Damn Penelope. The girl was as bad as the rest of these women, but he couldn't let it go. Pretend it was of no consequence. Damn it all.

In hindsight, his earlier boredom was a hell of a lot more

inviting than the prospect of persuading a recalcitrant wife to go home.

Certainly not a role he'd ever played before.

He glanced back at the mysterious Mrs Travenor and caught her frowning gaze and his blood rose to the challenge.

Fiend seize it. Two women under one roof, likely to give him nothing but trouble.

Outwardly composed, inside, Rosabella Cavendish trembled like an aspen. For the first time in her life, she didn't know what to think. One glance from those dark, coolly insolent eyes and her heart had drummed so hard and so loud her body shook. Why? He was no different from the rest of Lady Keswick's male guests. Rakish. Confident. Handsome. All right, perhaps he was more handsome than the rest, with his lean athletic body and saturnine aristocratic features. His smile when he bent over the dog had been heart-stoppingly sweet.

None of that was what had sent her blood pounding in her veins, though. It was the way he had looked at her. Really looked at her. Most of them presumed her a poor widow forced to earn a living as a paid companion and their gazes moved on. He'd looked at her as if he saw her innermost secrets. She had the feeling that for the price of his smile, she'd tell him anything he wanted to know. Clearly the man was downright dangerous.

'Striking-looking devil, ain't he?' Lady Keswick said, watching him shake hands with the men and greet the ladies to their obvious pleasure.

'I hadn't noticed,' Rosa said, breathing deeply to settle her heart into its proper rhythm.

'Don't look at me with those innocent brown eyes, my dear. You'd have to be dead not to notice Stanford. Be warned, though, he's an out-and-out rogue. Never settles on one woman when two will do.'

Facing Lady Smythe and Mrs Mallow, his spare elegant form in a dark coat and buff unmentionables a foil for their pastel gowns and fluttering ribbons, she sensed a wildness about him, a hard edge. Rosa's insides fluttered with what could only be fear.

Sensible terror.

It certainly was not envy of the two beautiful ladies so obviously entranced by his company.

Beside the fashionable lush-figured Mrs Mallow in prim-rose, Lady Smythe looked ethereal in a gown of pale leaf green, the scalloped hem finely embroidered with flowering vines and her face framed within a leghorn bonnet adorned with a profusion of roses at the crown. The ruffled lace at her throat gave her an air of modesty out of place among Lady Keswick's flashy company. A pearl among diamonds who, according to Lady Keswick, had been snapped up in her first Season by a man destined for political greatness. Every man at the house had been paying her attention from the moment she had arrived this morning. A woman who already had a husband, too.

A stab of something sharp in her chest stopped her breath. Surely she didn't envy the young woman her attentive male court? A bunch of rakes and Stanford the worst of them?

The *grande dame* narrowed her eyes. 'He seems to have got Lady Smythe all of a fluster. I won't have him upsetting my guests.'

Lady Smythe did indeed look a little panicked, the colour in her cheeks a bright flag. Perhaps she wasn't so charmed by the rake after all.

Despite the gossip, Lady Keswick ensured nothing hap-pened under her roof that both parties didn't want. It was a point of honour with the hostess to the wickeder element of the *ton*. As she'd earlier explained, a woman needed some freedom in her life. Freedom without consequences for widows and women who had married for convenience. Women like Lady Smythe, Rosa assumed.

Her heart ached for the delicate-looking lady. A marriage without love was no marriage at all, her mother had always said.

'Bah!' Lady Keswick pronounced. 'Stanford's trouble. Has been since he arrived on the town. No girl, decent or otherwise, is safe once he has her in his sights. Take my advice, Rose, keep well clear of him. You are far too innocent for a man of his ilk.'

Did innocence show on one's face? She hoped not or her game would be up.

A cry went up from the watchers. The race must be over.

'Who won?' Lady Keswick asked. 'I had five guineas on my gardeners.'

The men on the balcony doubled up with laughter. Jeers rang out across the lawn. 'I think your money is safe,' Rosa said.

'Go and see, child.'

With a swift intake of breath, Rosa left her shadowy corner, edged around the laughing group, mentally shaking her head at her cowardice as she made for the stone railing far from Lord Stanford.

On the grass, Mr Fitzwilliam and Lord Bannerby were collapsed in a heap two-thirds of the way down the course, while the gardeners, at the finish line, toasted them with mugs of ale and huge grins.

'Did you win?' a low dark voice said in her ear.

She jumped, heat flashing through her, and turned to find Lord Stanford smiling down at her. His gaze flicked from her head to her feet the way it had when they were introduced. As she had then, she felt exposed, vulnerable.

Fortunately, her skin didn't blush pink the way most pale

English ladies did. He couldn't possibly know of the quickening of her heart or the sudden clench in her belly. She backed up until the carved-stone rail pressed against the small of her back.

Dark as the devil, out here in the sun his eyes were obsidian, his cheekbones and jaw carved in hard angular lines, his hair a shade darker than chocolate. But darkest of all was his aura of danger.

No wonder Lady Smythe's eyes turned his way the moment she thought he wasn't watching.

'I do not gamble,' she said. How self-righteous she sounded. How priggish in this company that denied itself nothing. Yet it was the truth. She had no money for frivolities. 'Lady Keswick has an interest in the outcome.'

He leaned one elbow on the rail, effectively cutting her off from the rest of the company. Deliberate? Naturally. He was a man who did nothing without a purpose. What purpose could he have with respect to her? A tremor ran through her frame. Fear. Excitement. She quelled the rush of sensation and presented a calm expression. 'If you would excuse me?' She moved to step around him.

He shifted and blocked her path. 'I would excuse you anything at all,' he said with a dark smile. 'What is your offence?'

'I say, Stanford,' called Mr Phillips, a man so pale he looked as if he had never stepped in the sun, pale eyes, pale thinning hair, pale skin. 'They are setting up the butts. Time to make good on your boast.'

The crowd on the balcony were drifting down the steps at the far end, heading for the lawn.

A flicker of emotion passed over his face. Annoyance at the interruption? Before he could say more, Rosa ducked around him and hurried to Lady Keswick's side, her heart beating far faster than she wanted to admit. 'You win, my lady.' Her voice sounded breathless as if she'd run a mile. She drew in a steadying breath. 'The gardeners were indeed too much of a match for the gentlemen.'

'Fifty guineas isn't a bad profit for indolence,' Lady Keswick said with twinkling eyes. 'Hapton is a fool with his money. Tell Jonas to see that the lads get a shilling each for their effort. Will you join the guests at the butts?'

'I have no skill with a bow and prefer to watch from up here. Would you like to move closer to the balcony for a better view?'

Lady Keswick reached out and patted her hand. 'You are a good girl, Rose. And you have talent. By summer's end I am sure I can find you a place in the opera.'

The end of the summer might be too late. Triggs was beginning to press for his money.

Rosa pushed the old lady towards the terrace wall. 'Has no one replied?'

'Have patience. They are busy people. One of them will come through, I am sure.'

It was their agreement. Rosa would help entertain the guests over the next few weeks, and Lady Keswick would help her find a role in an opera company.

Only things were not going quite as she'd planned. The money she was earning as a companion was not enough for her urgent needs. It was beginning to look as if she might need to find something more lucrative. A role in an opera seemed as if it might be her best option.

To date, though, there had been no one interested in hiring an unknown singer, in spite of Lady Keswick's unqualified praise.

Hopefully, Rosa wouldn't need to fall back on her talent. Hopefully, she would find what she needed tonight and all her worries would be solved.

'I am grateful for your help.'

'Pshaw,' the old lady said as she looked down at the company gathered on the lawn. 'Did I tell you I was considered the best female archer in all of Sussex in my girlhood?'

Many times. 'How did that come about?' Rosa opened her parasol, shading them both from the afternoon sun.

'It was in seventy-eight,' Lady Keswick mused. Then scrunched up her face. 'Or was it seventy-nine? No matter. Keswick was present, you know. He always said that was the day he learned about love...'

Love. Wasn't it love that had brought Rosa to Sussex and to the house of a woman with a less-than-stellar reputation? An actress who had married an elderly nobleman. When Rosa saw Lady Keswick's advertisement for a companion at this house, so close to where Rosa had grown up, the opportunity had seemed heaven-sent.

And if she was wrong about her father's love? What then? Her hands clenched inside her gloves. She would not let such doubts enter her head. The idea was too painful to contemplate.

'Oh, I say, nice shot!' Lady Keswick cried, dragging Rosa's attention back to the contest. Lady Smythe had hit the bull and was now laughing up at Lord Bannerby. It was the first time she'd seen the young woman look even moderately happy since she'd arrived. Bannerby tucked a loose strand of copper hair behind a shell-like ear with a grin that said his intentions were all bad, while Stanford glowered at the pair from the sidelines as if he wanted to challenge Bannerby to a duel for that touch.

Jealousy between rival males. Something in Rosa's chest felt uncomfortable, the way a pebble in a shoe felt. A painful irritation.

She really didn't belong in this house. The sooner she left the better. And tonight's search would end all her difficulties. It must.

* * *

Garth stared up at the haloed moon and drew on his cigar. He sent a stream of smoke upwards to form a cloud above his head. A fluky gust of wind whipped it away. He enjoyed a smoke before bed, yet hated the smell of stale cigars first thing in the morning. So here he stood on the terrace to blow a cloud after the rest of the guests had retired. Some to their own rooms. Some to those of other guests.

He grinned as he recalled Bannerby's obvious confusion when he'd chased him away from Penelope's door. Hopefully that would be an end to the man's ambition.

His lip curled. All he needed to do now was get the foolish wench to go home before a braver man than Bannerby tried his luck. Hapton, for example.

Garth turned the cigar in his fingers and observed the glowing tip through narrowed eyes. If he could get her out of here quickly, perhaps Mark need never know.

A scandal of that sort would make life for Mark unbearable. Unsupportable. The stupid wench.

He drew hard on his cheroot, fury at her deception a low fire in his stomach.

The sky turned dark. Rain spattered on his shoulders and in his hair, left dark spots on the terrace flags in a sudden rush of wind. The shower ceased. The cloud cleared, leaving the moonlit landscape grey and full of shadows. He gazed at that telltale ring of moisture around the moon and the increasing number of clouds floating by. *More rain to come.*

A door opened and closed somewhere around the corner. Someone coming in or going out? Mildly curious, he stubbed out his cigar and strolled down the steps. As he rounded the corner, he glimpsed the back of a figure enveloped in a black cloak. A woman, he thought from the slender shape and quick short steps. A chambermaid off to meet her beau in the village? He frowned. If he remembered correctly, the village lay in the other direction. There was something familiar about the hurrying figure. One of the guests?

A smile pulled at his lips. Intrigue was rife in this house, but why would one of the guests need to leave the comfort of a well-appointed bed in pursuit of bliss? Tantalised, he followed and caught another glimpse of the quick-paced shadow disappearing into the woodland to the east of the house, then a whiff of jasmine.

Mrs Travenor? Rose. Her height should have given her away, but she was the last female he would have expected to see scurrying off to an assignation. Was he, then, so naïve? Hardly.

She might have purity in her face, but beneath her still surface, she was as wicked as any woman. A pang of disappointment stilled him. No, he wasn't disappointed. He was glad. It meant his instincts about her were right. He would only be disappointed if she'd proved to be virtuous.

Arriving at the entrance to the woods a few moments later, Garth saw no sign of the woman. Paths led in three directions and, with no sound to guide him, he halted.

He inhaled. Was it imagination, or did a trace of her perfume linger on the rich damp air? Where was she going? It was not a good night to meet a man out of doors unless there was some handily placed folly somewhere in the grounds. A vision of the exotic Mrs Travenor in the arms of one of the burly gardeners filled his mind. Or might she prefer the cheeky butler? Neither image fit. Unease rolled through him.

A suspicion rose that the quiet widow might be up to something nefarious. If she was meeting a servant, or even one of the guests, she would not be heading into the woods. There were too many other convenient places, dry places, within doors or nearby. No, the lady had some other less straightforward purpose.

His jaw clenched. He lifted his face as rain pelted down.

He felt the sting of it on his cheeks and eyelids and mentally shrugged. It was none of his business what Lady Keswick's temptress-nun-come-companion did with her nights, no matter how much she aroused his curiosity.

Hell, she aroused more than that, he realized, as his blood thickened and an image rampaged through his mind of her dressed as a nun pressed up against a marble column with him filling her body. No wonder he was hard within the tight confines of his pantaloons.

Moonlight speared through a gap in the clouds, revealing nothing but trees and lawn.

A wry chuckle escaped his throat. Another lying little baggage keeping secrets. It would behove him, for the sake of his hostess, to find out what they were.

She'd gone out by the side door, and he did not doubt she would come back the same way.

Rosa stopped to listen. Had she heard footsteps on the flagstones behind her? A shiver ran down her back at the thought of one of Lady Keswick's dissolute guests finding her out here alone in the dark. Whoever or whatever she'd heard, there was no sound of them now. Aside from the wind in the trees, the whole world seemed remarkably quiet. Any creature with any sense was huddled somewhere out of the wind and rain. She pulled her cloak tighter around her and continued on.

Since she arrived two weeks ago, she'd several times walked this way in daylight, familiarising herself with the paths meandering through the park, ostensibly exercising Lady Keswick's pug, Digger. The fat little thing hated to walk and in the end he'd sat down and refused to budge beyond the edge of the lawn. Now she was resorting to night-time expeditions.

On one of her earlier rambles, she'd found the shortcut

leading to the woods belonging to Gorham Place, the square red-bricked mansion where she'd lived out her childhood. She trudged on.

Deep in the forest, at the edge of Lady Keswick's estate, the sharp sound of fast-flowing water cut through the muffling effect of her hood. A fence blocked her path. In one of the brief moments of moonlight, she found the stile, an ancient right of way, leading to the bridge across the stream meandering between the two estates.

While the bridge was in a poor state of repair, she'd crossed back and forth several times during one of her daytime forays and knew it would safely hold her weight. Darkness slowed her steps to a crawl. She looked up at the sky, waiting for the moon to reappear and light her way. Rain slapped her in the face and she turned away, holding the hood close while the wind tugged at her skirts. As the cloud drifted on, she could see where the muddy footpath changed to the slippery wooden slats of the bridge.

Carefully holding the rough wooden railing, she crossed the shaky structure, testing her weight on each rotting plank before stepping forwards. At this rate it would take her all night to reach the house. Perhaps she should turn back and try on another evening, one with better weather.

Gritting her teeth, she pressed on. She couldn't bear the thought of going back without at least looking upon the house where she had spent the happiest years of her life. In those days, she'd been secure in the knowledge of her parents' affections. Now, as she crossed six feet of rotting wood, the doubts crowded in. She forced them to the back of her mind and hurried on, emerging from the trees and crossing the expanse of ill-kept lawn until she reached the drive. Stray moonbeams bounced off darkened windows revealing the house. Gorham Place.

Dear old house. So full of happy memories. Idle enquiry

in the village had revealed no one lived here. The house had been let for a while after her father remarried, but now it lay empty and abandoned, with only a gardener employed to see to its maintenance. A man who would know her. But would he let her inside to search?

Her wet hem clinging to her ankles, she strode quickly to the walled courtyard around the back. A light flickered in an upper window of a cottage adjoining the stables.

Taking courage from a swift deep breath, she lifted the cottage's iron knocker and let it fall with a loud bang. The sound echoed through the night.

Chapter Two

Heavy steps coming downstairs emanated from within. And then the echo of a chest-rattling cough. 'Who is it?' a voice wheezed.

'Mr Inchbold,' Rosa said. 'It is Rosa Cavendish. Do you remember me?' She held her breath, fearful and excited all at once. When she'd heard in the village of the guardian left here to mind the place, the familiar name had given her hope.

A bolt rasped in its hasp and the heavy oak door swung creaking back. 'Lady Rosabella?' the white-haired and bent old man said querulously. 'Is it really you?'

Relief rushed through her in a warm flood of memories. 'Yes. It is me. It was more than I dared hope to find our dear old Inchbold still here after all this time.'

Dim muddy eyes peered at her. The wrinkled face cracked a smile. 'Welcome home, my lady. Welcome.'

It seemed so odd to be called my lady after weeks of being plain Mrs Travenor. 'Thank you. I'm so happy you are here. Are you well?'

The gnarled hand holding the lantern on high trembled weakly. Not surprisingly. Inchbold had been ancient the last time she saw him, eight years before. 'Well enough, my lady. Am I to open the gate? If you've a carriage, there are no grooms, no servants. Best if ye go to the inn in the village. Come back in the morning. Is your grandfather with you?'

She swallowed. 'No carriage. Only me. I wondered if you might let me in the house?'

A gust of wind whipped around the corner of the cottage, bringing another smattering of rain. The lantern flickered and died to no more than a glow, then flared up.

'Come in, child, come in. No sense in standing out in the rain.' He turned and led the way down a short passage past the stairs into a small square parlour stuffed full of old furniture. He brushed half-heartedly at a chair, sending a cloud of dust upwards. 'Sit down, dear girl.'

She perched on the chair edge just as she had as a small child, while he set the lamp on the table. He peered down at her, his bushy white brows drawing together over his hooked nose. The lines on his face had deepened and spread out over his face. Shiny pink scalp covered his head, apart from the odd tuft of thin white hair. 'What brings you to Gorham Place at this time of night after all these years, my lady?'

Even bent as he was, and trembling, shades of the man he'd been clung to his shoulders. As steward and trusted retainer, he'd been kindly but firm to his master's daughters.

'I really did not expect to find you here after all this time,' she said. 'When they mentioned your name in the village, I had to see for myself.'

He gave a gusty sigh. 'When your grandfather closed up the house and took the knocker off the door last year, I thought of applying for a new position elsewhere, but he needed someone to keep an eye on the place, maintain the grounds, like, so I offered. Too old to start again. But why are you here?'

She clenched her hands in her lap. 'My father's will was never found. This is the only place I can think to look.'

Inchbold frowned, his lined face a map of crevasses. 'Your grandfather searched, my lady. He went through everything in the house.'

Disappointment, sorrow, bitter defeat tangled in her chest, leaving her breathless from the pain. She stared at her twisting fingers, blinking away a hot rush of moisture. Finally, she drew a breath around the lump in her throat. 'I see.'

When she could bring herself to raise her gaze, Inchbold's brown eyes regarded her sadly. 'There is one thing I recall. I didn't mention it to your grandfather. It didn't seem important at the time.'

She forced herself not to hope. 'What is it?'

'Not long after your ma died, I had occasion to visit your father in his study. He had me and the footman, William, that was here then, sign a paper. Witness to his signature.'

Hope unfurled a tentative shoot. 'You think it was a will?'

He shook his head. 'It could have been anything. Not my business to ask.'

'Then I must search for myself.'

At his expression of shock, she clenched her hands together. 'It is too important to trust anyone else. I can't believe Father did not make provision for me and my sisters.'

'How are Lady Meg and Lady Sam?'

'Well,' she said, lying to save the old man's feelings. Sam had never recovered from an ague caught out in the rain and Meg was losing hope. She leaned forwards, closing the distance between her and the old man, looking into his dull brown eyes. 'Dear Inchbold, won't you let me in the house for old times' sake? I promise Grandfather will never know.'

He shook his head.

Rosa wanted to scream. To throw herself at his feet and beg. She straightened her spine. 'Why not?'

'The woman who comes to dust once a week has the key.'

She frowned. 'But you can get it?'

Unwillingly, he nodded. 'Tomorrow, I can. But last week Barrington, your grandfather's solicitor, came down from London and showed a gentleman around. He's leased the house starting the first of the month.'

Her stomach dropped. She'd wasted too much time, hesitating in fear of finding nothing, preferring to dream of a perfect answer to her problems. She shot up from the chair and paced to the window. 'Then I must begin right away. Tomorrow night.'

All this time, she'd held on to the flicker of hope their father had kept his word, despite every derogatory thing her grandfather had said about his feckless fanciful heir and his dreadful foreign first wife. Rosa had clung to the belief that sooner or later the will would be found. She'd worked and schemed so she could search for herself and then she'd hesitated.

Such a coward.

She turned to face him, looking into his worried face. 'Please, dear Mr Inchbold. It won't take long. A few hours at most.'

'All right. I'll get the key, tomorrow. Where will I find you?'

'At the Grange. I am employed as Lady Keswick's companion.'

Horrified, he gaped at her. 'You are staying at that den of iniquity? The parish is up in arms about her buying the place. The gentry won't have nothing to do with her. Oh, my lady, how could you?'

Rosa drew herself up straight. 'How could I what, Mr Inchbold?'

He stared at her, his eyes wide, his jaw slack. 'Did anyone tell you, you are just like your mother?'

'Frequently. But not as a compliment.'

He winced. 'Well, you should be proud, you should. She was a fine woman, your mother. A proper lady, no matter what they said.'

'She was an opera singer from Italy, Mr Inchbold. The reason my grandfather cut my father off without a penny until she died.' And now he was doing the same to her daughters.

He looked sad. 'His lordship would never leave you and your sisters with nothing. While 'tis more than my job is worth to help you search, I'll turn a blind eye.'

Relief flooded through her. At last someone who cared. 'Thank you, Inchbold.' She rose to her feet and hesitated, pressing her lips together. 'You won't tell Grandfather you've seen me, will you?'

A wheezy cackle ended in a cough. 'Lord, my lady, your grandpa don't come nigh or near this place. He certainly doesn't communicate with the likes of me. Nor I with him. Just with old Barrington.'

Naturally. Grandfather was far too high in the instep to have anything to do with servants or the children of an opera singer, even if they were his own flesh and blood.

She smiled and patted his hand. 'Thank you, dear Mr Inchbold. I will return tomorrow evening. Oh, and by the way, I go by the name of Mrs Rose Travenor.'

His frown deepened. 'Be careful, my lady. Your Grandpa is not a man to cross.'

As her parents had discovered.

Only the torches at the doors gave off any light as Rosa approached The Grange. As it should be. She slipped quietly around to the side door she'd left open. Her heart picked up speed. What if someone had come along and locked it?

Slowly she lifted the latch and pushed. The door swung back on silent hinges.

She let go a sigh of relief and stepped over the threshold.

A large warm body smelling of cigars and sandalwood blocked her way. A man. She leapt back.

The man grabbed her arm and raised a lamp high. She blinked in the glare shining on her face, unable to see her assailant. 'Back so soon, Mrs Travenor?' he mocked. 'Whoever you are meeting can't be much good if he is finished already.'

Stanford. She recognised his voice. A flash of heat followed by the cold of dread left her breathless. She drew herself up to her full height. 'Stand aside, Lord Stanford.'

He hung the lamp on a hook on the wall. It cast eerie shadows on his harsh features. She shivered. 'Please, let me pass.' She made to push by him.

He put a hand against the wall, blocking her way.

She could feel the heat of his body only inches from hers, his dark insolent gaze raking her face. 'Where have you been?'

Her heart rattled. Her breath quickened. 'Out for a walk.'

'At this time of night?' He made no attempt to hide his disbelief.

'Where I go is none of your business.'

'Perhaps not,' he mused, not moving an inch. 'But Lady Keswick might be interested to hear about her little companion's forays into the night. Or does she already know?' The amused smile on his lips made her want to hit him.

He lifted a hand and brushed back the hood of her cloak, trailed a finger down the side of her face. 'Who are you meeting, hmm? A lover? Or some man you must meet in secret because…he has mischief on his mind?'

Inwardly, she trembled. She hated how weak he made her feel, as if her knees had no more substance than overcooked asparagus. She straightened her shoulders and forced herself to meet his dark gaze and saw more than she expected. Heat.

She drew in a shaky breath. 'Lady Keswick has no interest in what I do in my free time.'

He laughed. A cruel low chuckle, full of arrogance. 'And if I tell her I suspect you are up to no good, if I tell her I suspect you have some criminal intent sneaking out at night? What then, do you think?'

She edged back, away from the heat of his body, free of his overbearing presence that seemed to scramble every thought in her head. 'Why are you wandering the halls at night?' she asked haughtily.

His smile broadened. 'Waiting for you.' His low murmur was a silky stroke to her ear. 'I saw you leave.'

A shiver slid down her spine, far too pleasant to be entirely fear driven. The thought of such a man waiting for her was far too distracting. Her brain seemed full of him, instead of coming up with a reasonable explanation.

'Well, here I am,' she said, lifting her chin and meeting that penetrating gaze full on. Pride that her voice held steady, despite the trembles rushing through her body, gave her courage. 'And you can tell Lady Keswick whatever you wish. Now if you would excuse me, I would like to retire.'

His eyes widened a fraction. He turned sideways and leaned against the wall, tipping his dark head back. 'Not until you tell me where you were.'

'Why?'

'Let us say I am curious.'

She swallowed. 'I told you, I went for a walk.'

He turned to face her, his eyes gleaming. 'In the woods, in the pouring rain?'

'I couldn't sleep. I find the fresh air helps.'

'I know an excellent cure for insomnia I'd be willing to share.'

The salacious undertone in his voice sent shivers across her shoulders. 'No,' she whispered. 'Thank you.'

He chuckled softly. 'Such a polite little nun. And yet I do think you are tempted.' He leaned closer.

Tempted? She stared up at him, staring at the smile on his sensual mouth a mere whisper away, the scent of brandy and cigars filling her nostrils. If she leaned forwards just a fraction, she had the feeling he would kiss her.

Her lips tingled at the thought of how his mouth might feel on her lips. Her body ached to be held close to that magnificent breadth of chest. A moan of longing rose in her throat and only by dint of will did she stop from giving it voice.

Heaven help her, he was tempting. The man was a rake and a libertine and he thought her a widow. An experienced woman.

Her heart banged a fearful tattoo against her ribs. Her blood ran in rivers of molten lava. Did he know the effect he was having? A swift glance into his eyes told her he had no doubt about what he was doing. He was playing with her. Tormenting her the way a cat toyed with a mouse.

'Let me pass,' she said, knowing she was begging for release, not from physical restraint, but from the spell holding her enthralled.

'Tell me where you went and I will let you pass. If you are sure you really want to go.'

She swallowed. 'How many times must I repeat myself before you believe me?'

His smile turned hard. He stepped back and bowed. He gestured for her to continue on. 'Then I must bid you good-night and hope you find sleep.'

A breath she didn't know she'd been holding rushed from her parted lips. Ignominiously, she ducked her head and scuttled past him. For some reason, she felt curiously disappointed.

Oh, dear. It seemed she really had wanted that kiss.

* * *

The showers of last evening had turned into a steady drizzling rain overnight. Most of the company gathered in the library around two in the afternoon. Tucked in a quiet corner at her employer's elbow with her needlework, Rosa forced herself to hide her impatience for the day to be over and her night of searching to begin.

Her only fear was Stanford saying something to Lady Keswick and preventing her from going back to Gorham Place tonight. He couldn't.

Digger snuffled and snorted through his dreams, using her feet as his own special pillow.

While the men conversed about the sports news in desultory tones, the elegant ladies compared notes on various creams and potions designed to improve their complexions. Lady Smythe and Lord Stanford had yet to put in an appearance.

Every so often, Lord Bannerby kept looking at the door with a frown. Poor man. He was clearly suffering.

The door opened and Lady Smythe sauntered in dressed in a morning gown of blue muslin with rows and rows of diamond-pointed lace at the hem and cuff. Her copper-coloured curls created a halo around her head. She looked like a fairy queen. 'It is still raining,' she announced.

Observant as well as beautiful. Oh, dear. Was the acerbic wit of these ladies rubbing off? It wasn't Lady Smythe's fault her petite beauty made Rosa feel ungainly.

The various groups scattered around the room looked up and offered greetings.

'What on earth will we do now?' Lady Smythe said. Her rosy lips formed tragic lines. 'We were to go riding. I had my outfit all picked out. It took me ages to find something else.'

An excuse for her tardiness? And still no sign of Lord Stanford.

Bannerby leapt to his feet to kiss her hand and lead her to his recently occupied chair. 'My dear Lady Smythe, we were only waiting for you before we decided on the entertainment for the day.'

Clever Lord Bannerby elicited a brilliant, if brittle, smile. 'What did you have in mind?'

As if there had been some unseen signal, the company slowly gathered around her.

Lady Keswick cast her newspaper aside. She'd chosen a blond wig today, with ringlets above the ears and tiny curls across her forehead. 'Now we will see some liveliness.' Her smile turned her cheeks into rouge-painted apples. 'I like to see young people enjoying themselves.'

'Why don't we put on a play? Daniel has several he is working on.' Mrs Phillips, a buxom brunette just past her first bloom, looked adoringly at her aesthetic playwright husband. For all his severe appearance, he was a nice man, if rather led around by the nose by his wife. He was always courteous to Rosa, who would have liked to have talked to him more about the theatre. His wife's glares kept her at bay.

'Charades is better,' Fitzwilliam said. 'A play requires the learning of lines and will take more than a week of hard work.' He smothered a yawn behind his hand. 'Who knows, it might be fine tomorrow and then all the work will be for naught.'

Several of the men muttered agreement with the sentiment and voices were raised on each side of the question.

'Good day, Lady Keswick, Mrs Travenor.' Rosa jumped, instantly recognising Stanford's deep rich voice. Heat rushed through her body. She closed her eyes against the invading warmth as the image of his mouth close to hers danced in her vision. She took a deep calming breath and attempted a serene smile.

Lady Keswick gave him her hand. 'Stanford. I see you are

not among the early risers.' Her gaze darted to Lady Smythe. 'Made a late night of it, I suppose.'

Stanford grinned good-naturedly, his eyes finding Rosa with a gleam of wickedness. 'I like to walk before retiring as an aid to sleep, though the rain last night was not conducive to long ramblings.' His gaze rested upon Rosa's face. 'How about you, Mrs Travenor? Did you sleep well?'

A breath caught in Rosa's throat. There was no doubt in her mind he was threatening exposure as he looked at her, his eyes issuing a challenge.

She raised her chin. 'I always take a short walk every evening, rain or no, Lord Stanford.'

He blinked at her intimation that only a weakling would let rain keep him indoors. With a triumphant smile at his obvious surprise, she gestured to the dog at her feet. 'I usually take Digger for his nightly perambulation. But, like you, he preferred to remain indoors last evening.'

Stanford hunkered down at her feet and scratched behind the pug's ear. The dog opened one eye and wriggled with pleasure as the strong long fingers moved with assurance over its flanks. The dog grunted its bliss and rolled on its back.

Stanford tickled the dog's underside and tipped his face up to meet her gaze. The individual lashes around his eyes were long and thick and veiled his thoughts, but not his mocking smile. 'He's a lucky fellow to have such a considerate attendant, but you really should not wander the grounds alone at night, Mrs Travenor. Anything might happen. I beg you allow me to accompany you in future.'

A warning. He was not going to say anything this time. A spurt of relief left her feeling weak. She really didn't want to make up any more lies. Nor did she want to have to explain to her employer.

Lady Keswick's plucked eyebrows drew sharply together.

'Are you implying Mrs Travenor is not safe in my grounds, Stanford?'

His smile turned cynical. He straightened to his full height and once more she was aware of just how large he was, despite his sparseness of frame. 'I am sure she is as safe here as anywhere, Lady Keswick.'

Not safe at all with men like Stanford on the prowl.

'Hmmph,' the old lady said, eyeing her guests, who had devolved into a heated discussion about the relative merits of a play or charades. She picked up the cane beside her chair and rapped it sharply on the floor. Silence descended as all eyes turned on their hostess. Rosa shrank into the shadows of her corner.

Not that she need have bothered. None of them were looking at her. They were all looking at Lady Keswick.

A wicked grin spread over Stanford's face. He kept his eyes fixed on Rosa's face as he spoke, though he raised his voice to include the whole company. 'I suggest a game of hide and go seek. The gentlemen will find, while the ladies hide. Ladies, if you are caught, you will forfeit a kiss.'

One of the women squealed her excitement. Mrs Mallow, Rosa thought.

'Stanford,' Lady Smythe said in objecting tones. 'How can we hide if we do not know our way around the house?'

'Don't worry, Lady Smythe,' Mrs Mallow said. 'Stay with me. I am good at this.'

A flicker of something passed across Stanford's face. Dismay? How could that be? This was all his idea. He turned to Mrs Mallow, his smile turning wolfish. 'Have no doubt, I will find you.'

And he would. His kind knew such things by instinct.

Lady Smythe cast him an anxious glance, which seemed a little odd. Unless she worried that Stanford might not find her.

Rosa bit her lip until it hurt. Better that than feel envy for

Lady Smythe. Envy? Surely not? What had got into her head? The kind of fun proposed by Lord Stanford would keep the guests busy for the rest of the afternoon. A good thing, from her perspective.

Stanford glanced down at her. 'Would you care to join us, Mrs Travenor?'

Dear Lord, had he read her thoughts? She really must be more careful around him. He was far too observant for a man so apparently indolent.

'Certainly not,' Lady Keswick put in. 'Mrs Travenor has other duties.'

Rescued. She lifted her chin, shooting Stanford a look of triumph.

He shrugged. His dark eyes gleamed wicked encouragement. 'Too bad.'

Lady Keswick's eyes lit up. 'And before you ask me, I am far too old, but it sounds like just the right sort of thing for a rainy day. Feel free to use the whole of this floor, but do not go upsetting my servants.' She reached out a hand. 'Come, Rose, you shall help me to my chamber. I have correspondence to write.'

Lady Keswick heaved herself to her feet with Rosa's help. Digger, tongue lolling, got his short legs beneath him. 'Dinner will be served at six in the dining room,' the countess announced and headed for the door.

Hapton strolled to her side and offered his arm. 'May I escort you, Lady Keswick?'

She beamed. 'Now you are what in my day we called a cavalier.' She took his arm. 'You can see me as far as the stairs. Clarence will take me the rest of the way.'

Rosa trailed in their wake, oddly aware of Stanford's gaze on her back. The very thought of it made her legs feel wooden and her movements stiff. It was only by practising a great feat of will that she did not turn around to ask him to stop.

The footman stationed at the foot of the stairs took over escort duties from Mr Hapton, whose granite-grey eyes ran over Rosa for a moment. 'I keep thinking we have met before, Mrs Travenor,' he said as she passed him to climb the stairs.

Rosa shook her head. 'I don't believe so.'

'Then you remind me of someone.'

A cold feeling settled in the pit of her stomach. Everyone said she looked like her mother. An Italian opera singer famous in Rome and London before she married, she had been much admired for her voice and her opulent figure. Many painters had daubed her likeness, some showing her in the scandalous costumes of the opera house. One reason Grandfather had been so opposed to her parents' marriage. The reason for their years of estrangement.

Hapton must have seen one of her mother's likenesses somewhere. The thought he might put two and two together made her queasy. Not because she was ashamed of her mother, but because she did not want word of her presence in the area to reach her grandfather. Not yet. Not until she found the will. 'I can't think who it might be, Mr Hapton,' she said coolly and followed Lady Keswick and Clarence up the stairs.

At the door to his mistress's chamber, the footman waited while Rosa fetched the wheeled chair. Lady Keswick collapsed into it with a deep sigh as Rosa wheeled her inside.

Stone-faced, but with beads of sweat on his upper lip and forehead, Clarence closed the door from the other side.

'You should really think about a bedroom on the ground floor,' Rosa said gently.

'Pshaw. I'm not dead yet, girl. Nor yet an invalid.'

'Indeed no,' Rosa said. 'I was thinking more of your footman. Didn't you see how red Clarence's face was by the time he reached the top of the stairs?'

Lady Keswick grinned. 'Naughty puss. Trying to appeal

to my soft heart.' She sighed. 'Very well, I will consider it. But not until these guests of ours are gone. Time was when I would be playing hide and go seek with the best of them. Are you sure you don't wish to join in the fun? An amorous adventure might be just the thing to cheer you up. You can't remain in mourning forever. Fitz is a nice young man and without a brain in his handsome head. You'd twist him round your little finger in a trice. I'd be wary of the rest, though. Bad men, the lot of them.'

Despite the horrid feeling in the pit of her stomach each time Lady Keswick mentioned her widowhood, Rosa laughed at the old lady's character assassination of her guests. 'A man would interfere with my plans.'

Lady Keswick shook her head. 'You gels today, so independent minded. Very well, I will write again to my friend with connections at the Haymarket. Meanwhile, you can practise on my guests tonight. It would be to your advantage to gain the Phillipses' approval, if nothing else.'

Mr Phillips had lots of connections with the theatrical community in London. He would be useful, if she did not find the will. But she had so much hope in her heart, she really didn't want to think about her option of last resort. Not today.

Yet, it was wise to be prepared. 'I will look forward to singing tonight.' She just hoped the nerves that always assailed her when singing to an audience would not change Lady Keswick's view of her talent.

Rosa tied the length of cord attached to the bell pull around the arm of Lady Keswick's chair. 'Ring if you need anything.'

'There is one thing. Tell Jonas I want the best burgundy served tonight. I can't abide the dreadful stuff he served last evening.'

Rosa sighed. Lady Keswick's servants could be a little slack sometimes and she had a feeling the butler watered the wine, but the old lady wouldn't hear a word against him, so all she could do was pass along the message.

Leaving Lady Keswick scratching away with her pen, Rosa ran down the nearest servants' staircase and along the corridor on the first floor, only to find the pantry empty. He must be below. She headed for the cellars.

An arm shot out from a cupboard, jerked her inside, up against a man's body.

Rosa screamed.

A hand covered her mouth, the palm damp and smelling of snuff. 'Hush, you little fool.' Hapton.

He swung her around to face him, pushing her deeper into the small space lined with shelves full of table linen and lit by a small window high on one wall.

She pulled free and stared at his sly grin. 'Mr Hapton, you know very well I am not playing your game.'

He leaned against the door frame, his arms crossed over his chest with a rather chilling smile. 'You are now.'

'Let me pass. I am on an errand for Lady Keswick.' She stepped towards him, but he remained blocking the doorway.

'The price of release is a kiss,' he said.

Her heart thundered. She felt as if all the air had been squeezed from her lungs. Another man who wanted to kiss her. But unlike last night, she felt not the slightest bit tempted. What she felt was disgust. She backed away until a shelf prevented further retreat. 'You should not be here. Her ladyship offered you the second floor for your game.'

'I play to win,' he murmured. 'And today you are the prize.'

'Is there something wrong with your intellect? I made it

quite clear in the library that I did not intend to join your festivities this morning. Now, please excuse me.'

'Not without my kiss.' He lunged at her. She dodged his pursed lips and ended up jammed in the corner.

Now what was she to do? Men like Hapton saw anyone in the servant class as an easy target.

'You will let me pass, sir,' she said in a low voice. 'Or Lady Keswick will hear about your ungentlemanly conduct.'

He crooked a finger beneath her chin. Forced to look up, she glared into his cold grey eyes and repressed a shudder. Showing fear would only make things worse.

'Come now, Mrs Travenor, we both know her ladyship cares nothing for convention. And I've remembered where I've seen your face. On a theatrical broadsheet. Does Lady Keswick know your true calling?'

The idiot had mistaken her for her mother. Her chest tightened. If he thought her an actress, would he refuse to listen to her objections? 'You are mistaken, sir. And you will unhand me.'

'Now here's a pretty picture,' a darkly dangerous voice said from the doorway. 'Plaguing the hired help now, Hapton? Not getting anywhere with Mrs Mallow?'

Hapton cursed softly and turned to greet the newcomer. 'Am I treading on your turf, Stanford? Sorry, old chap, the last I saw you were hard on the heels of Lady Smythe. A little greedy, even for you.'

Stanford merely cocked a brow. 'Lady Smythe is in the library along with Bannerby, Mrs Mallow and Mrs De Lacy. It appears you have wandered off course. Unless I am mistaken and Mrs Travenor has changed her mind about joining us?' He cocked a questioning brow in her direction.

Rosa glared at him. 'As I told Mr Hapton, I am not a participant, Lord Stanford.'

A cool smile curled his lips and made him look darker and less friendly than she could have imagined. 'If that is the case, do feel free to be about your business, Mrs Travenor.' His ice-cold stare moved to Hapton and he stepped back with a gesture inviting them both to depart.

She had never felt so mortified in her life as she followed Mr Hapton into the corridor. There was something in Stanford's mocking gaze that made her feel like a scullery maid caught with her skirts over her head, instead of a victim of a man who ought to know better.

But then she could hardly expect him to fight a duel for her honour. He also saw her as ripe for amorous adventure.

Face scalding, she glared at both of them. 'You were given the run of the second floor by your hostess. Please do not come down here again.' Shoulders straight, she spun away and marched through the door leading to the basement, slamming it pointedly behind her.

Horrid men. Just because they had the morals of tomcats on the prowl, did they have to assume everyone else was the same?

And if Mr Hapton told his tales to Lady Keswick, he would catch a cold. While she hadn't given the lady any names, the dowager countess knew about Rosa's family connections to the opera. It was how she had secured this position. Lady Keswick liked to help those in the theatre down on their luck.

She took a deep breath and realised she was trembling from head to toe. Hapton had made her afraid. And Stanford's considering gaze had made her angry. Both for the same reason. No matter how drably she dressed or how prim and properly she behaved, men took one look at her foreign appearance and decided the worst.

Luckily, her two younger sisters took after their father, neither of them having their Italian mother's dark complexion or jet-black hair. Neither of them, as her grandfather was fond of saying, looked like dirty gypsies.

Heart still pounding, face still full of heat, she headed for the kitchen in search of Jonas.

Chapter Three

Restlessness felt like maggots under Garth's skin. Watching Penelope playing the harpsichord, while a solicitous Bannerby turned the pages of her music, was enough to turn his stomach.

After hours of ridiculous games in the afternoon and a dinner consisting of inane conversation, he really had to wonder if he'd survive the next few days without calling someone out. Someone like Hapton. He glared across the drawing room at the languid dandy and his fingers curled into his palms. He'd wanted to choke the life out of the ageing tulip of fashion this afternoon, and he would have, if he'd been certain Mrs Travenor hadn't welcomed the man's advances.

They'd looked very cosy in the linen cupboard. And she'd looked devastatingly flustered. Much as she'd looked the previous evening trapped in the passage. She'd certainly been angry when he interrupted them, but whether it was because he'd disturbed a *tête-à-tête*, or Hapton's importunities, he had no way of knowing. Unless he asked.

He glanced her way. As usual she was sitting calmly at

her embroidery beside Lady Keswick, looking thoroughly nunnish and utterly desirable. Her tapered, skilful fingers moved with a delicate precision. He imagined those fingers in his hair, or on various parts of his body. Most of all, he wondered how those lush courtesan-lips would feel beneath his own in the throes of passion.

He'd almost found out last night. Yet something, some chivalrous instinct, had held him back. An instinct he now heartily regretted after finding her with Hapton.

A stab of jealously twisted in his gut. For Hapton? Damn it all. What was he? A fifteen-year-old with a crush on his governess? He could have any one of the other women in this room at a snap of his fingers and the promise of a diamond necklace. And if he'd wanted, he could have had Mrs Travenor. He'd seen the longing in her eyes.

She might look like a nun, but his initial instincts had been correct: the woman was like all the others here. Available to the right man.

His gaze swung back to Penelope. Could he have her? Not that he wanted her. He didn't. He would never touch another man's wife, not even to prove a point to Mark, who deserved so much better.

No. Her he would chase back to London. Infuriatingly, Maria Mallow was sticking to her like a limpet to a rock and he'd yet to get Penelope alone and convince her to see reason.

Bannerby leaned over to turn the sheet of music. Didn't the silly chit know he was looking down the front of her gown? Perhaps she didn't care. Perhaps she wanted him to look.

Mark would be devastated if he learned of her perfidy. Why the hell hadn't he made sure she stayed at home? Locked her in. Or, better yet, taken her with him wherever he'd gone. That was a man besotted for you. They saw what they wanted to see. Mark had forgotten how easily women gave in to temptation. Either that or the poor sap thought his wife was different.

Which left the field open to men like Bannerby and Hapton. Men who didn't give a damn if a woman was married or not. They were curs. And the women who succumbed were no better.

He gritted his teeth and forced the thought aside, letting his idle gaze drift to Mrs Mallow. The woman pouted. He pretended not to notice. His gaze once more fell on Hapton, who was lounging, eyes half-closed as if listening to the music, when in reality he was also watching the companion ply her needle.

Garth kept his hands relaxed and his gaze moving. Mrs De Lacy and Mrs Phillips had commandeered the window seat furthest from the harpsichord and were exchanging remarks about their dress and yawning copiously.

All the while their plump hostess sat beaming happily.

For a house rumoured to be seething with carnal sin and every kind of vice known to man, he had never been so bored in his life.

He pushed to his feet as Penelope played the closing notes of the piece of music. Applauding loudly, he strolled to her side. Others politely joined him. Penelope blushed, rose to her feet and dipped a curtsy.

Garth took her hand and led her away from the instrument. 'Let us take a turn about the room. You have been wearing your fingers to the bone, my lady. Perhaps there is someone else who would like to play or sing for us?'

Her gaze when it met his contained resentment. He gave her his most charming smile.

Lady Keswick said something to her companion, too low to be heard, and Mrs Travenor nodded and rose to her feet.

Hapton sat up. 'Why, I believe Mrs Travenor has been hiding her light under a bushel.'

The lady in question stiffened, but kept walking.

'How delightful,' Mrs Mallow said.

'Mrs Travenor has a beautiful voice,' Lady Keswick said. 'Will someone play while she sings?'

'I will,' Mrs De Lacy said from the window. She was one of the kindest of the racy females here. The ardent expression on Mrs Phillips's face indicated a hope that the beautiful widow would sing like the old crow whose feathers she emulated in her dress. Garth found himself wincing. He had no wish to see Mrs Travenor embarrassed.

He guided Penelope to a chair and perched one hip on the arm, blocking her from any possible intrusion. Garth bared his teeth at the approaching Bannerby and the man gave him a sour look and with a huff took the seat vacated by Mrs De Lacy.

Rose—Mrs Travenor, Garth corrected himself—glided to stand beside the instrument. Black suited her. It emphasised the warm tones of her skin, the beauty of her stunningly expressive eyes and the lush ripeness of her lips. Most women looked washed out in black, their skin deadened. She looked dramatic, like an exotic fruit that could taste either gloriously sweet or surprisingly bitter.

Every muscle, every sinew, every blood beat inside him, wanted to taste, to savour, to learn her unique flavour. He curled his lip at his body's state of arousal. These days most of the thrill lay in the chase, not in the capture.

He doubted this one would be any different.

In which case, why bother?

And yet…

Mrs Travenor gave Mrs De Lacy her music and stood at her right shoulder.

'Why are you doing this?' Penelope hissed up at him.

'Adoring you?' he murmured back. 'Isn't that what you want?'

'No.'

He raised a brow and for a moment Penelope looked ready to scream. He curbed a smile. Adoring swains did not find the tantrums of their adored ones amusing, though he dearly wanted to laugh at her chagrin.

Mark would not appreciate his being amused. Probably wouldn't appreciate his methods either. But that was his friend's fault. He should better guard what was his instead of being so trusting. Had he learned nothing during his years on the town?

The first notes from Mrs Travenor's throat were low and hoarse. Panic filled her gaze and he winced, expecting the worst. She dragged in another quick breath and her voice steadied; at first barely audible, it grew in volume. Everyone paused mid-breath the better to hear. Even Garth. Then her voice swelled with astonishing depth and strength. The room vibrated with its power.

Not a weak tinny soprano, after all, this dark exotic female. A stunning contralto. She'd chosen Handel's *'Ombra Mai Fu'*, a distinctly odd choice. Originally composed for a castrato, it was often performed as a female trouser role. Her tones were rich with passion and dark with mystery.

There wasn't a man in the room who wasn't wholly focused on her. A feral odour of lust and excitement filled the room, when all she was singing about was sitting beneath the shade of a tree.

As the last notes died away, male applause thundered. Bannerby cried, *'Bravo.'*

Garth rose to his feet. *'Encore.'*

Hapton followed suit, as did Fitz and Phillips.

The women smiled and clapped, any sound deadened by their gloves.

Mrs Travenor curtsied and brought Mrs De Lacy to her feet. Both women curtsied together. Garth narrowed his eyes.

So the mysterious young widow was wont to perform. In drawing rooms? Or on the stage? The professional manner, the confidence—hell, the skill—said she was no amateur. What a surprise. An opera singer who left the house in the dead of night.

What the hell was she up to?

Despite the calls for more, Mrs Travenor shook her head and returned to the shadows behind her employer, who said cheerfully, 'Be still, you rascals. She will sing for us again another day. Will you play for us, Mrs Mallow, or will you sing?'

Mrs Mallow's irritation in being asked to follow such a performance could not have been more obvious.

Garth leaned forwards to whisper in Penelope's ear, 'Be glad she did not call on you.'

Penelope's expression said she was very glad indeed. She shrugged an impatient shoulder.

A glance at Mrs Travenor revealed no expression at all. The woman was an actress *par excellence*. First she played the nun and now the siren. His curiosity had been thoroughly roused. Along with a decidedly unruly part of his anatomy.

The woman presented a challenge. His blood stirred at the realisation. Very well. He'd pick up the gauntlet and find out exactly what she was about. Honest or nefarious. Virtuous or clever whore. The truth would out.

Mrs Mallow elected to play rather than sing. No fool, Maria Mallow. She never had been. She'd landed an ancient earl at the age of sixteen, buried him not long afterwards and spent most of her adult life as a rich and very indulged widow. She was the sort of woman he'd have been only too delighted to pursue at this kind of party, if his interest hadn't been diverted.

Boredom had dissipated. He felt enervated. All because of Mrs Travenor. Fiend seize it, his quarry would be a whole lot easier to catch if he didn't have to play nursemaid to Penelope.

He gulped down half of his wine and gave Penelope a toothsome smile.

She glowered over her fan. 'Why can't you bother someone else?'

'Go home and I won't bother you at all.'

Like the spoiled miss she was, Penelope slumped in her chair and gazed at the piano, her pretty mouth in a pout. What the hell was Mark thinking marrying such a girl? Obviously thought hadn't entered into his decision. Thank God Bannerby was too much of a coward to challenge Garth head-on for what he wanted, the puny weakling.

Another warning would probably do it, despite Penelope's encouragement. Not that she seemed particularly encouraging today. More sulky and unhappy.

No doubt because Garth was getting in the way. Well, she should have picked a man with a stiffer spine.

Hapton was a different proposition altogether. He took what he wanted and got away with it. Of all the men here, he presented the most danger to the pretty bride should he bestir himself in her direction. Fortunately, he seemed more taken with the lady companion. Garth suppressed the urge to warn him off there, too.

To Hapton that would be an irresistible dare.

While Mrs Mallow played competently, if without inspiration, the rest of the party listened politely or chatted softly. 'This is so dull,' Penelope whispered.

'What were you expecting?' Garth asked. 'An orgy?'

Penelope's cheeks turned pink. 'You are disgusting.' Married she might be, but she was no sophisticate.

'You said you were bored,' he said mildly.

The pout grew more pronounced. 'And all you think about is…is…' Now her face was fire red.

'It is all any man thinks of.'

Pain filled her pretty green eyes. Tears welled. 'I know that now.'

Why the hell was she crying? Mark was the one being betrayed. 'What is going on, Penelope?'

She blinked a couple of times, teardrops clinging to her lashes. She dashed them away. 'Why would you care?' she muttered. 'You are just like him.' She turned her face away.

'Penelope?' he said.

She rose swiftly to her feet with her fingertips pressed to her temples. 'Please excuse me,' she said to the room at large. 'I have a headache.' She almost ran from the room.

Mrs Travenor leaned forwards and whispered something in Lady Keswick's ear. The old lady nodded and Rose came to her feet and disappeared from the room.

She looked tired, he noticed, as if singing had tapped her strength. Or was her late-night excursion wearing her down? Would she go out again tonight? If she did, he would be right behind her.

Mrs Mallow finished her piece and the guests applauded.

Lady Keswick got to her feet, smiling broadly. 'Come along, everyone. Rose has arranged for card tables in the drawing room.'

Cards had been an inspired idea. Rosa closed the door on a buzz of conversation and laughter. While the guests, including Lord Stanford, gambled away their wealth, Rosa had something else in mind.

She smiled at Jonas coming the other way with more port for the gentlemen. 'Goodnight, Jonas. I hope they don't keep you up too late.'

'I'm used to it, Mrs Travenor. Got a note for you.' He nodded at his tray. A white folded square of paper lay on its edge against one of the bottles. Who on earth would be writing to her? No one knew she was here, except her sisters. She nipped the paper between finger and thumb, smiled her thanks and ran off up the servants' stairs, the missive a dead weight in her hand.

Inside her room, she opened the letter.

The spidery handwriting was unfamiliar, but the signature was not. She sat on the bed to read.

Inchbold's note relayed the worst possible news. Her grandfather would arrive in two days' time to ensure all was in readiness for the new tenants. Inchbold had been ordered off to Rye to procure supplies and servants and he would not be back until the day after tomorrow. Just in time to meet her grandfather. The dear sweet man had left her the key under a stone beside the door into the kitchen.

She only had two nights for her search.

Something hard and heavy weighed down her chest. Fear.

Fear that Grandfather's blistering rant the day he came to the school to inform her of Father's death was the truth. Fear her father had forgotten his daughters.

She got up from the desk and went to the window, fingers laced so tight her skin burned. She would not give up. She would prove Grandfather wrong.

Whirling around, she grabbed up her cloak and fled, pausing only long enough to pick up the small lantern she'd placed beneath the table near the side door earlier in the day. She lit it from one of the candles on the hall table and ducked out into a light drizzle.

Cloud cover made finding the path through the woods difficult. She shielded her light from the house with her body and held her skirts as high as possible with her other hand. The scent of wet leaf mould and greenery washed clean filled her nostrils. A friendly scent, unlike the heavy perfumes of Lady Keswick's female guests.

She spun around at a sound. Could someone have followed

her? Stanford? Hapton? She shuddered at the thought it might be the latter. She stood stock-still, not breathing and hearing nothing but the pounding of her heart and the rain pattering on soft earth. It must have been raindrops dripping from the trees that she'd heard. Or a nocturnal creature about its business. A badger or a fox. She waited a moment more. Waited for her heart to calm. Then hurried on, crossing the bridge in reckless haste, splashing through puddles and mud. She only had a few hours before she must return. It would not do for any of the early-rising servants to see her coming in.

She found the key as promised by Inchbold, unlocked the door and stepped into a kitchen that seemed oddly chill, when it had always been a warm friendly place in Rosa's memories.

Where to start?

Her father's chamber. Mother and Father had always shared a room and Rosa had visited them there in the mornings. To go there in the knowledge they would never be there again clawed at her heart. For her, there was some joy in the sadness. At least she remembered Mother and Father and how happy they were. The girls struggled to remember their faces and Grandfather had insisted that all pictures of their mother be destroyed.

On the way up the well-remembered flight of stairs to the second floor, memories flooded back. The pictures on the walls, all gone now, the pale green paint picked out in white replaced with Chinese silk. She flung open the chamber door, fearing the worst. If the pictures were gone, would the furniture be gone, too?

Everything was covered in holland covers—chairs, chests, tables. Hardly daring to hope, she lifted the corner of a sheet and discovered her father's desk in its usual place. A cloud of dust rose in the air. She sneezed. The woman who dusted clearly didn't make a very good job of it.

She smiled at the desk she remembered so well. Her father's escritoire, inlaid with gilt and rosewood flowers and birds. She'd sat on his lap while he wrote his personal letters. She also remembered the secret drawer beneath the lid.

Could it be this simple? Could what she sought be right here, tucked away and forgotten? If it was going to be anywhere, would it not be here where he must have known she would look?

It had to be.

Chapter Four

Breath held, fingers trembling with hope, Rosa felt far at the back for the catch inside on the roof of the pigeon-hole. A small raised knob. It was easier to twist as a child. It slipped from between her thumb and forefinger. She huffed. Tried again. It turned. A faint click.

A drawer slid out from the elegant carving above the writing surface. She peered in. Nothing.

Either someone had found it already, or... Neither scenario boded well for her quest. She refused to give room to her doubts. He must have put it elsewhere.

She would not lose hope. For her sisters' sake, she must search everywhere.

She glanced around the room. Under the bed?

She crawled on the floor, but found only dust.

Perhaps another secret hiding place. One she did not know about. She walked around the room and its adjoining dressing room, pushing and twisting any projection or seeming oddity in the hearth and the panelling until her fingers were sore.

A loose floorboard squeaked beneath her feet. She

snatched up the poker and pried it up. An old mouse's nest, full of bits of wool and fluff, met her gaze.

Rosa shuddered.

Despair rose in her throat. Hot moisture burned the backs of her eyes. She swallowed hard. She'd been so sure it would be in the desk.

She sucked in a breath. She'd try the other bedrooms on this floor and then the library, and after that, she'd try every other room in the house. And if she didn't find it tonight, she'd come back tomorrow.

Oh, please let her find it tonight.

Garth wanted to curse. He would never have believed the woman could slip out of a house so quickly. He'd had to run to catch her up. Or at least to catch up to the sight of her lantern willow-wisping ahead to who knew where.

Thank heavens for the lack of a moon, though he could have done without the rain.

The lantern danced ahead like a glow worm. Or a naughty little wood sprite of children's stories. Except there was nothing of the wood sprite in Mrs Travenor. Far from it. She looked like an innocent and sang like a siren, an erotic siren. As exotic as an eastern princess.

The lantern stopped bobbing.

Damn. She'd heard him. He remained still, not breathing, staring into the dark, listening to the sound of the rain splattering on leaves, on his hat and his shoulders. The rain itself was of the fine drizzling sort, a kind of irritating mist, but the leaves harboured the foggy stuff, releasing it in big fat drops.

The twinkle moved on. Faster this time. He increased the length of his stride, determined not to lose her. In his mind's eye, he tried to guess her destination. There was nothing out here, except woods. He'd checked with the gardeners.

A new sound, the sound of running water, overpowered the pattering of the rain on the leafy floor. A small stream, if he recalled the map, with a narrow footbridge. It defined the boundary of the neighbouring estate.

The progress of the lantern slowed to a crawl. He drew closer, catching glimpses of ancient wooden rails in the swinging circle of light. Why would she risk life and limb crossing such a rickety structure?

He waited until she was clear and approached the stream. Feeling the slick boards beneath his feet and the shake in the timbers in his grip, he crossed slowly.

Wherever she was going, it had to be important to risk traversing this bridge.

By the time he reached the other side, all sign of her lantern had disappeared. Cursing under his breath, he wandered around seeking a path. Without her light to guide him, it took him a good few minutes to find the track, only to discover he'd gone in a circle ending back at the bridge. This time he used his brain and sparked his tinderbox. In the brief flash it provided, he found her footprints in the mud, heading off to the right.

He pressed on through the tangle of brambles. A wet branch slapped him in the face. He grabbed for his hat. He cursed at the trickle of chilly rain running down between his collar and his skin. Any owner of a property who let his woods grow wild ought to be shot.

The woods ended at a lawn. And beyond the lawn there had to be a house.

Got you!

He frowned. Why so much secrecy? He couldn't imagine Lady Keswick caring if her lady companion had a special friend at her neighbour's house. He could even imagine the old girl encouraging the lass.

Perhaps she had. Then why not admit it?

He forged on. The house was there, he knew, he'd seen it on the map, but strangely, it was utterly dark. Even if all the occupants were abed, which they couldn't be if she was meeting someone there, then there ought to be some light in the corridors and stairways.

The house must be empty.

The crunching of gravel beneath his feet signified he'd reached a drive, albeit a rather weedy one. And at the end of the drive, he found a house. Of Mrs Travenor there was no sign. How far ahead of him was she? He must have lost sight of her at least a half an hour before. He went around to the back of the house and stopped.

Here were the lights he sought. A lantern hanging beside a back entrance to the house. It bounced off slick cobbles.

Of Mrs Travenor there was no sign.

He crossed the courtyard, searching for a clue to her whereabouts. He scanned the back of the house. There. A light. On the second floor. It wasn't very bright, but it had to be her.

She'd gone inside. It was the only explanation.

What in hell's name was she doing?

He walked carefully up to what was clearly the kitchen door and put his ear to the crack at the jamb. Nothing.

Slowly, he depressed the latch. The door opened silently. He stilled, breath held. No cry of alarm. No footsteps coming his way. He opened the door enough to allow his body to slide through and closed it behind him.

Now he really was in the dark. In the pitch-black, with the echoing sound of footsteps somewhere deeper in the house.

It seemed Mrs Travenor was up to no good.

A sense of disappointment slid through him, bitter edged and sharp. He hesitated. He could just walk away and forget what he'd seen. Or he could catch her in the act and, damn it, see her brought to justice. Clearly she'd been using Lady

Keswick as her dupe to gain access to this empty house and now was about to make off with some sort of loot. His gut knotted. He almost preferred to think of her in the arms of a lover than this.

He fumbled around as quietly as possible until he found the stub of a candle. Taking his time in order not to alert her to his presence, he lit the wick. The light revealed an abandoned kitchen. Clean. Tidy, but definitely not used recently. A narrow set of stairs led upwards. Perfect. He'd take the servants' stairs to the second floor, where he'd seen the light, and catch her in the act.

This was impossible, Rosa thought, staring around the library at chairs and tables covered in sheets and walls lined with empty bookshelves. Where did she start?

She set her lantern down on the red-leather-covered rent table in the middle of the room. It had a keyhole within its central circular section. Would her father have hidden his will in there? It seemed unlikely. Any fool would look there first, and Grandfather wasn't a fool.

She pulled on the knob beside the keyhole. It lifted easily. She groped inside, feeling nothing but dust under her nails. Ugh.

Walking around the table, Rosa pulled open the three drawers beneath its top where Father would have kept his records of rents paid and collected. More emptiness.

She turned in a circle. This room still had all of its pictures. Perhaps they disguised a hiding place.

She pulled one of the straight-backed wooden chairs underneath a hunting scene adjacent to the hearth.

She hopped up on the chair. The picture shifted easily enough to reveal blank plaster painted blue like the rest of the walls. Disappointed, but not surprised, she slid the picture back in place. Something gave way with a snap. The picture slid through her hands. It was going to smash to the floor. She clutched it, wobbling on the chair.

'Blast!'

'Well, well,' a menacing voice said from the doorway. 'I had no idea you were an art lover, Mrs Travenor.'

Rosa gasped and almost dropped the picture. 'Lord Stanford?' Oh, no. What was he doing here?

He strolled to her chair and looked up at her. 'It seems a call on the magistrate is in order.'

'You followed me.' Gripping the picture frame, she stared at the cynical twist to his mouth and the suspicion rampant in his dark eyes.

'As well I did,' he said. 'Or you'd be making off with someone else's property.' He moved in close, too close, and grasped the picture by the frame. 'I'm afraid I can't allow you to steal this.' He took the frame from her grasp and set it down, one edge on the floor, the other leaning against the wall.

He put his hands around her waist and lifted her. His hands were large and warm; he smelled of rain and cigars, and sandalwood. He set her down lightly, as if she weighed nothing at all. 'Now then, madam, what are you up to?'

How to explain without giving too much away? 'I know this doesn't look good, but I am looking for something that belongs to me. I did not intend for the picture to come down off the wall.'

Stanford laughed. 'Smooth, Mrs Travenor. Very smooth. You must think I'm an idiot.'

'Then why do you think I have the key to the door?'

He frowned. Looked a little nonplussed. 'Perhaps you have an accomplice.'

Her heart sank. She certainly did not want to implicate Mr Inchbold. Brazen it out. It was the best way—she'd learned that during her long years at school. And more recently in dealing with the doctor who had come to attend her sister, Sam. 'I have the key, my lord, because I have every right to be here. I used to live here with my father and I believe he left something behind.'

If anything, the curl to his lip increased. 'Money? Of course. You are looking for a safe. Expecting to find the family jewels, perhaps?'

'There are no family jewels here.' They had all gone to her stepmama. Even those her father bought for her mother. Blast Lord Stanford—why couldn't he just stick to playing cards instead of chasing after her?

It was that business with Hapton in the linen closet, no doubt. A blush crept up her face. He thought she was no better than she should be. Apparently in more ways than one. 'This really is none of your business.'

'It is every man's business to protect his fellow from thieves and burglars.' He gave a rather nasty laugh. 'Indeed, I'll have you know I am sworn to uphold the law in my role as a member of the House of Lords.'

She gave him a sour look. 'God help England.'

He cracked a laugh. 'Indeed.'

Dare she trust him? She heaved a sigh. 'Perhaps if I explain…'

He nodded, his eyes wary. 'I'll listen. But stick to the truth. I will know if you are lying.'

Not telling everything was not lying. All she had to do was convince him she wasn't a thief. 'As I said, I lived here once.'

He threw back his head and laughed. 'Mrs Travenor, you are the most outrageous female I have ever met.'

'It's true. There is a servant here who can vouch for me.'

'Where is this servant?'

She winced. 'He had to go to Rye, but he will be back and

he will confirm that my father was a tenant here before he died. We had to leave in a hurry.'

The laughter left his face, replaced by a swift frown. 'Debts?'

Well, there were debts. Just not her father's. 'Yes.'

His mouth twisted in that cynical smile. 'And what do you expect to find behind the pictures?'

He didn't believe her. She swallowed. She couldn't tell him about the will because then he would want to know the names of her relatives. If any word got back to her grandfather about her search, he would no doubt ban her from the house and Inchbold would be in terrible trouble.

She clasped her hands together, a prayer for his trust. 'A miniature of my mother. It was only after he died that I realised it was missing from his effects.' It wasn't completely a lie. Change the word miniature for will and it was as close to the truth as she dared get.

He looked unconvinced.

'In two days the house will be rented again. This is my last chance to search.' She couldn't stop the pleading note in her voice. Not that she thought pleading would do any good, judging by his forbidding expression.

'Are you sure it is here?'

'It cannot be anywhere else.'

'Why sneak about in the night? Why not just ask the owner for permission to look?'

Did he have to be so logical? 'The owner is unlikely to grant me permission, given the cloud we left under. Surely you won't stop me from looking for what is mine? It has no value to anyone except me and my sisters.'

His expression remained doubtful.

She swallowed the dryness in her throat. 'You can stay and watch if you wish.'

'Good God, woman, it is long past midnight. A time when honest people are heading for their beds.'

'I have other duties to perform during the day, as you know.'

He muttered something under his breath. 'All right. Search. But you will not remove anything from the property without the owner's express permission.' He folded his arms across his chest and leant against the wall.

It was the best she could hope for. Besides, if she did find the will, she would be able to put paid to his suspicions in an instant.

She stared at the picture on the other side of the fireplace, another hunting scene. She dragged her chair around the hearth and stepped up. Taking care not to put any pressure on the cord, she pushed the picture aside. Nothing here either. Skirts in hand in preparation of jumping down, she glanced over at Stanford. He was staring at her ankles. When she didn't move, he raised his gaze to her face. She glared. 'Do you mind?'

'Not in the slightest.'

Heat flooded her body at his lazy mocking smile. They locked gazes for a moment and then finally he shrugged and looked away. She leapt from the chair.

There was another picture, this time a Scottish scene, complete with a gillie and his dogs out amid the heather. A console table stood beneath it. It looked sturdy enough to hold her weight, but she needed the chair to climb up. She turned to pick it up.

'Allow me.'

The velvety voice in her ear caused her heart to leap into her throat. She drew back. 'Certainly. Over there by the window, if you please.'

'That is not the kind of wall where one would locate a safe.'

'I want to look.'

'Well, we don't need the chair.' He strode to the picture, reached up, grasped the frame and shifted the picture at an angle. Nothing. His expression was long suffering. 'As I said. Can we now put an end to this nonsense?'

Damnation. He was going to try to rush her out of here. 'If you don't want to help, sit down and leave me to it.' She walked over to the bookshelves and tried twisting and turning any ornate projection she could see.

He let go a heavy sigh and did the same for the ones above her head. Lord, but the man was tall. When they were finished there, she peeled back the large rug covering the middle of the floor and started on the floorboards.

'What is so important about this picture anyway?' he grumbled while he tested the boards at the other end of the room.

'It is the only picture we had of my mother.'

'Why would someone hide it away?'

The man just couldn't leave well alone. 'My father couldn't bear to look at it after she died. He put it away in a safe place for us. When we left, it was forgotten.'

'It sounds like a very bad play,' he said. 'Who can't bear to look at a picture?'

'My father loved my mother very much.'

'As I said, a very bad play,' he scoffed.

She frowned at him. His gaze was fixed on the floor, but the smile on his lips was not merely mocking, it was bitterly cynical.

'I suppose you are one of those men who does not believe in love,' she said, flipping down one corner of the rug and moving to another carpet corner on her side of the room.

'Love is a fairy tale created by females with nothing better to do than create fantastical events in their heads.'

'Don't you love anyone? Your family? Is there no woman you have ever loved?'

'Family is a duty. I fulfil my responsibilities. I believe in friendship. It also has responsibilities.' He looked up, his dark gaze shadowed and unfathomable. 'But all this emotional talk and poetry about hearing music, the sky being brighter, because you love someone is just so much claptrap. It isn't possible.'

The vehemence in his tone took her aback. 'I will admit there are different kinds of love. Love of family is quite different from romantic love. But why would so many people, men and women, write about it, if they have never experienced it?'

'Because they are in lust. People don't like to think of their baser urges as the same as unthinking beasts, so they call it another name.'

She gasped. Baser urges. Is that how he saw love? 'Then what about familial love?'

'Family members care about each other as long as it benefits them. If it doesn't, then they don't.'

Never had she heard anything so cold. What on earth could have caused such a chilly outlook? She flung the carpet back in place and put her hands on her hips. 'I feel sorry for you, Lord Stanford, if that is how you feel.'

He kicked his corner of the carpet flat. A puff of dust rose up. 'Indeed, Mrs Travenor. Well, I am not the one searching a stranger's home for a stray picture that a widower no longer wanted to look at and promptly forgot about because he probably married again to assuage his baser instincts.'

How had he guessed Father had married again? 'My father never forgot my mother. Never.'

He gave her a dark glance. 'Are we done here? Are there any other hiding places you can think of?'

'The study.'

He groaned and pulled out his fob watch, bringing it close to the lantern on the table. 'It is almost two. After the study, we will leave.'

'After the study, there is nowhere else to look.' She'd searched all the other rooms. Oh, how she hoped the study held the answer.

She blew out the candles she'd lit, picked up her lantern and marched along the corridor, all too aware of Stanford trailing behind.

She was aware of his presence all the time. It was like having the devil sitting on your shoulder, whispering tempting words in your ear, because she kept remembering their almost-kiss, kept feeling a glimmer of the heat that had ripped through her body, each time their gazes met. And she had the distinct impression, when he looked at her, that he was remembering it, too.

'You certainly seem to know your way around,' he said as she went to the study and flung back the door.

'Because I lived here,' she said, not quite disguising the triumph in her voice.

'Or because this is not the first time you have searched.'

The room was bare of furniture. Not even one picture remained.

'Oh,' she said, recalling her father's oak desk and the heavy wooden chairs. 'Where is everything?'

Stanford shrugged.

If only Inchbold was here, he would know. She glanced around the oak-panelled walls. Could they hide a secret place? She tried tapping on the wall nearest the door.

Stanford groaned. 'This is ridiculous.'

'Not to me, it isn't,' she said fiercely. Her sisters were depending on her to find the will. They all were. The debts were mounting by the day. Debts to the school. Debts to the doctor. She'd managed to stave them off, but she had borrowed against the certain knowledge they would inherit something by way of her father. When no will was found, everything had gone to his new wife and their son and the debts had remained. Growing more crushing by the day as interest piled on top of interest. She clenched her hands. She would not believe her father had broken his promise.

'If you want to help, then do so. If not, please stand back.'

She pushed past him to get to the wall on the other side of the door. Her tapping revealed nothing out of the ordinary. With a long-suffering sigh, Stanford inspected the floor-boards.

'There's nothing here,' he said after he'd covered every inch of the floor and she had done the same with the walls. She'd even looked up the chimney, which was an old-fashioned one, probably built when the first house occupied the estate.

Her shoulders slumped as defeat washed through her. 'You are right. There is nothing here.' And disaster loomed closer.

He shot her a considering look.

She forced a careless shrug. 'He must have put it some-where else. Perhaps his second wife has it.'

His mouth tightened. 'I'm sorry.'

'Me, too. There is no point in searching any longer. It is time we went home to our beds.'

The hot look he sent her way seared her skin everywhere it touched and it roamed her at will. As if he'd like to eat her up. Or kiss her.

The thought of comfort in a pair of strong arms was very tempting right at this moment. It seemed like years since she'd had anyone to lean on. She forced her gaze away. 'Let us go.'

Outside, she locked the door and put the key in her pocket. 'I will return it to the servant tomorrow.' In an oppressive silence they walked across the lawn and into the woods, with only the light of the lantern to guide their steps.

'You don't believe me, do you?' she said. 'About the miniature?'

'No.'

'Why not?'

'Because it doesn't make sense. Why wouldn't the owner give you permission to look?'

'He took the furnishings in lieu of rent,' she said. 'He would say the miniature also belonged to him.'

'In that case, I'm afraid it does.'

She halted. 'Have you no compassion at all?'

His gaze searched her face, the light from the lantern emphasising the starkness of his features, the high cheekbones, the angular jaw. The bleakness in his eyes. 'None.'

'Heaven help you, then.'

He gave that short laugh of his. 'It won't.'

She wanted to shake him. Then realisation flooded through her. 'You are going to contact the owner, aren't you?'

'I'm afraid so.'

'Why?'

'Because you are lying.'

'How can you say that?'

His lips twisted. 'Do you want to know how I can tell when a woman is lying?'

She stared at him. 'How?'

'Her lips are moving.'

She recoiled. 'What cynicism, my lord. Perhaps you have been mixing with the wrong kind of women.'

He inclined his head a fraction. 'Perhaps.' He took her arm firmly and urged her forwards. 'But you are lying, nonetheless.'

Blast the man, she was, but not about what was important in this matter. 'What I seek is rightfully mine.'

'If so, you would not be sneaking around in the dark.'

Implacable. She jerked her arm free of his hand. 'If I had any other choice, do you think I wouldn't take it?'

Oh, dash it all, were those tears she heard in her voice? She despised tears. She swallowed the hot lump in her throat. 'Fine. Tell whoever you wish.' She broke into a run, slipping and sliding on the sodden ground, hearing his heavy steps behind her. Why couldn't he just leave her alone?

'Mrs Travenor,' he said in low impatient tones. 'Stop. You will fall and hurt yourself.'

She broke through the trees and saw the light of the house ahead. She lifted her skirts higher, ran faster.

A hand caught her arm. Swung her around. Held her upright. And then she was pressed against a hard wall of male chest. It rose and fell from running. As did hers. Heat invaded her breasts and thighs. She struggled to free her arms. He drew her closer, using only one hand, and lifted the lantern. Grim-faced he glared down at her. 'What in hell's name do you think you are doing?'

'Let go of me.'

If anything he tightened his grip. The heat of the day before swirled around them. She stared at his mouth. At the lips that once more tempted. She could not tear her gaze away.

'Rose,' he whispered.

He bent his head and took her mouth.

She grabbed his lapels, stood on tiptoes and pressed against him, kissed him back. It seemed the only way to quench the fire in her blood.

A groan rumbled up from his chest. Her breasts tingled and tightened. She put her arms around his neck.

On a gasp, he broke the kiss.

A sense of loss engulfed her. Longing.

Retaining his grip on her shoulders, he blew out the lantern and set it down. 'Now,' he murmured, 'where were we?' Both arms went around her, one hand at her nape, the other around her waist, and once more their lips melded.

She felt as if she was flying ten feet off the ground. A dizzying, exciting sensation. Her body hummed with a longing to burrow against him. His tongue slipped through her parted lips and into her mouth. Her limbs became heavy and languid, her mind empty of all but the heat and the hunger. When his tongue retreated, she followed it with her own, tasting the darkness of his mouth, the brandy and pleasure.

His hand cupped her buttocks, lifting her, pressing her hard against him. Something hard, demanding, pressed against her belly.

He broke away on a groan. 'My room or yours?' he whispered, his voice hoarse and urgent against her neck.

She froze. He thought… He wanted… She'd misled him into thinking she was like all the other women under Lady Keswick's roof. Of course he did. And, heaven help her, she was terribly tempted to ease the hot thrumming in her body, to learn what it meant to lie in a man's arms. Ruin was literally staring her in the face, a fallen angel ready to lead her astray. This was why mothers didn't leave daughters alone with handsome young men. Her body trembled with longing. If she was ruined, her life would be changed forever. There would be no hope left.

'No,' she said pushing backwards with her palms flat against his chest.

'You are jesting?'

She shook her head. 'I— No, I am not.'

She couldn't see his face clearly, only hear the harshness of his breathing and feel the warmth radiating from his body.

'Oh, now I have it.' The note of cynicism was back in his voice, the sneer so audible, she could hear the curl of his lip, see it in her mind's eye. 'You want something in exchange.'

What on earth was he talking about?

'You want to name your price. What is it? My silence about tonight? Money?'

She did want his silence. She didn't want her grandfather learning about her search. But what he was suggesting was… was wrong. Against everything she believed in. This bargain he suggested was cold and calculating, without love or any deeper affection. It had nothing to do with feelings or emotions. This was all about lust.

Base urges paid for in some sort of coin.

She touched a finger to her lips and shook her head. 'You have nothing I want.'

'I'm sure I can think of something given time.' The teasing note in his voice, the velvet purr, did nothing to soften his meaning, the implication that every woman could be had for a price. She'd been right not to trust him with her story.

She backed up a couple of steps, shaking her head. 'No, thank you. I must bid you goodnight.' With a fine show of bravado, she straightened her shoulders, swung around and ran for the house.

Chapter Five

What the hell had happened? His breathing just as ragged as that of a boxer who'd received a blow to the solar plexus, Garth bent down for the lantern and strode for the house. The kiss had been good. Better than good, it had been perfect. All right, perhaps he should have been more subtle about asking her what she wanted, but she'd been the one spouting nonsense about romantic love. He wasn't going to pretend he felt something he didn't.

He had felt something stir in his chest, though. A strong desire to possess as their bodies melded. She'd responded beautifully to his kiss. Even better than he'd anticipated. She'd kissed him like a courtesan and run off like a terrified virgin.

Women. Every time you thought you understood them, they shied off in another start. Perhaps she thought she had him fooled with that innocent face, as if he was some green boy new on the town.

A smile crossed his lips. Perhaps this was all part of her game. He'd encountered them all in his time, bold ones, shy ones and everything in between. Very few of them didn't end up in his bed once he understood the direction of their carnal desires.

This one would be no different. In the end. One thing he wouldn't do was chase after her. He would give her time, let her decide her next move.

He entered the house. There was no sign of Mrs Travenor, not even wet footprints. No doubt the sly little wretch had removed her shoes from the slender feet he'd noticed when she stood on the chair and deliberately teased him with glimpses of her ankles. Damn her.

She'd probably spent most of her married life sneaking out of her husband's house to meet some man or other. Another womanly trait. Lord knew, he'd had enough of them offer to slide out and meet him in his time, and seen their disappointment when he'd refused.

Damn it to hell. Now he needed a brandy or he would never sleep. Because right now a certain part of his anatomy was expecting something it wasn't going to get.

He cursed low and with feeling.

And then he recalled his other problem. Penelope.

He strolled up the main staircase and along the corridor leading to his room.

A burst of hope fired off in his chest at the sight of a figure lurking outside his door. Blast. The figure was male and was trying Penelope's door.

'Going somewhere, Bannerby?' he drawled.

The man shot upright. 'God, man, don't you ever sleep?'

Garth smiled a nasty smile. 'Not when there are profligates like you around.'

Bannerby glanced at the door and back at Garth. 'I was worried about her. I thought to ask her if her headache had improved.'

'At four in the morning?'

'Her maid wouldn't let me in earlier.'

Garth's gut stirred with foreboding. 'Did she make an assignation with you, through her maid?'

The other man grinned. 'Is that any of your business?'

Damn the woman. Damn him for not keeping a closer watch on her. Damn him for being distracted by the thieving Mrs Travenor, actually, when he should have been doing something about Mark's wife. He reached out and tried the door handle. The door remained firmly locked.

A door further down the corridor opened. Modestly wrapped in a heavy robe, Mrs Travenor stepped into the passageway. 'If you gentleman don't mind, some of us are trying to sleep.'

He almost laughed at her brazenness. He bowed instead. 'Our apologies, Mrs Travenor.'

Her gaze dropped to his hand still on the doorknob. 'As I understand it, Lady Smythe is not receiving at the moment. She is unwell.'

He wanted to curse. Instead he glared at his companion 'That is also my understanding. Is it yours, Bannerby?'

The man shot him a glare and strode off down the corridor.

The light from the candle in the wall sconce caught the expression on Mrs Travenor's face. Chagrin? She must have thought he and Bannerby were arguing over Lady Smythe.

He felt the urge to explain. Good God, he never explained himself to a female. Clearly, he was going to have to take swift action to get this one woman out of his blood. There was only one way to do break a woman's hold. Get her into his bed. Once conquered, they lost their allure. 'Goodnight, Mrs Travenor,' he said silkily. 'That is unless you wished to invite me in?'

She ducked back into her room and closed the door, a flimsy panelled block of wood transformed into castle wall, but the challenge lingered and they both knew it.

Something to look forward to on the morrow. He retreated
to his chamber and poured a glass of brandy.

The next morning, Garth stood in the corridor, puzzling
over the noises emanating from Penelope's room. They
sounded oddly hushed. His jaw tightened. Had she, despite
his careful warding off of Bannerby, found a way to lure him
into her bed?

He eyed the doorknob. Should he burst in and reveal her
treachery once and for all? And if he did, would Mark believe
him? His friend was remarkably obtuse when it came to his
wife. And he used to be such a sensible chap.

The door opened. Garth prepared to confront the scoun-
drel.

Lil, Lady Smythe's maid, stepped out into the corridor,
closing the door softly behind her.

'Lady Smythe not up yet?' Garth asked.

Lil gasped, putting her hand to her chest. 'You gave me
a proper turn, my lord.' She lowered her voice. 'Got one of
her headaches, she has. Started last night it did. Sometimes
they last for days, they do. But this one don't seem so bad.'

Really? Or was it a ruse? It wouldn't be the first time she
had faked one of her so-called headaches. It was how she had
captured his friend. Sneaking out, when everyone thought
she was ill in her bed, then getting caught so Mark had no
choice but to do the right thing.

She had caught his friend in the parson's mousetrap; Garth
would be damned if she'd use the same trick to cuckold him.
He pulled a silver shilling from his pocket and tossed it in
the air.

Lil's eyes followed the spinning coin.

'I want the truth,' he said sternly. 'And this is yours. If you
lie, I will know it and see you dismissed without a reference.'

The girl swallowed and pressed her hand to her heart. 'I

swear it, my lord. Couldn't bear me drawing the curtains to let in the light, this morn. She's always like that when the weather changes, poor little thing.'

The poor little thing had made mincemeat of his friend. 'Are you sure?'

'Her ladyship heard she was ill,' Lil said, tossing her head. 'She sent Mrs Travenor with some of her powders. She came by with them and that nasty little dog. You can ask her when she comes back from the village.'

Could he now? Something inside him smiled at the thought of asking Rose anything. It was the oddest sensation. He flipped the coin into the outstretched palm. 'Let me know when your mistress feels better.'

'Hopefully by this afternoon, my lord.' The maid bobbed a curtsy and scurried off.

Did he believe her? Lil had been with Lady Smythe for years. He did not discount female loyalty as some men did, even if it was often misguided or plain wrong, but he knew lies when he heard them. Lil had been speaking the truth.

A smile pulled at his lips as he realised he had a morning to do as he pleased. And a fine morning it was, too. The sun was shining for once. The sky clear. And Mrs Travenor had walked to the village. Alone.

He kept remembering the little flashes of ankle beneath her skirts as she had vaulted on and off the chair. Pretty well-turned ankles and glimpses of elegant calf. Not to mention the way the echo of her kiss had left him tossing and turning for what had remained of last night. No doubt her intention. He looked forward to their next meeting alone.

Energised in a way he hadn't felt in a long time, he ran lightly down the stairs and out of the front door. A whistle came to his lips and a sense of well-being buoyed his spirits. The woman delighted him enough, he didn't care that she was a liar and possibly a thief.

* * *

After an easy half-hour stroll along a winding lane with high hedgerows full of cheerful birds, the first of a cluster of cottages heralded his arrival at the village. Still no sign of Mrs Travenor. Had he missed her?

He narrowed his eyes against the glare of the sun. If he remembered correctly, the post office lay at the centre of the small hamlet, and since there was only one road through it, she could not have returned without him seeing her. Unless she had taken a short cut across the fields.

Damn.

He had seen a stile leading to a footpath a short way back. And she did seem to know her way around the surrounding woods and fields. Perhaps that part of her story was true and she had lived near here as a child. He huffed out an impatient breath. Meeting her on the road was one thing, following her along a little-travelled path was so obvious as to be pathetic.

Yet the chance to tease her was simply just too tempting. And besides, he needed to keep an eye on her, find out what she was really up to.

He increased the length of his stride and soon leapt the stile he'd passed earlier. A barely discernible path led around the edge of a golden hayfield, which a few days before would have been ready for the scythe, but was now flattened here and there by last night's rain.

The sweet scent reminded him of boyhood jaunts in Sussex with Christopher. Those times with his brother had been good. And there would have been more, if Christopher hadn't been so sickly as a boy and Garth hadn't been such a devil. In those days, he'd accepted their differences. Only later had he realised the truth. The truth of what he was and what that meant for his brother.

He shrugged off the unwelcome intrusion, instead focusing ahead for sounds of his quarry. He paused at the sound of excited yapping and then a yelp. He grinned. It seemed the dog was on his side.

The next stile led him into a field of young bullocks all crowded in a corner on the far side. Above their brown bovine heads he saw a wildly waving parasol.

Sweet Hades, it just got better and better. He broke into a run.

The young bullocks turned at the sound of his yell. Ruminative brown eyes took him in. As one they turned in his direction. He knew what they wanted. Food. 'Off. Be gone, you stupid beasts.' He slapped the closest one on the rump and it kicked out and took off. The rest followed blindly at a lumbering run, leaving a dishevelled Mrs Travenor, her bonnet askew, clutching the grinning pug to her chest.

Right now he'd like to change places with the dog. He lifted his hat. 'Good day, Mrs Travenor.'

Her olive skin deepened in colour, her version of a blush. Hopefully because she remembered their encounter the previous evening and not because she'd been fleeing a herd of bullocks.

Her gaze wandered somewhere off over his left shoulder, as if she was trying to think of what to say. Her back straightened. 'Thank you, my lord. I don't know how many times we have passed through this field without any problem. This morning, Digger decided he didn't like the look of one of those cows and ran at it.' She closed her eyes. 'I wasn't watching and he pulled the leash out of my hand. I thought he was going to be trampled.'

'I heard him yelp. Don't tell me, you rushed in to save him. Very courageous.' It was. He couldn't imagine one of the women back at the house risking life and limb for a dog.

She gave an uncomfortable wave of her hand. 'I should have been more careful.' She looked up at him. She'd been crying. His fingers itched to touch her skin where tears had left a shiny trail on her face. He was afraid she might shy away, the way she had last night. The more he thought about it, the more he'd realised he'd rushed his fences.

The attraction between them was obvious, it was simply a question of slowing the seduction.

Garth reached out and tickled behind the dog's ears. It closed its eyes in ecstasy. 'Bad boy,' Garth said. The creature wagged its stubby tail.

'Stupid creatures. No matter how much I yelled they wouldn't go away. Then you come along and off they trot as nice as you please.'

He almost laughed at the resentment in her voice. 'I'm sorry. I am sure you would have prevailed in the end. Once they realised you didn't have a bale of hay tucked away on your person, they would have become bored and wandered off. Perhaps I should have left you to it.'

'Lord, no.' She gave him a rather chagrined look. 'I was glad to see you.'

The admission warmed him. 'I think you would have been glad to see anyone.'

She chuckled. 'You are right.'

'I'm wounded.' He put a hand to his heart. 'You are supposed to say only I could have vanquished the beasts.'

She laughed outright then. A low husky sound in the back of her throat. It caressed his skin, sent his blood flowing south while his brain seized.

With some difficulty he managed to signify they should start walking.

She put the dog down and brushed at the mud on her black skirts. 'What brings you out here so early in the morning?'

'The sun,' Garth said, watching her reveal the outline of her legs with each stroke of her gloved hand. 'The country air. I must say I am surprised to see you up and about so early.'

'I went to collect the post.' She sounded oddly defensive.

A basket lay in the grass at her feet. It contained several letters, one of them open.

She picked it up and let go a sigh. 'I was reading and didn't hear the cows approach.'

'Bullocks,' he said. 'Young males who have…er…lost their maleness.'

She looked at him blankly, then lowered her gaze, long black lashes shielding her eyes, but he was sure he saw the glimmer of that lovely smile of hers twitching at the corner of her mouth. 'Oh. I see.'

A sign she wasn't so averse to him as she made out. She certainly wasn't averse to his kisses. He held out his arm. 'May I escort you back to The Grange?'

She darted what he thought was a regretful glance at the open letter, but nodded and placed her hand lightly on his forearm.

The touch seared through his coat like nothing he'd ever experienced. His blood headed south again. He should find something to do with his hands or he might do more than offer his arm. 'I'll take the dog.' He grabbed the leash half-way down and she let it go.

'Thank you.'

'I'm surprised they don't send a footman for the mail,' he said as they approached the next stile.

'I have to walk the dog anyway.'

'And it means you don't have to wait to read your own mail.'

She bit her lip. 'My sisters write once a week. I am always anxious for news from them.'

He helped her over the stile. 'Perhaps you prefer to be alone to finish your letter.' Now why the hell had he given her the chance to be rid of him? Perhaps it was the anxiety he saw in her eyes.

'Oh, no, I had just finished when we encountered those...
bullocks.'

'Bad news?'

She glanced up at him from beneath the brim of her ugly
black bonnet. Somehow it made her seem all the more alluring. Like a badly wrapped parcel with intriguing hints of the
contents showing at the corners.

'It is not important.'

A lie. He could see it in the flash of panic in her eyes as
her thoughts went back to the letter. He hesitated, confused
by a wish she would confide in him, by the desire to help.
Surely his desires were all physical. 'If there is anything I
can do...' he found himself saying.

The shake of her head was a disappointment. 'They are at
school in the north.' Her hand flexed on his sleeve, a small
movement, a slight tightening of fingers quickly relaxed, but
it spoke of anxiety.

'Are they not treated well?'

'Well enough. I went there myself before...'

'Before you were married,' he finished. She glanced up
at him, her almond-shaped eyes startled and large.

'I— Yes.' She swallowed.

Damn it to hell. She was lying again.

Those tears he'd seen had not been from the encounter
with the bullocks. They had dried on her cheeks. His gaze
dropped to the letter. The contents of the missive had made
her cry. His lip curled. Was it sisters who wrote to her, or a
lover?

It wouldn't take much to discover the truth.

'How many sisters do you have?'

She sighed. 'Two.'

'Younger than you, obviously, if they are still at school.
Surely your parents...'

'My parents are dead.' She bit her lip. 'I am responsible for their...for them until they are of age.'

For their what? He frowned at the almost imperceptible change in what she had been going to say. 'An odd situation for a woman of your age, surely?' He calculated her age at no more than twenty-three or four. 'There must be other members of your family better situated to take on such a burden?'

She shook her head. 'No one I trust.' If anything, she sounded a little bitter as if there was someone, but they had failed in some way.

This time, she was telling the truth. Apart from that one small hesitation, every word rang true. The anxiety had been there all the time, he realised, a shadow in her eyes when he first saw her, and while she searched the house, but today it had developed into dread.

Bad news had arrived in that letter.

And she wasn't going to confide in him. Not yet. If ever. He wasn't the sort of man women trusted with anything important. A bitter taste filled his mouth at what he'd once taken pride in.

They paused while the dog halted to investigate a fallen tree stump. It lifted its back leg and then waddled on.

She took a deep breath, straightened her shoulders and smiled calmly. It was like watching someone draw down a screen, blurring the sharp edges of what lay behind. The smile was a mask. 'Digger likes you,' she said. 'You are honoured. He hates everyone, except Lady Keswick.'

He had no choice but to follow her lead, to step back from her private life and return to civil conversation. 'He likes you, too.'

'He tolerates me. He has bitten the ankles of every gentleman who passed through the front door, except you.'

'Wise dog.' He bared his teeth. 'He knew I'd bite him back.'

She laughed. The sound was a punch to his stomach, because he felt proud of that laugh. Because whatever troubled her, he'd managed to dispel the cloud for a moment. He'd felt this feeling before, but not for years. And never as strong.

Saints above, what was it about this woman that had him half-seas over? Dizzy like a drunkard because she had laughed at something he'd said. So what if she kissed like an angel and sang like one, too. There were hundreds of beautiful women in London and he'd sampled a good few of them without wanting to fall at their feet.

In the end, they'd all succumbed to his advances. This one was the only one who'd offered a challenge in years.

They broke into a clearing. Sun shafted down through the gaps in the canopy and bathed the grass and the cornflowers in golden light.

'How pretty,' she exclaimed. 'None of these was open yesterday.'

She let go of his arm and strolled about, picking the flowers, her face glowing.

How on earth could he have thought her akin to a crow, or a nun? Never in his life had he seen anything quite so alluring.

He folded his arms and leaned against a handy oak tree, content to watch.

What on earth was she doing? Rosa picked yet another of the tough fibrous stalks and added the bright blue flowers to her growing bunch. Encountering him on her walk was the worst of luck. It had been ages before she'd been able to fall asleep after their kiss. Every sound outside her door had brought her upright in her bed with the fear he'd somehow arrive in her bedchamber. Fearing…or hoping?

She glanced at him out of the corner of her eye. A dark

presence watching her pick wild flowers with heavy eyelids and a cynical smile. The bunch she had gathered looked scrawny and thin. She could hardly give up now, yet this was the last thing she wanted to be doing.

So why was she? Because he'd made her feel as if her skin didn't fit, as if she needed to do something with her hands or find them back on his shoulders while she offered her mouth to be kissed. Because it had all felt so wonderful and made her forget.

His kisses made her feel hot all over and dizzy. For those few moments she had forgotten all her worries.

She still didn't know what he planned with regard to her search of Gorham Place. If he was going to report her to the local authorities, surely he would have done so first thing this morning? At the very least, he would have already spoken to Lady Keswick. He'd done neither, which meant she was safe. For now.

She glanced down at the letter in her basket, the rounded handwriting of her sister, the crossed and recrossed lines spattered with inkblots revealing her agitation. Everything that could go wrong had done so. She'd gone to the post office, hoping Lady Keswick might have heard from her friend and found a terrified letter from her sister instead.

Why, oh, why had she borrowed that money?

Her heart stopped beating. She stared at the flowers trembling in her hand as she fought against the roiling in her stomach. She didn't want to be picking flowers. She wanted to run. To hide.

But she couldn't. She needed money. Lots of money.

Mechanically she picked another handful of flowers.

She'd known borrowing money was a risk, but the school fees were due and the doctor had refused to attend Sam without some payment on his account. With Grandfather deaf to her pleas for help and her certainty that Father would leave her well provided for, the decision had been simple.

That was months ago. Now the usurer had gone to the school demanding payment, waving the note she'd signed under the headmistress's nose and threatening debtors' prison for them all.

Meg's letter was frantic.

Why had Father broken his promise? She understood why he'd married again, but he'd promised he'd take care of his first family. She'd looked everywhere in that house. Everywhere.

A flash of something passed through her mind. A long narrow staircase leading down into the dark. The cellar. She hadn't looked in the cellar. Or the attic.

Could she possibly have missed the most obvious places after all? Grandfather would never go in the cellars or the attics. Father might not have been very practical, but he wasn't a fool.

The urge to run and look swept through her. She could be there and back in a flash.

'Are you done, Mrs Travenor?'

She whirled around. Stanford. She'd forgotten all about him. And Digger. She couldn't go haring off to Gorham Place in the middle of the day; she'd be missed. And she could not for a moment let Stanford know she planned to go back. She had to let him think he'd won. That she was happy with her lot and enjoying his company. It was the only way to allay his suspicions.

She looked down at the flowers. 'Yes. Yes, I'm almost done.'

She inhaled deeply, drawing in the air for the strength to get through one more day, the way she had when Father left them at the school, the way she had when he died.

Swiftly, she snapped off another stem and another. Added

some greenery. Bound the bouquet with a twisted length of columbine. She marched back to the man watching her from beneath lowered lids. Her heart gave a lurch. He was just so blasted attractive. If her life had taken a different turn, they might have met in a ballroom in London. He might even have become her suitor.

Something hot and uncomfortable filled the back of her throat. Tears? Over a man like Stanford? Never. She was worried about her predicament. About her sisters.

And whatever it took, she would get them out of this mess.

Stanford straightened at her approach. He flicked a blossom with a dismissive finger. 'Pretty enough, but not nearly exotic enough for you.'

A thrill raced through her blood. Unwanted heat, because she knew it meant nothing. He was amusing himself with a drab widow. For now, she'd play his game. She held his gaze and smiled boldly. 'Flattery, my lord?'

He blinked as if startled, but recovered swiftly, flashing her that suave smile. 'Never.'

She grinned at him. 'Save it for Lady Keswick. She loves that kind of thing.'

'And you don't?'

The velvet was back in his voice. The soft teasing that drove something inside her into a wild flutter. Calm. She must remain in control, not let him get too close, while letting him think she might succumb to his charm.

And hoping she didn't.

She cast him an admonishing look and started walking. 'What woman does not like a compliment or two, my lord?' she responded airily. 'Or man for that matter. When it is sincerely given.'

He fell in by her side, leading the dog. 'Are you saying I am insincere, Mrs Travenor?'

'With you, I think it is hard to tell.'

His brow furrowed. 'So you think I am sincere some of the time, or never at all?'

She laughed. 'I think you reveal very little of your real thoughts, to be honest.'

His expression was arrested, sharp. 'Nor do you, I think.'

She inclined her head in acknowledgement. 'We all have things we prefer to keep private.'

'I suppose you are wondering what I will do about last night?'

His directness startled a gasp from her lips. She shot him a quick glance. 'I suppose I am.'

They reached the other side of the clearing and entered the cool of the woods.

'I'm no telltale, Mrs Travenor. You found nothing. You took nothing. You assured me your search is over. So why don't we forget all about it and enjoy what appears to be shaping up as a perfect summer's day?'

Her stomach dipped to her shoes. She felt nauseous. He'd said exactly what she wanted him to say and she felt sickened by yet more falsehood.

They emerged on the lawn at the back of the house. She stopped and turned to face him, forcing herself to smile. 'Thank you.'

Dark eyes gleamed wickedly. 'Gratitude is a good place to start, Mrs Travenor.' His mouth curved in a sensual smile.

Staring at that mouth, she swallowed, unable to move. He was warning her he wasn't done with her. Reminding her that she only had to lean forwards a little to experience all those wonderful sensations in his arms.

She turned her head away, seeking to break his spell, but nothing shielded her from his heat, or the scent of his sandalwood cologne, a deep sensual musky scent that teased at her senses. She backed up, stumbling over Digger, who growled. 'Then we can be friends?'

A soft laugh greeted her words. 'It's not friendship I want, my dear Rose. But it will do for now.'

Her heart rattled back to life. It seemed they'd reached some sort of understanding. He would chase and she would run. Oh, how she wished she could stand still.

By two in the afternoon, all the guests, including a rather wan-looking Lady Smythe, gathered in the drawing room looking for something to do. There would be no escape for Rosa today.

'It is such a lovely day, why not ride out to some local beauty spot?' Mrs Mallow suggested.

'Why not a picnic?' Fitzwilliam said, his round face beaming. 'On the shore.'

The sea was a bare two miles away. 'I love the sea,' Mrs Phillips enthused.

'There are no bathing machines there, old girl,' her husband said.

'A walk on the beach would be pleasant,' Mrs De Lacy said. 'After a day indoors.' She turned to Lady Smythe. 'That is, if you feel well enough?'

Lady Smythe smiled. 'I thought I was going to have one of my sick headaches, but the powders Lady Keswick sent along did the trick. I am feeling much more the thing.'

'Then it is agreed,' Lady Keswick said, beaming. 'A picnic on the shore it is. Rose, please ask Cook to put up some baskets. Have two carriages prepared. The ladies can drive, the men can ride. A sea breeze will do us all good.'

'I must change,' Lady Smythe said.

'I'll need my parasol,' Mrs De Lacy announced.

The party broke up to prepare and Rosa started off to complete her tasks. 'A moment, Rose, if you please.'

She had never heard such a stern note in her employer's voice. Had Lord Stanford broken his word? Oh, why had she trusted the man? She should have gone to Lady Keswick first thing this morning and owned up. With sinking heart she went to stand before her employer. 'Yes, my lady.'

The elderly lady peered up at her. 'Are you quite well? You have dark shadows beneath your eyes.'

Lack of sleep. 'I am fine.'

Lady Keswick frowned. 'It's not one of these young reprobates upsetting you, is it? You are worth ten of any of them.'

If only it was something so simple. She shook her head. 'Perhaps, like Lady Smythe, I was affected by the stormy weather.' Hope sprang into her mind. 'Though I would prefer to stay at home today and rest, if I may.' She could slip out to Gorham Place.

'Nonsense, young lady. A sea breeze will put colour in those pale cheeks of yours.'

No point in arguing. Her employer never listened.

Lady Keswick cocked her head on one side. 'And don't wear black. You will be far too hot. I must say, I really am tired of those widow's weeds of yours. Too gloomy by half.'

'But—'

'Your husband passed on more than a year ago. It is time you came out of mourning. You impressed Phillips with your singing yesterday, now impress him with your looks. Ellie told me you have other gowns.'

The maid assigned to help her dress. Rosa bobbed a curtsy. What could she say? And Lady Keswick was right. Because if she didn't find the will, she needed a way to make more money than she would ever make as a companion.

Impressing Mr Phillips might indeed be the best course of action. Not that he would think her any great beauty.

Chapter Six

It was a surprisingly short time before the company was ready to leave, the ladies in the carriages and the gentlemen on horseback. If anyone was surprised to see Rosa dressed in a muslin of pale peach and a chip-straw bonnet instead of her usual black, they were too polite to say. Or perhaps no one had noticed. After all, she was barely more than a servant in this house.

Happily, all seemed in high spirits—even Lady Smythe seemed to have regained some of her colour. She had chosen to wear a white muslin sprigged with forget-me-nots and looked less like a married woman and more like a young débutante. She allowed Lord Bannerby to pay her outrageous compliments as he helped her into the carriage. Stanford had merely raised a careless eyebrow.

Was the young matron trying to make him jealous? If so, it wasn't working. And for some reason, Rosa felt glad as he rode along beside the carriage which she, Lady Keswick and Mrs De Lacy occupied. Mr Fitzwilliam rode on their other side and the rest of the gentlemen accompanied the second carriage. Two liveried grooms sat behind each carriage, their

role to carry the baskets and blankets to the chosen spot on
the beach and help Lady Keswick into her chair.

After half an hour, the carriages turned a corner and the
sparkling blue of the sea spread out before them. The white
sails of ships plying the coast added to the charming picture.

'Did I not tell you Camber Sands was one of the loveliest
spots in all of England, Mrs De Lacy?' Lady Keswick said.
'It was the reason I bought The Grange. I love the sea.'

The widow smiled. 'You did, my lady. And you were
right.'

The coachman drew the carriage off the road and into
the sand dunes. 'It is lovely,' Rosa agreed. She'd known that
before they set out. Another reason she had thought to cry
off. Too many memories.

'Charming,' Mrs Phillips said, joining them as they
walked across the dunes to the beach. 'Simply delightful.'

While the footmen unpacked the food, the sunshades
and the blankets under Lady Keswick's eagle eye, the party
walked to where the sea lapped on the long stretch of golden
sand.

Gulls wheeled overhead in anticipation of crumbs. Rosa
had the urge to take off her sandals and paddle as she had as
a child when her parents visited this beach.

Happy times and, surprisingly, looking back was not as
painful as she had expected.

'May I say how delectable you look,' a dark voice murmured behind her.

Delectable. He made her sound edible. A thrill of something dark ran through her as she swung around to meet Lord
Stanford's mocking gaze.

'I am delighted to see you out of mourning.'

'At Lady Keswick's request. She thought I would find the
heat of the sun unbearable.' Why explain? From the look on

his face, he thought she had dressed for his benefit, and to her shame, she had wondered about his reaction as Ellie had helped her dress.

'Then we have the sun to thank for a lovely sight,' he said smoothly.

The man was a practised rake and seducer. Such pleasantries would drip from his tongue for any female on whom he set his sights, but still, the compliment pleased her. More fool she. Because no matter how she tried to retain a calm appearance, her passions ran hot beneath her skin. Why shouldn't she enjoy the attentions of a handsome man for one afternoon? As of tonight, her time here was done. Just for one day she would like to forget her troubles, pretend she was an ordinary young woman out on a picnic with her peers.

She twirled her sunshade and smiled at him. 'You are very kind.'

His expression warmed. 'Shall we walk?' He held out his arm. She rested her hand on it and strolled beside him.

The party wandered in twos and threes along the beach, while Lady Keswick sat queenlike in her wheeled chair beneath a sunshade.

'Is this not just divine?' Mrs Mallow called out as she strolled towards them on Mr Hapton's arm. Her peacock-blue muslin gown left nothing of her lower limbs to the imagination as the wind moulded it to her form.

'It is, indeed,' Stanford said, raising his voice to carry over the hiss of breaking wavelets. 'The sand is so flat when the tide is out, I thought we might play a game of cricket after lunch. The ladies against the gentlemen.'

'Capital idea,' Fitzwilliam said, bringing Mrs De Lacy to join them.

The widow hooked her arm through Rosa's. 'You do play, don't you, Mrs Travenor? And may I say, it is so good to see you out of black. Not that it didn't suit you,' she added hastily. 'But that shade of blush looks stunning on you.'

'I couldn't agree more,' Lord Stanford said with a wink and a devastating smile.

Her heart picked up speed. Her breathing shortened. She felt as if she was in a runaway carriage heading downhill. Dash it all, no matter what her head was telling her about him, her stupid heart basked in his approval.

Lunch over, most of the party once more dispersed along the beach. Garth remained stretched out on the sand, peeling an orange for Lady Smythe. He'd deliberately chosen to sit beside her on the blankets, hoping for a quiet word. Penelope had looked thoroughly nervous when he sat down. And so she should.

Mrs Travenor, on the other hand, didn't know the meaning of fear. He glanced at her seated beside Lady Keswick, her fingers drawing patterns in the sand, her thoughts clearly far away.

In her dreary blacks, she had been exotically unattainable. In peach-coloured muslin, it was as if an orchid had bloomed. His first sight of her waiting to board the carriage had taken away his breath. She'd dressed her hair differently, too, no doubt to accommodate the fetching straw bonnet's low crown and wide brim. Black curls framed her face, and a low knot of thick black ropes nestled at her nape.

He wanted to see that hair unbound. Spread around her shoulders. Preferably her naked shoulders.

He handed another orange segment to Lady Smythe, aware of Rose's darting glances and puzzled expression.

Inwardly, he cursed.

It wasn't that he couldn't keep two women dangling, but he would have preferred to devote his whole attention to Mrs Travenor. Penelope was a self-imposed duty, but one he could not abandon. Not and look at himself in the mirror, at any rate.

'You don't look well, Penelope,' he murmured so no one else could hear. 'You don't belong here. Why not go home?'

She bit her lip, then lowered her voice. 'Home to what? Mark has gone away on business.'

He wanted to curse.

She twisted the ends of her bonnet's ribbons around her fingers. 'Mark doesn't care what I do and I don't care what he does.'

He blinked at the bitterness in her voice. And the hurt.

It occurred to him that the blame wasn't all on one side. Not once in the year of Penelope's come out had she behaved with anything but utmost decorum until she met Mark. For all her brave smiles, she was clearly out of her element here. Why hadn't he seen that? 'What did Mark do?'

She turned her face away. 'Why would I tell you?' she said in a low voice. 'You are his friend. You would just take his part.'

A cold fist clenched in his gut. Dear God, was she about to cry? He looked around desperately for some help. Rose studiously avoided his gaze, though Lady Keswick was watching him with narrowed eyes.

'Look, Penelope, I don't know what Mark did, but—'

She pushed to her feet. 'I'm going for a walk. And no, I don't want your company. Or anyone else's.' There really were tears in her eyes.

Damnation. He didn't deal with crying women. They cried. He gave them diamonds and left.

'Go with her, Rose,' Lady Keswick said, suddenly.

Garth glanced at her in surprise.

'See if you can find out what is wrong with the poor dear,' the old lady said. 'You know how these things are for young brides.'

A frowning Rosa got to her feet. 'I—'

'Go on,' Lady Keswick urged. 'Before Bannerby sees she's alone.'

'She doesn't belong here,' Garth said, watching Rose catch Penelope and walk by her side.

The old lady looked at him for a moment. 'I know. Where on earth is that husband of hers? He should have been here by now.'

Right. Where was Mark? He'd taken to disappearing quite a bit over the past year. Garth swallowed. Surely his friend didn't have a mistress? He'd seemed so happy with his wife. 'I don't know where he is.'

'Well, if he doesn't arrive soon, he'll have a good deal of trouble on his hands. Perhaps Rose can find out what is going on.'

Rose. A woman who searched other people's houses at night. He wasn't sure how she could possibly be of help. He wasn't sure he ought to let her anywhere near Mark's wife and yet he trusted her a good deal more than he trusted any of the rest of them.

A surprising admission.

Penelope was such a dainty little flower. To Rosa she looked as if she might fly away in a high wind. Fortunately today was calm. Rosa hesitated, her stomach churning even as the question formed in her mind. 'Did Lord Stanford do something?'

Lady Smythe gazed out across the waves. 'No.'

Gladness rushed through her. Good Lord, had that horrid feeling in her stomach been jealousy? Surely not? 'Was it someone else? Lady Keswick will speak to them if one of the men…' Oh, goodness, what on earth did one say? 'I mean. If one of them…'

'It is nothing so simple.' Lady Smythe turned her head and looked at Rosa, her bottom lip trembled, her clear green eyes filled with tears. 'It is Mark, my husband. He went away with another woman. I saw them together at the coaching house.'

'Oh,' Rosa said, nonplussed. 'You are sure it was your husband?'

A tear rolled down her face and she dashed it away. 'Positive.'

'Might he have been with a friend or a relative? Someone he was seeing off?' Rosa felt as if she had one foot in a very rocky boat.

'He followed her in. He was going to S-Scotland.'

'Did you suspect something was wrong? Is that why you followed him?'

'No.' She sounded so woebegone, Rosa couldn't help but put an arm around her shoulders. The slight body shuddered beneath her arm. 'I knew he was going away. On business. We had an argument and I w-wouldn't k-kiss him goodbye. But I felt so bad I went to tell him I was sorry before he left and I s-saw him.'

Rosa winced. 'Did he see you?'

'No. I turned and ran.'

'You know, there might be some reasonable explanation.'

Lady Smythe started walking again, her gaze fixed on her feet. 'He was expected home two days ago. I thought he would come. I thought he would come riding up and explain it all. And say he was sorry. Now I'm stuck here with all these horrid men.'

'No, you are not,' Rosa said. 'You don't have to stay.'

'What if there really is an innocent explanation? I've ruined everything. It's my temper.' She touched her hair. 'He'll never believe nothing happened.'

'You love him.'

'Yes.'

'And he loves you.'

'I thought he did. He said he did. Mrs Mallow said all men are like that. They marry for gain and abandon their wives.'

'Not all of them.' Her father didn't abandon his wife, even when society turned their backs. And that's why she wouldn't believe he'd abandoned his daughters. 'If he loves you, he will believe you.'

'If I had known Stanford would be here, I never would have come here in the first place.'

None of this was making any sense. The nasty feeling had returned. 'You said he didn't do anything.'

'He's Mark's best friend. He keeps telling me to go home.'

Rosa felt her jaw drop. Never would she have imagined Stanford with such chivalric tendencies. 'He's right, you know. Better to face the music than have your husband come and fetch you away.'

'Do you think so? I thought it would be romantic.'

'Like a knight on a white charger?'

She nodded.

Rosa huffed out a breath, because she honestly didn't know. She didn't have any experience at all. She'd been locked up in a girls' school until a month ago. 'You know your husband better than anyone. It is something you must decide. Or perhaps talk to Lady Keswick. She's very…shrewd about the ways of the world.'

Lady Smythe stopped walking and turned to face Rosa with a tentative smile. 'Thank you. It is such a relief to have someone to talk to.'

'I'm glad I could help.' If only her own problems were as easily solved. Not that she thought Lady Smythe would have an easy time of it, but if her husband truly loved her, it would surely work out in the end. Rosa, on the other hand, knew in her heart that she was putting off confronting her deepest fears.

They continued walking in silence. Rosa bent and picked

up a cockle shell, striped orange and white on the outside. It was pale pink on the inside. 'This is pretty, don't you think?'

'Y-yes.' She took a shuddering little breath and pointed with her toe. 'There is another. I don't think I have ever seen a shell that shade of lilac before.'

Rosa picked it up and handed it to her. Lady Smythe gazed at her with a measure of composure. 'I beg you will not say anything to Mrs Mallow about what we discussed.' She waved a hand. 'She would think me such a ninny.'

Rosa nodded. 'Not a word.'

A shout took her gaze back down the beach. Mr Fitzwilliam, waving them back. The rest of the party were wending their way to what had become a cricket pitch. Rosa was surprised to see how far they had walked from the site of the picnic. 'It seems they are ready for our game. Do you play cricket?'

'I don't have the heart for it.'

'Then perhaps you won't mind serving as the umpire.'

As was only polite, the ladies were up to bat first, and the gentlemen were in the field. Since Mrs Mallow and Mrs Phillips had drawn first in the batting order, Rosa had nothing else to do but sit on the sidelines and watch.

All the gentlemen had discarded their coats, but none looked so fine in shirtsleeves as Lord Stanford preparing to bowl. He wasn't as broad shouldered and brawny as Mr Fitzwilliam, but he had no sign of the paunch the lean Mr Phillips carried around his middle.

No, indeed. Lean and lithe, he moved with the lethal grace one observed in a predator. He reminded her of a great cat, a sleek black panther lazing in the sun, but ready to strike at a moment's notice.

Mrs Mallow defended her wicket, while the other gentlemen stood ready. Stanford drew his arm back, let the ball fly and sent it whizzing down the pitch with a grin.

In that moment, he looked younger, less dissipated, perhaps even boyish. Her heart tumbled over and over, a wild fluttering starting up in her belly as the memory of his kisses tingled on her lips.

She forced herself to look away.

A crack of the bat and Rosa whipped her head around to see the ball speed past Hapton and into the waves. He splashed into the surf, retrieved the ball and tossed it back to the wicketkeeper, one of Lady Keswick's footmen who had happily agreed to join the game.

Two runs.

'Stanford bowls well,' Rosa said to Lady Smythe.

'He threw the ball at her bat,' Lady Smythe said, her voice thickening. 'My husband does the same for me. Oh, look. Stanford is ready to bowl again.'

For all her good intentions, Rosa could not resist watching his long stride, the flexing of muscle in his shoulders and his strong thighs. The man had a pure male animalistic fire. He stole her breath.

'You like him, don't you?' Lady Smythe said.

She swallowed, hating to be caught out. She shrugged. 'I like to see a man bowl well.'

'That wasn't—'

'Howzat?' one of the fielders yelled. The stump lay on the sand behind Mrs Mallow.

'Oh, dear,' Lady Smythe said. 'She knocked it with the bat when she swung.' She signalled the out.

Rosa stood with a feeling of dread. Now it was her turn to face the bowler. She set her shoulders. She'd played cricket at school. All the girls did. And she'd been one of the best players. She wasn't going to let Lord Stanford intimidate her.

No indeed. She'd think of the ball as his head, and she'd be sure to hit it for six.

'Rotten luck,' she said to Mrs Mallow as they passed and the other woman handed her the bat.

Rosa took her place, standing facing the bowler. The grin, which had enchanted her on the sidelines, now hit her with full force, melted her from the inside out. Her heart faltered. A tremble rippled through her body.

She tightened her grip on the bat, took a deep breath and nodded her readiness.

A dark eyebrow shot up and he started to run. The thud of his steps on the hard sand travelled through the soles of her feet and up her legs in a most extraordinary manner. Seeing him running those few steps towards her was far more unnerving than seeing bullocks chasing Digger. She adjusted her grip. Kept her eye on the ball, stepped into it and swung.

Thwack. Wood on leather. A satisfying sound. The ball took flight into the dunes, heading straight at Fitzwilliam. 'Run,' Mrs Phillips yelled.

Picking up her skirts, she dashed for the other end of the pitch, where Stanford waited for the ball's return. 'Well done,' he said at her arrival in the crease. His voice dropped to a low sensual murmur. 'It is rare to find a woman who runs like a gazelle as you do. Such a pleasure to watch.' His eyes gleamed wickedly and dropped to her heaving bosom.

Rogue. He was trying to put her off.

Fitzwilliam fumbled his throw. She grinned at Stanford. 'Then watch from behind.' She started running and passed a red-faced Mrs Phillips in the middle. 'Good Lord, another two,' the other woman panted.

At the other end, Rosa turned. Still no sign of Fitzwilliam with the ball, but Stanford had moved up to cover the gap and the other men were running in.

Should she run again? She started forwards. Her partner shook her head and Rosa stayed where she was. Glad of it, too, when the ball came whizzing back to Stanford, who spun around ready to throw them out.

'Well played,' he called to her with that cheeky smile.

The other men must have thought so, too, because they had rearranged themselves to cover off the left side of the field.

They were in for a surprise. This time, Stanford didn't seem nearly as intimidating, despite that rakish grin as he ran a couple of steps before he let the ball fly. She kept her face deliberately blank as the ball came at her, much faster this time. He was showing a little respect. At the last possible moment, she altered the angle of her bat and fired the ball into the sea.

Groans of despair from the men and cheers from the women. Lady Smythe was on her feet, clapping. Not the actions of an impartial umpire at all.

Three runs. A panting Rosa stood in the crease at Lord Stanford's end of the pitch with Mrs Phillips readying her bat.

'Aren't you full of surprises?' Stanford said, tossing the ball in the air and giving her a jaunty smile.

'As are you,' she said. 'That last ball had an odd sort of curve.'

He grinned. 'Spotted it, did you?'

'I almost didn't hit it.'

'I wonder what your partner will make of it.'

The beet-faced Mrs Phillips wielded her bat more like a battledore. Rosa inwardly groaned.

He leaned closer. 'I'll go easy on her for a kiss.'

Startled, she recoiled.

He laughed. 'All's fair,' he said with a wicked lift of his brow.

His smile was infectious. Disarming. Playful. She grinned back. 'Eat your heart out, Stanford.'

He leaned closer. 'I am. For you.' He tossed the ball in the air and strode off to take up his position.

Heart racing, Rosa stared after him. A softness filled her chest. Sweet and tender. She liked him, she realised with shock. He was funny and teasing when he was not playing the sardonic rake. Something in him reached out to her. And it shouldn't. Because he was the worst sort of man.

She forced herself to focus on the game, to watch her team member, to ready herself for the ball.

Stanford bowled fast and hard. The ball hit the stump.

'You're out,' Fitzwilliam yelled from the top of a dune.

Stanford winked at Rosa. 'See. You should have kissed me,' he whispered, dark eyes dancing.

And she wished she had. Not because she cared about winning, but because there was a yearning in her heart to have him hold her close and work his magic with his mouth.

Mrs De Lacy strolled out to take Mrs Phillips's place. She proved to be an excellent player.

By the time the ladies were all out, they had racked up a nice fifteen runs and Lady Keswick had refreshments waiting, small beer for the men and fruit punch for the ladies.

'You seem to know what you are doing,' Mrs De Lacy said to Rosa. 'Will you bowl for our team?'

'If you wish.'

Mrs Phillips fanned her face. 'It is so hot.' She raised her eyes to the clear blue sky. 'Perhaps we should just declare in their favour.'

'I should think not,' Mrs Mallow said. 'You be wicket-keeper, then you don't have to run. I'll field on the water side, the grooms can cover the dunes, and Mrs De Lacy can fill in any gap.'

The men huddled off in a group. 'Planning their strategy, no doubt,' Lady Keswick said. 'Ladies, my money is on you.'

'Money?' Rosa gasped.

'I made a bet with Stanford.'

Rosa narrowed her eyes. Was that what they were doing over there, gambling on the outcome?

She marched over to Stanford and tapped him on the shoulder. He turned and smiled when he saw her. Lord, the man was tall up close. Every time she got this close she suddenly felt tiny and dainty. Which was ridiculous for a woman of her height.

'A guinea, if you please, on the ladies.'

His eyes gleamed wickedly. 'A guinea it is, but I warn you, I do not intend to let you win.'

'Let us? Sir, are you intimating that our score is not honestly achieved?'

His eyes flickered a fraction as he realised she'd caught him left footed. He inclined his head in acknowledgement. 'Indeed not, Mrs Travenor. I am happy to take your money.'

Fitzwilliam slapped him on the back.

Rosa marched back to her team-mates. 'We are going to win this game.'

'That's the spirit,' Lady Keswick said and covered her face with her handkerchief. 'I am sure you won't mind if I take a nap.'

The ladies took their positions in the field. Rosa cursed her skirts and petticoats, grasping them in one hand, and the ball in the other. She surged forwards and set her ball pelting down the pitch at Mr Phillips.

The ball hit the wicket.

'Out,' Lady Smythe called with a little more glee than was seemly.

'I wasn't ready,' Mr Phillips said, his pale face turning the shade of a newly peeled beet.

'The umpire called out,' Stanford said, lounging on a blanket. 'You should stop dreaming about your next play and focus on reality.' Phillips stomped off and sprawled on the sand.

Hapton walked to the crease to take his place. She wasn't going to catch him unawares, she could see that by the determined expression on his face. She settled into her stride.

The men's team made heavy inroads on the ladies' score; they were up to twelve, when by some lucky fluke a ball went straight up in the air. Mrs De Lacy put up her hands and closed her eyes and...unbelievably...she caught it. She opened her eyes and stared in surprise. 'You are out,' she said.

Both teams clapped.

Well, it really had been the most amazing piece of luck.

Rosa bowled out Fitzwilliam. One of her best efforts. And then she was facing Stanford.

He readied his bat. He handled it like a man who played professional cricket. She'd seen such a game once, when the school lent the local team their field because of flooding in the village. The men had been rough and ready and wore expressions just like Stanford's.

A smile curved her lips. She'd saved him a surprise.

He tapped his bat in the crease and wriggled his hips. A breath caught in her throat. He flashed her a grin and heat rose up to her hairline in a scalding rush. Wretched man. She really must stop reacting to his flirting.

Three long strides, one small hop to make sure her feet remained behind the crease and her weight was balanced, then she let the ball go, with a twist of her wrist. Too much. She realised it as soon as the ball left her hand. It careened off to the left.

'Wide,' the umpire said.

Blast. She'd let him unnerve her.

'Too bad,' Stanford said, granted a walk to her end of the pitch because of her mistake.

'It won't happen again,' she said, waiting for the ball's return. She frowned when she realised he was staring at her feet. 'Is something wrong?'

The corner of his mouth kicked up in a private smile. 'No. Just admiring your sandals.'

Strange man. There was nothing at all unusual about her shoes, except maybe that she wasn't wearing stockings. 'Incorrigible,' she muttered.

He laughed and she shook her head at him.

One of the grooms threw her the ball and she strode back to her position. She gripped the ball firmly and sent it down the pitch. It curved. Bannerby altered his position only to discover the ball straightening. It went between him and his bat and knocked the wicket askew.

'Out!' Mrs De Lacy jumped up and down in excitement.

'Very nice,' Stanford muttered as he waited for the next man to come out: Albert, the groom on the men's side. 'Where did you learn that little trick?'

'Trick?' she said innocently. 'Now what will you give me, so I won't make you lose?'

'A kiss?' he said.

She glanced at him over her shoulder with a small chuckle. 'I think not.'

She signalled her fielders to draw in close. Their only chance to win was to stump one of them out, which meant fielding the ball close to the wickets.

'Last desperate measure?' Stanford called.

'Sorry it is you at this end instead of the other?' she replied.

He laughed ruefully. 'How right you are.'

Once she was sure her ladies were in the best spots, she bowled her ball. A nice slow easy ball. Seeing his chance, Albert struck hard. It ran along the ground and bypassed Mrs Mallow. The men ran. Mrs De Lacy somehow scooped up the ball and threw it to Rosa. With a grin at the desperate face of the running groom, she knocked the stump down with the ball. 'Out,' she cried. 'We won.'

'No,' Fitzwilliam said grinning. 'It is a draw. Stanford made it to his end before you hit the stump.

A tie. A perfect ending. Though she could have used winning some money, not losing any was nearly as good. They gathered bats and balls and stumps and returned to Lady Keswick. 'Who won?' she asked, opening her eyes.

'A tie,' Stanford said. 'Which deserves a toast.' The footmen quickly distributed glasses of wine.

'To the ladies,' he toasted.

They drank in high good humour.

The sun went behind a cloud. Rosa looked up. The sky which had been clear earlier, was now filled with ominous clouds coming in from the east.

'Oh, dear,' Mrs De Lacy said. 'Do you think it will rain?'

Stanford studied the clouds for a moment. 'I shouldn't be at all surprised if we weren't in for a storm.'

As if to confirm his words, they heard the roll of thunder in the distance.

'We had best make haste,' Rosa said, and hurried off to help the grooms get Lady Keswick into her carriage.

Chapter Seven

The clock had struck one in the morning before Rosa dared make her way out of the house and into a storm that seemed to have no interest in abating. The edges of her cloak whipped out of her fingers and flew apart. Driving rain soaked the front of her gown. She put down her lantern and retied the strings tighter. She glanced back. No sign of anyone following.

This really was her last chance. She wished she'd thought of the cellars and the attic yesterday. Going out tonight was a huge risk after telling Stanford she was done searching. All evening she'd been picturing her and her sisters out on the street, or, worse yet, in a debtors' prison. If she didn't find the will tonight, she'd have to make a new plan. Not even her dream of working in the theatre would help her. She needed money now, right away.

And she'd spent the afternoon playing cricket. Flirting with Stanford. Offering advice to a woman who had never lacked for a penny in her life. Could things get any more ridiculous?

Thank goodness Stanford believed her when she said she

wasn't going to look any more. Well, there was no reason why he would not. She had meant it last night. He certainly wouldn't be looking for her to go out on a night like tonight.

She plunged into the forest. The wind dropped dramatically, though it howled in the canopy overhead. She picked up her skirts in one hand and, holding the lantern high, ran along the path, avoiding the mud as best she could.

The river sounded much louder than usual. She paused at the centre of the bridge, looking at the dark swirling water in the circle of light from her lantern. It looked angry.

She hurried on, flinching at each clap of thunder, blinking against the flashes of lightning. No light shone from Inchbold's cottage. Nor did she expect it, but it would have been nice to see his cheerful face. She soon had the back door open and stepped inside. The wind rattled the windows and shrieked down the chimney. She shivered. An empty house in a storm was a lonely place indeed.

Cellars first, or attic? The thought of the cellars made her shiver again. Then that was where she must start or she might avoid them altogether, although she really didn't think her father would have kept important papers down there. She really had her hopes pinned on the attic.

She took a deep breath. Cellars first.

A low arched door led to the cellars from the kitchen. She'd never been down the stairs, but she'd known of their existence.

She lifted the latch and opened the door and gasped at the smell of mould and damp. A set of stone steps twisted downwards into darkness. Holding her lantern high with one hand and the wooden balustrade with the other, she marched boldly down the steps.

A narrow passageway led past a series of archways, some of them with doors that were open, some with no doors at all. The cellars were ancient and the ceilings low. As she peered into all the empty spaces a feeling of hopelessness filled her chest. A fool's errand. She had to stop hoping, it was just too painful each time her hopes were dashed.

Footsteps. Loud. On the steps. She whirled around, her lantern casting dizzying shadows. Another lantern twinkled at the far end near the stairs. Her stomach did a belly flop. 'Who is it?'

'Find anything?' a cool mocking voice asked.

'Stanford,' she gasped over the sound of her pounding heart. 'You scared me. What are you doing here?'

'Thought you'd give me the slip, did you?' He had to bend his neck to prevent hitting his head on the arching ceiling.

She bit her lip. 'Yes.'

His laugh echoed off the walls. 'Well, I have bad news for you.'

'You found me.'

'That's not the worst of it. The bridge is out.'

She stared at him, then, as he lowered his lantern, she saw that he was soaked to the waist and dripping water in a puddle all round him.

'Oh, no. You fell in the river. You could have drowned.'

'Wouldn't that have solved your problems?'

'Hardly. What sort of person would wish another drowned? Why did you follow me? I told you I was done here.'

He stared at her silently for a moment. 'And like a fool I believed you.'

He sounded a little bitter. She recalled his opinion of women as liars with an odd sinking feeling that she'd proved him right in her case, too. 'Oh.'

'It's a good thing I saw you from the library window, or you might have found yourself in the river on the way home.'

He was right, dash it. 'Then I must be glad you are here.' She did feel glad. Far happier than she had a moment ago. Because even though she'd found nothing in the cellar, the feeling of despair had receded, as if the light of his lantern had driven it back.

'Did you find anything?'

'There is nothing down here but some empty barrels, dust and a heap of coal.

He walked past her down the passageway, peering in the empty cellars much as she had. 'Not much of a cellar.'

'I think they were built for the original house. It burned down in the seventeenth century.'

He turned and came back to her. 'You know a lot about this house.' He sounded suspicious again.

She shrugged. 'I told you. I lived here. You learn things about a house when you live in it.'

'I suppose you do. Are you done down here?'

She sighed. 'Yes. I can't imagine anyone keeping anything of value down here. It is too damp.'

'And cold,' he said with a shiver.

'Perhaps we should light a fire and get you dry?'

His eyes widened. 'Why, Mrs Travenor, are you asking me to remove my clothes?'

Heat enveloped her. 'Of c-course n-not,' she stuttered.

'Then you are thinking of parking me beside a nice warm fire while you go off and search on your own. I don't think so.'

Horrid suspicious man. Dash it, let him think what he liked. 'Suit yourself. But if you come down with the ague, don't complain to me.'

'I wouldn't dream of it. Shall we?'

He escorted her back up the steps into the kitchen.

'The servants' stairs to the attic is this way,' she said.

'After you,' he said.

The sound of squelching followed her up the stairs.

'Perhaps if you took off your boots,' she suggested, imagining how uncomfortable he must feel.

'I'll keep them on,' he said.

Stubborn idiot.

'Did you say something?' he asked.

Oh, Lord, had she spoken aloud? 'No. Not a word.' She continued the climb, past the first, second and third floors. The stairs came to an end on the fourth floor. She opened the small door at the top. 'These are the servants' quarters,' she said. 'At least, those of the lower servants—the housekeeper and butler have rooms on the ground floor since there is no room for them in the cellar.'

'You think this picture is in the servants' rooms?'

'No. There is storage at the end.' She walked quickly past the cramped chambers where the female servants would have slept in twos and threes. 'Through here.' Another small door barred their way.

She tried the handle. 'It's locked.'

'Because the owner doesn't want anyone going in there,' he said drily.

'Or because he doesn't want the female servants sneaking through here to visit the men,' she said equally drily.

'Good Lord, is that how to keep them apart?'

He was laughing at her. This really wasn't an appropriate topic of conversation, was it? 'I need to get in here.'

'Do you want me to break down the door?'

'Do you think you could?'

'No. It is solid oak.'

She gazed at the heavy wooden door. 'Then why offer? Perhaps we should try from the other side.'

'There might be a key in the kitchen.'

So there might. They trailed back down the stairs. A quick search through the drawers in the dresser beside the hearth revealed a bunch of keys.

'The housekeeper must have left them here.'

'How very obliging,' Stanford drawled.

'Are you insinuating I knew of their existence?'

'You do have a key to the back door.'

'Yes, I do. The groundskeeper gave it to me. He said nothing about this set of keys.'

'Oh, yes, your accomplice.'

'Accomplice? Oh, that is really too much. You still think I am here to steal.'

'My dear Mrs Travenor. I don't think, I know. You already told me you are.'

'I only want what belongs to me. Nothing else.' She glared at him and saw that he still didn't believe her. 'Oh, never mind. Come on, let us see if one of these keys work, but quite honestly you would be better off making a fire and getting yourself dry.'

She stomped out of the kitchen and back upstairs. He followed in silence.

Blast him, she hoped he froze to death. It would serve him right.

After a few tries, she found the key that fitted the lock and the door swung back. The room was stuffed full of tables and chairs and carpets.

Over against the wall where the roof came down almost to the floor, almost buried by a huge rug and behind an assortment of pictures, she spotted her father's desk. The one that had once been in the study. 'There,' she said. 'The desk.'

'Wouldn't the miniature more likely be with the pictures?' he asked.

'It's small. He would have put it somewhere safe.'

'And I suppose you want me to move everything so you can rifle through the drawers.'

'It would give you a purpose for being here.'

He laughed and set his lantern down. The first thing he grabbed was the rug. A cloud of dust rose. They both started coughing.

Stanford flung it to one side. More dust flew. He picked up a portrait, the frame gilded and heavily carved. 'It weighs as much as a pony,' he grunted, setting it up against the rug.

Rosa moved some of the smaller pictures and set them on one side and moved a lamp out of the way.

The desk was clear, but the drawers were obstructed.

'We'll have to pull it out.'

Stanford heaved the heavy oak piece as if it weighed nothing, though he did make a grunt in his throat.

'That's far enough,' she said. Quickly, she opened the lid. It had assorted drawers and little pigeon-holes, but as she felt around with her fingers she discovered nothing like the catch in the escritoire. No secret compartments.

She pulled out the drawers each side of the knee hole. The desk was completely empty.

She felt around again, hoping against hope she had missed something. Not a knot or indentation did she feel.

Her stomach slid sideways. Her knees felt weak.

It wasn't here. A lump formed in her throat. Hot moisture stung the backs of her eyes. Grandfather was right. Father hadn't cared.

All hope fled.

She'd have to write to Grandfather again. On behalf of the girls. She didn't care about herself.

She glanced up to find Stanford watching her intently.

'It's not here,' she said, trying to sound casual, and failing miserably as her voice broke.

'I'm sorry.' He sounded sorry. And uncomfortable.

She turned to put back the drawers and surreptitiously wiped her eyes. He didn't need to know how hard this blow had hit. 'I suppose we should put this back where we found it.'

'I doubt anyone will care. Is there anywhere else you want to look? There's a chest over in that corner. I could dig it out.'

Surprised, she darted a glance at his face. For once he looked genuinely concerned. Almost as if he believed her.

She looked at the chest, brown leather and bound in brass. It wasn't something she recognised. 'I suppose we could look inside.'

Once more he cleared a path through the items piled up in the room. Dust flew up in clouds while the rain drummed on the roof, inches above their heads.

Thankfully the chest wasn't locked and she easily lifted the lid.

'Oh,' she said, realising instantly what she was seeing. The tools of her mother's trade. Wigs and feathers and face paint. Even a costume or two.

Stanford leaned over her shoulder. 'Any luck?'

It was possible her father had hidden the will in here. Of all the places her grandfather was likely to look, this would be the last. Anything to do with her mother's lowly profession made him shudder with revulsion.

Carefully she lifted out a pair of old-fashioned green leather shoes with paste buckles, faded ribbons and paper stuffed in the toes.

'I say,' Stanford said, leaning over her. 'Look at this.' He pulled out a mask. The kind revellers wore in Venice, turquoise, with fancy embroidery, a pointed beak and feathers. A peacock's face.

'It is beautiful.' She set the shoes aside.

He dropped the mask on top of them. 'Hah, what about this one?' He placed the scary devil mask against his face, his eyes gleaming through the eyeholes. 'Am I a handsome fellow?'

'Much better looking than usual.'

'Oh, a wisty caster,' he said with a wink.

She lifted out a diaphanous piece of fabric covered in spangles. At first she thought it must be a shawl, then when she looked closer, she realized it was a gown. Something her mother had worn on stage.

'Very nice,' Stanford said, his eyes dancing. 'Would you care to try it on?'

Mortified, she folded it carefully and added it to the pile beside the chest. She lifted out the rest of the costumes without investigating what they were until the bottom of the chest sat bare before them. 'It's not here,' she said.

'I see that.' He glanced around. 'There doesn't seem to anything else that might contain a hiding place.

Rosa couldn't take her gaze from Mama's trunk. She hadn't even known it existed. She would love to have been able to keep it. To look through it properly. Reluctantly she put everything back and closed the lid. No doubt Grandfather would throw it away if he saw it and its contents. She had the feeling that once that happened it would be as if Mama never existed.

Sadness squeezed her heart. And not just because Father had forgotten her and her sisters. It seemed he'd also forgotten their mother. The woman for whom he'd been prepared to give up everything. Perhaps in the end he'd decided he'd made a mistake.

With a sigh she rose to her feet and let her gaze sweep the cramped space. 'I don't think there is anywhere else to look.'

Saying the words brought her situation home with the force of a gale. Her hopes were built on a foundation of sand and everything was about to tumble down around her ears.

Now what should she do? Write to Grandfather again? Beg him to look after the girls, even if he wouldn't lift a finger for her? It wasn't their fault she'd borrowed the money. If he wouldn't help, they would have to fend for themselves.

She was the one who had incurred the debt. She was the one who would have to go to prison.

Even if she landed a role as an opera singer in London, it

might be weeks before she earned enough to pay off the debt unless the moneylender would accept something on account. It was a hopeful thought.

'Mrs Travenor?'

She glanced up. 'I'm sorry. Did you say something?'

'I was wondering if you would like me to unroll the carpets?'

He looked sorry, caring, as if he'd like to help. There was nothing he could do.

She shook her head with a brief smile. 'The carpets would have been taken up long after we left.' She squared her shoulders as she thought of the task in front of her. 'It isn't here. I'll leave the back-door key with these others in the kitchen. I won't need it again.'

Stanford must have seen her distress, much as she tried to hide it, because he gave her an encouraging smile. 'We could try the other rooms again. I don't think we'll be leaving here tonight.'

She stared at him aghast. 'Not leave?'

'I told you, the bridge is down.'

She had to leave. Grandfather would arrive in the morning. She could not be found here with Stanford. 'We will go around by the lane.'

'We could try,' he agreed. 'But it's a three-mile walk and, if you hadn't noticed, it's raining cats and dogs. Who is to say that the lane isn't flooded? There are three bridges between here and The Grange according to the map I saw.'

'Three miles? How can it be? It takes fifteen minutes to walk here through the woods.'

His lips thinned as if she'd called him a liar. 'I assure you it is. The lane goes around the woods to the village, just as the lane to The Grange goes around the fields in the other direction to the village. There is no lane between the two houses apart from the path through the woods and, as I mentioned, the bridge is down.'

'Well, there is no need to be unpleasant about it.'

He took a step towards her, as if he'd like to shake her, but he'd forgotten the low ceiling. He banged his head. 'Blast.'

The shock on his face made her giggle. The small laugh released some of the pressure on her chest. Got her mind working again, instead of going around and around in the same old circle.

He gave her a sour look, rubbing his forehead, then he grinned. 'Trust me, it is a three-mile walk.'

She sighed. 'Oh, I believe you.' Well, of course she did. If anything could go wrong, it did. 'Then we had best get started.'

He shook his head. 'No. Not in the dark in a raging storm.' As if to confirm his words, a thunderclap reverberated through the house, making her jump. It grumbled into silence, leaving the sound of rain beating against the roof. 'We will light a fire, get dry and set off at first light.'

Spend the night? 'What will people say?'

His jaw dropped. 'What people?'

She twisted her hands together. 'The owner is due here tomorrow. That is why I came again tonight. What if he finds us here in the morning?'

He glanced down at the hem of her gown, mired in mud and the dust from the floors. 'We will leave at first light. Long before anyone is on the road.'

'If you are too fine to get a little damp, I will go by myself.'

At that moment her lantern winked out, leaving only his alight.

'Good luck in the dark,' he said. 'Unless you know the whereabouts of a supply of oil.'

Negotiating a country lane would be hard enough with a

lantern when there wasn't a storm. To do so on a night like tonight would be foolish.

'Very well, but we will have to leave the moment it is light.'

'The instant, I promise. Let's get downstairs to the kitchen before my light goes out. I noticed a stack of wood on the hearth in the kitchen. We can light the fire.'

'So *now* you want to light a fire.' She huffed out a breath.

He looked down at her and there was a strange expression on his face. He hesitated, then smiled his devil-may-care smile. 'After you.'

She hurried down the stairs to the kitchen. In short order they had kindling on the fire and a merry blaze. But there weren't many logs and they would soon burn through them.

'I'll fetch some of that coal up from the cellar while you get out of those wet clothes,' she said.

He nodded. He looked a bit demonic in the light from the fire, all axe-hard angles and shadowed hollows. Not scary, though. Just terribly wicked. Her stomach gave a funny little lurch.

'Now there is a suggestion I never thought I would hear pass your lips.'

Uncomprehending, she blinked. Then his words made sense and heat flooded her face. 'Wretch. This is no time for jokes.'

'Well, I just thought I'd mention that once my clothes are off, I will be naked.'

Oh, right. 'Wait a moment.'

She went into the drawing room and pulled the covers off a couple of chairs. She brought them back to the kitchen. 'They might be a bit dusty, but you can use one as a towel and the other one as a robe.' She grabbed the coal scuttle beside the hearth, and the lantern. 'I'll get the coal before we lose the last of our light.' She ran down the stairs, trying not to imagine him removing his garments.

She shovelled coal into the bucket. He'd looked fine in his shirtsleeves this afternoon. Naked, he'd probably look like one of the many statues littering The Grange. 'Really, Rosabella,' she muttered, 'have you no shame? Just because you pretend to be a widow, doesn't mean you should think like one.' She picked up the heavy scuttle and staggered back to the stairs.

A white apparition stood at the top. She gave a little squeak.

'Give me the coal,' the apparition said, running down to help.

When he entered the light cast by her lantern, he looked more like a mummy than a Greek god.

With a nervous giggle she handed him the bucket and went ahead up the stairs. 'Thank you,' she said when they reached the top. 'That bucket was heavy.'

It didn't look heavy in his hands; his naked arms were beautifully formed. So were his shoulders. She couldn't take her eyes off their sculpted curves and the way they flexed as he set the bucket down on the hearth. Her fingers longed to touch the swell of flesh on his upper arm, to see if it was hard or soft. His forearms were huge and dusted with dark hair. By comparison her arms looked like twigs. He was... delicious.

Embarrassed, she turned away. 'I should hang up my cloak to dry,' she said, then pressed her lips together at the hoarse sound of her voice as if sand lined her throat. She swallowed hard.

'Take off your shoes and stockings, too,' he said. 'Your feet must be as damp as mine.'

Her head jerked around.

He wasn't looking at her, he was busy placing lumps of

coal on the fire with tongs. There was nothing salacious in his voice, just plain practicality, but her heart was pounding like the hooves of a runaway horse.

When she didn't answer, he turned his head to look at her. Firelight danced in his eyes and lit his full sensual mouth. Lips that had enslaved her body to his will.

He stood up, hands on hips. The fire outlined his shape. She could…oh, saints above, she could see the outline of his legs where he stood with them wide apart. She forced her gaze to move to his face, not to take stock of the way the sheet clung to his hips, or the bulge between his thighs. But even lifting her gaze wasn't safe when she encountered his broad chest, or the wide shoulders emerging from the white fabric.

He glared at her. 'Do you think I would take advantage of you?'

Her stomach did a little dance of hopeful glee. She took a quick breath to still it. 'I— No, of course not.'

She grabbed her cloak from the chair where she had flung it when she came in and shook out its folds. 'If we move the chair closer, we can use it as a drying horse.'

'Good idea,' he replied, though there was a bit of mockery in his voice. 'It will make a good place to dry your stockings.'

He was right. Her feet were wet. In her anxiety to search, she really hadn't noticed the physical discomfort, but now there was no hope to buoy her spirits, the damp was creeping into her bones. It was also creeping cold and chill into her heart, but there was nothing she could do about that. Nothing at all.

She went behind the chair and removed her footwear and then her stockings while he continued building the fire. She hung the stockings over the chair back and put her shoes on the hearth. He glanced around and nodded. 'I'll get another chair for my things.' He dragged two more chairs forwards, making a semicircle around the hearth, and draped his clothes over them. 'Hmm. Something is missing. Sit down beside the fire. I'll be back in a moment.' He picked up the lantern and disappeared.

Already the fire had a nice red glow in the middle. Its warmth permeated through her skirts. The scent of burning wood and coal filled the room. Cosy. Intimate. Comforting.

How could she be comforted with a man wearing nothing but a sheet? A man she found far too attractive for her own good. A man renowned for his powers of seduction.

Despite his assertions, given her weakness where he was concerned, she'd be a fool not to think him dangerous.

Forewarned was forearmed. Wasn't it?

Chapter Eight

'Here we are.' She looked up to find Stanford with his arms full of red velvet cushions. 'I remembered seeing these in the library. More comfortable than sitting on the floor.'

He spread them around until they looked like a bed.

Feeling a little foolish, she sat on one edge. He was right, it was more comfortable. She hugged her arms around her knees, careful to keep her feet well covered, and gazed into the fire, while he settled himself beside her.

The lamp wavered and went out. Now all they had was the glow from the fire to see by. There might be some remnants of candles in the library, she recalled, but they wouldn't last long. And why would they need more light? There was nothing to do.

It was a bit like being in a cave; with the ladder-back chairs draped in clothes behind them and the stone chimney breast with its fire in front, she could almost imagine them spending the night on the side of a mountain, isolated from the world, living in their cave with no one to bother them.

Startled by her odd thoughts, she blinked and broke the flame's hold on her vision.

'This is cosy,' he said dreamily, as if he, too, were caught in another world. 'Too bad I don't have a deck of cards.'

'It is too dark to play cards.'

He grunted. 'Then what shall we do to pass the time while we dry?'

She shrugged.

'I know. You can tell me all about yourself.'

'Nothing to tell,' she said, suddenly wary.

'Where did you grow up?'

'Here. I told you that.'

'And when you left?'

'I went to school. I told you that, too.'

'What about Mr Travenor? How did you meet him?'

Blankly, she stared at him.

'Your husband,' he said with a frown.

Good heavens, she'd almost forgotten her invented husband. She struggled to remember the tale she had told Lady Keswick when she applied for the position of companion last month. She'd read that the elderly woman had bought the house next to Gorham Place in *The Times*. Then she'd seen her advertisement for a companion.

'I'm sorry.' His deep voice held compassion. 'If it is too painful for you to talk about him, please don't think you must. I should not have asked.'

She looked away, unable to look him in the eyes and tell untruths. 'I do prefer not to talk about him.' That at least was a half-truth. Who would want to talk about a man who existed only in her imagination? In her mind she'd created the perfect husband, honourable, faithful, the image of her father. Only the image now seemed tarnished.

Father had changed. The man she recalled with such fondness would never have married another woman, never have sent his beloved girls to a school far away in the north, and never have not visited them.

For years, she had waited for him to visit.

She could not put the two men together. The laughing man who had spun her around and who had put her on her first pony—

Stanford muttered something under his breath.

She turned her head. 'I'm sorry.'

'I said I'm an idiot. My callous question upset you.'

'Oh,' she said. 'I wasn't thinking about Mr Travenor. I was remembering growing up in this house.'

'More sad memories?'

'Not at all. They were the best times of my life. My father was kind, my mother adored him. He spoiled his girls, as he called us. We were happy here.'

'You were lucky, then.'

'Yes. There was always lots of laughter in this house. And singing.' She bit the inside of her lip. It was wrong to be ashamed of Mama. She'd been a beautiful woman and had a truly exceptional voice. She deserved her daughters' pride. 'My mother was an opera singer before she met my father. She sang on the stage in Venice. My father fell in love with her the first time he saw her.'

Stanford straightened. 'Good lord, and he married her?'

She smiled. 'Much to his father's annoyance. As my mother told it, Grandfather tried to have their marriage annulled because it was celebrated in a Roman Catholic church. My father simply obtained a special licence and married her again.'

She sighed. 'They didn't care what people thought. They were happy here, together.'

'But she died.'

She nodded. 'She died giving birth to a son. Father was devastated. I think he blamed himself.'

'You inherited your mother's voice.'

She chuckled softly. 'Mother was thrilled. I can remember

performing in the drawing room for the few friends who stuck by Father after his marriage. Mother loved to sing and we would all take part in productions. *Rinaldo* was her favourite, for she got to play the man. My voice is very much like hers. I have sometimes thought I might like to go on the stage. Quite shocking, I know.'

'With that voice, and…' he hesitated '…and your face and figure, you would take London by storm, though it is hardly a respectable profession.'

'I would make lots of money.'

'Is that what you want?'

'I'm not sure I am good enough. My voice isn't trained. I would need to take lessons.' It would all take far too long.

She really needed to think of something else. It was not what her parents had wanted for her, but then they hadn't expected her to end up in debt.

If Mama had lived, or Papa had abided by his promise to see them well cared for, then the idea of becoming an opera singer would never have entered her head.

'Did your husband leave you nothing?'

'He earned very little as a curate.'

A silence descended. She glanced at his brooding expression as he stared into the fire. He seemed to have withdrawn into himself. Perhaps he also saw the past in the flames.

'Where did you grow up?' she asked.

'Not far from here, actually,' he said, lifting his head to look at her. Hot hunger lit his eyes and sent a *frisson* of awareness through her body. A longing to be consumed by the fires. Desire. She had no illusions. His powers of seduction were legendary and she had already learned she had no armour against him. Partly because she liked him more than she should. Much more.

He blinked and his eyes cooled, leaving only a smile. The sweet boyish one that pulled at her heart and left her in disarray. It was like a glimpse behind a mask at the real man. Or perhaps it was yet another mask, the one designed for seduction. She wished she knew for certain which, but since she did not, she must remain wary.

'I grew up not far from Brighton,' he said.

'Do you have brothers or sisters?'

His face took on a cynical expression. 'One younger brother.' His lashes swept down, hiding his eyes. 'Half-brother, in truth.'

'Your father married again?'

'I would that were the case,' he said rather mysteriously. 'My brother did well for himself as a shipowner. Recently he married a duke's daughter and went to America. They are expecting their first child. My mother is in alt.' He sounded bitter.

'You aren't pleased at your brother's good fortune?'

He drew himself upright. 'I am delighted for Kit. He's a good man. *He* deserves all that is good and more.'

'But you don't?' She didn't know what made her ask that question, except for the emphasis on the word *he*. When his gaze shot to capture hers she truly wished she hadn't opened her mouth, because the evidence was there in his eyes. A bleakness she'd never noticed before. It chilled her.

'Do you think you can read minds?' he mocked. 'See into other people's souls?'

She recoiled. Clearly she'd trod where angels feared to go. 'I beg your pardon. I did not mean anything. Idle chatter.'

'It seems neither of us is good at small talk.' His tone had gentled and his brows went up quizzically.

No sense in taking umbrage under the circumstances. They were caught here, together. She should try to get along with him. She smiled. 'In truth, I can't say I have had a great deal of practice.'

He chuckled softly 'You are a surprising woman, Mrs

Travenor. Or may I call you Rose?' He glanced down at himself. 'It is hard to retain formality when sitting wrapped in nothing but a sheet beside a fire with a beautiful woman. My name is Garth, by the way.' The seductive note softened his voice. A hot shiver ran down her spine to land low in her belly. The rake had returned. Now she must truly be on her guard.

'Sheet or no, I expect you to be a gentleman.'

He inclined his head, but amusement played about his lips. 'I promise nothing will happen that you do not want.'

Want. She was full of wants and all of them confusing. Another hot shiver. She had no way of dealing with him. No quick repartee or double-edged sally. Why had he come here? All he wanted to do was flirt. Or worse. Meanwhile her life teetered on the brink of disaster.

Panic rose in her throat. She'd have to go north. Present herself to the bailiffs. Prison. Meg and Sam would have to find work as governesses, lady companions, teachers. Meg would be fine. She was strong and would manage. Sam was just so sickly.

Perhaps if she wrote to Grandfather again and—

'I did want to thank you for talking to Lady Smythe this afternoon.' The sound of his voice made her jump. 'Did she say why she left London?'

Lady Smythe. She closed her eyes, pictured the tearful woman on the beach. 'I think she plans to go home.'

He let go a long sigh. 'Thank God.' He shifted, angling towards her. 'Now I can focus all my attention on you.'

His smile caused an ache deep in her chest. 'I'd really prefer you didn't.'

'You are a very beautiful woman, Rose.'

She couldn't resist that voice or that smile. Yet she should. 'And your intentions are less than honourable.' She could hear the smile in her voice.

'I make no pretence about my intentions.' His voice had dropped to a low seductive murmur. 'We would deal well together, you and I.'

Her body hummed in response. With all the worries pressing in on her, somehow, in this moment, he made her feel good. Far better about herself than anyone had ever made her feel for years. What would it be like to have such a man in her life? To share her burdens?

Stanford—no, Garth—wasn't offering marriage, or permanence or love. Although he hadn't said the words, she had no illusions. He was offering a *carte blanche*. The kind of relationship Grandfather would have happily accepted between her mother and father. It was the marriage he'd found objectionable.

How would he feel if he discovered his eldest granddaughter had gone down that road? He probably wouldn't care. Or he'd see it as proof he was right all along about her mother.

It was not the relationship she'd dreamed of for herself. She'd wanted a home, and children, and, most of all, love. The true love she'd seen in her parents' eyes.

True love was a luxury when you and your sisters were facing debtors' prison.

She really couldn't see any other option. And he really seemed to like her. Almost as much as she liked him, though she hadn't dare admit it.

Something had changed. Garth sensed it across his skin. The heat in the room had gone up as if the fire had doubled in size. Instead of Rose backing away as he'd half expected, she was looking at him the way a cat looked at a plump mouse who had wandered across its path.

Why would he be surprised? She was female, wasn't she? Worse yet, why the hell was he disappointed? He didn't harbour naïve notions about any of them. Especially not this one after all he'd learned about her.

He glanced down to discover her feet still primly tucked beneath the hem of her gown.

Prim. Even now, when desire perfumed the air, she was as prim as a nun. Was his hopeful imagination playing tricks?

As if sensing his question, her toes emerged, followed by the rest of her feet. Narrow feet, with high arches and long slender toes, except for the small one on her right foot. That one curled over. A tiny blemish on what were the prettiest feet he'd ever seen. And her ankles were nice, too, well turned and slender.

She brushed one against the other shyly.

His body hardened.

He dragged his gaze back to her face. Her gaze was fixed on his face. She licked her lips, making them moist.

Gently, so as not to scare her, he raised his fingertips to her chin and angled her face for easier access to those sweetly curved lips.

She swallowed and closed her eyes.

'Not scared, are you, sweeting?' he whispered against her mouth.

'No,' she whispered back, but her voice shook on the word.

A kiss or two wouldn't hurt. Although if the last kiss was anything to go by, he would have trouble stopping once he started. There was something about this woman that called to his most primal self. And it wasn't just the sight of her bare feet.

Indeed, they were the icing on an already delicious cake. A cake he should not be tasting if she was unwilling.

She leaned closer, making her desires known. Her mouth brushed his lips. Her tongue licked where her lips had touched.

He caught her nape and pressed his mouth to hers. She

turned into him, little sounds of approval coming from deep in her throat, her hands caressing his shoulders and arms.

She tasted sweet. Like honey or sugar and something far more exotic.

He breathed deep, inhaling her perfume. Jasmine.

Why was he questioning this? They were both adults, free to make their own decisions. And he'd been looking for this from the moment he had seen her. He would woo her, seduce her and show her a few things her curate husband wouldn't have known.

He deepened the kiss. Slowly she sank back against the cushions, her body soft and warm beneath him, her hands wandering his bare back in an erotically delicate, yet feverish, exploration.

He experienced a moment of shock as he realised just how much he wanted this woman. Not just carnally, which went without saying, but on some spiritual level, as if closeness with her could somehow beat back the darkness in his life.

A sigh of pleasure as his hand encompassed her breast through her gown drove the annoyingly awkward thought from his mind. His fingers tingled at the wild flutter of her heart beneath the soft flesh, and the rapid rise and fall of her chest with each breath. The desire to please shocked him, but since he wanted her, then he would ensure she wanted him with equal fervour. He would ply all his years of experience to drive this woman mad with longing until she begged for completion.

Slowly, gently, he lifted his lips from hers, lingering only to taste her lips lightly, then brought himself up on his elbows, one each side of her head. He gazed down into her lovely face gilded by firelight. *Beautiful* did not begin to describe the finely moulded bones beneath the warm-toned skin. There was haughtiness in the high cheekbones and the straight nose. Passion in the full lips reddened and pouting from his kisses. Untapped passion.

Her large dark eyes gazed back at him, heavy lidded and smoky. Lust clawed at his belly at the banked fires he saw in her steady even gaze.

He had the feeling that when those embers burst into flame, they would consume him.

He drew a deep unsteady breath and cradled her face in his hands. 'You are lovely,' he whispered.

She smiled her sultry smile and her even white teeth contrasted with the red of her lips. He rubbed his thumb across the fullness of her lower lip. She licked it.

His body clenched with pleasure.

With fingers that shook with the desire gripping his body, he traced the line of cheekbone and jaw. He brushed the back of his hand across the soft hollow of her cheek, pulled her hair free of its pins and speared his fingers in the luxurious black wings of hair at her temples. Soft and thick tresses haloed her face. The face of a temptress.

His body hardened to rock.

He shook his head at her. 'Who are you?'

Her eyes widened. Her lovely throat moved as she swallowed. 'Just a woman,' she said, her throaty voice rough.

'An unexpected gift,' he said and bent to plunder her mouth with his tongue.

The soft noise of pleasure from her throat urged him on. He slanted his head for better access to the hot recess of her mouth, and trailed one hand down her length, caressing the deep indent of her waist and the soft swell of her hip. Lovely womanly curves filled his palm and painted a picture of her beautiful body in his mind. He stroked her tongue and she tasted his with an eager enthusiasm that almost unmanned him.

He took a deep steadying breath and bunched the fabric

of her skirts, drawing them up to her hips. She gave a littl
gasp of surprise.

He lifted his head and glanced down at her, questionir

In that moment, he could have sworn she looked nervo
yet when she smiled and grabbed his shoulders, he decid
it was a trick of the light. That her gasp was pleasure, ot
surprise.

He palmed the long slender thigh, kneading and stro ng
in turn, slowly pressing his knee between hers.

She shifted beneath him, parting her thighs, welco ing
him into the cradle of her hips. Accommodating him as if
he belonged there. It felt so damned good. He nuzzled t her
neck, blew in her ear, heard her whimpers of ecstasy ithin
every bone and nerve in his body.

The urge to press into her heat plunged him i o hot
unthinking darkness. Only by force of will did he re in the
strength to take it slowly, because he had another riving
need: to ensure her climax. Anything less would unac-
ceptable.

He pressed kisses to the swells of her bosom ove her
gown, licking at the valley between them.

Her hips undulated against his shaft, sending ood, hot
and thick, coursing through him. He pulled at th ibbon at
the top of her bodice, untied the bow and pulled e bodice
down, revealing the top of a practical linen sh and her
stays. He traced the edge of the shift with a finge , dipping
beneath the fabric to brush a tightly budded ni le.

She drew in a hiss of breath

'You like that?' he murmured.

She nodded, her teeth worrying her bottom lip as if she
found it too hard to speak.

'You will like it better, if we remove your gown.'

A look of doubt crossed her face.

He wanted to curse. Had the curate-husband never pleasured her naked? No wonder she seemed almost innocent in her responses. The man had probably never bothered to do more than bring himself release without seeing to hers. Well, she wouldn't be the only widow he'd introduced to sensual delight.

'I promise you will be more than satisfied,' he whispered wickedly in her ear. She shivered.

He smiled.

Rosa had learned some things about the physical relations between a man and a woman since becoming Lady Keswick's companion. The married ladies in the company had been forthright in their discussions of bedsport among themselves. And in their acknowledgement of enjoyment.

If the thrills invading every part of her body were part of the experience, then she now knew whereof they spoke. Garth's kisses on her lips were wonderful, but now as he kissed the rise of her breast with his hot mouth, the heat in her blood and the pulses of sweet longing inside her resulted in the most delicious sensations deep inside her body.

She could hardly think while her body felt as if it was on fire. A fire only he could quench.

It wasn't wrong, this delight of the flesh. Her parents had clearly enjoyed their physical intimacy from the way they'd touched when thinking they were unobserved, and they had always shared a bed. But they'd been married.

They'd loved each other.

Not that love was a necessary component to passion. A married woman was entitled to take her pleasure where she willed as long as she was discreet, according to the women visiting Lady Keswick. Indeed, it seemed almost a point of pride with them.

A single woman would be ruined by such behaviour. Shunned.

Her heart gave a little squeeze for what would never be. Marriage. Family. Love. But very few people found love. Perhaps her sisters wouldn't reject her when they learned she had done this for their sake, to give them the chance of love, or at least a chance for a happy marriage.

He raised his head from tormenting her breast to look into her face. She keenly felt the loss of his mouth on her sensitised flesh.

He smoothed the hair back from her temples. 'Are you all right?'

Had he somehow sensed her roiling thoughts? Her inner fears?

He had a beautiful face. Sinister, yes. Even his smile was dark and dangerous, and the angles of his face were so hard they might have been cut with a blade. And yet he could be gentle, too, and fun. She smiled at him. 'I'm fine.'

'Only fine?' he growled, the smile on the lips belying the roughness in his voice. 'Then I am not at my best tonight.'

A chuckle rose in her throat; daring took hold of her tongue. 'Then you must try harder.'

His shoulders shook a little, and then he laughed deep in his chest. The rumble set up a pleasant vibration along her skin. 'Then we must be rid of this gown, my dear sweet Rose.'

Oh, how neatly he turned things to his advantage. A charming rogue. A practised seducer. A rake.

Which was all to her advantage, for no honourable man would let her use her body to buy her way out of her misfortune. Not if he knew her true identity.

Don't think of that now. The truth would not help her. She must manage with what she had.

She reached up and ran her hands across the breadth of his shoulders, smoothed the gilded flesh of arms sculpted as fine as any statue and sensually warm to the touch. She laughed. 'Then you need to rise, sir.'

'I, you saucy wench, am already well risen.' He tickled her chin, pressed a kiss to her mouth and stood up.

The sheet dropped to the floor. And there he was, outlined by the glow from the fire in all his male glory.

Open-mouthed, she stared at his large male part jutting up from the dark curls at his loins.

She knew what it was, and where it was supposed to go, but she had never expected it to be quite so substantial, or so stiff. Now the terms 'riding the pike' and 'mounting the pole' that the women had used as they discussed their adventures made more sense. The only male parts she had seen on statues were, though fascinating to her maidenly eyes, tiny wormlike appendages. They were nothing like this.

Nervously, her gaze shot up to his face. His expression was smug. 'Do I please you, sweet Rose?'

She swallowed. 'Yes.' Oh, dear, that sounded just a little more tentative than she had intended.

He tilted his head on one side and then silently reached out a hand. 'Come, let us have you out of that gown.' He easily pulled her to her feet and spun her around.

One hand came around her waist and pulled her back against him. She could feel his member hard against her buttocks. The heat of his body permeated through her gown. His other hand swept her hair from her neck and his lips nuzzled at her nape. She arched her back at the pleasurable sensation.

'So sensual,' he mumbled against her skin. 'I want to eat you all up.'

The words and the lick of his tongue across her nape sent shivers rampaging across her skin. Lovely shivers that penetrated her bones and reached deep inside her core.

He drew her closer, rocking against her, with a soft groan. His hand left her hair and slid down to squeeze and knead her bottom, and the hand at her waist moved up to cup her breast in a hot caress, as the rocking of his hips continued. 'So soft,' he murmured.

It felt lovely, but it was only a prelude to what was to come. And she must not remain passive or he would soon find her dull, as the friendly Mrs De Lacy had remarked during one of their discussions. Lady Smythe had turned a bright red, but had nodded as if she agreed.

She reached up and back to run her fingers through his hair. The movement brought her buttocks in closer contact to his groin and her breasts higher. His hand brushed back and forth across their peaks, making them tingle and ache.

He nipped her nape and stepped back. 'Witch. You'll have me finished before we start.'

His fingers attacked the fastenings of her gown while she mulled on his words.

Had he not liked her touching him? He hadn't sounded annoyed, but simply rueful, perhaps amused. She frowned. Was she doing something wrong?

The tugging at her back ceased. His large warm hands slipped over her shoulders and down her arms, pushing the sleeves free of her hands, sliding the fabric over her hips, until with nothing to keep it in place it fell to her feet with a whisper.

She let go her breath in a little huff. Her heart banged against her ribs in warning. She clenched her hands against the urge to run.

'Easy,' he breathed, kissing each of her shoulder blades in turn. His hands ran down her arms and clasped her hands, teasing her fingers open, while his mouth kissed the top of her shoulder. Fingers interlaced with his, she relaxed back against his broad warm chest.

'You've nothing to fear,' he murmured in softly. 'Only the best of little deaths, I promise.'

Her panic subsided, gentled by his touch and the dark

seduction of his voice. She took a deep breath and leaned into him, feeling his strength all down her back. A man like him had the power to protect the weak, or break them. She did not trust him to use his power well, but did she fear him? Not at this moment. For at this moment, she had something he wanted.

She gently freed her fingers and moved her hands backwards, explored the naked flesh of his flanks, so narrow and firm, and the rough-haired muscle of his thighs. More lean strength beneath warm skin.

His hips jerked against her bottom. He muttered something that sounded like a curse, then, 'Too many clothes.'

He gently pushed her forwards. 'Let me at these laces, girl,' he said softly. 'I would have you skin to skin.'

Her stomach clenched at the sensual whisper and the image it provoked.

His hands made short work of the ties of her stays. They, too, fell to the floor. Slowly, almost reverently, he drew her chemise up her body. She lifted her arms and he pulled it over her head and off. He spun her around to face him, his gaze raking her body, taking in her breasts and waist and the triangle of glossy black curls between her thighs, before travelling back to her face.

Did he approve of what he saw? Or would he see the low-class foreignness in her blood as something to scorn or mock as her grandfather had avowed when offering her the horridest of old men as a husband?

There was an expression on his face, something in his eyes, but she couldn't read it.

She dropped her gaze, fearing what she might see. What he would say.

'Gorgeous,' he whispered. 'Truly lovely. I never thought the beauty of your body would outmatch a most delicious pair of feet.'

She looked up quickly and saw nothing mocking in his face. Indeed, there was a kind of wondering awe. The amazement in his eyes was unquestionably sincere.

She managed a tremulous smile, even as the heat of embarrassment at his outrageous praise flooded her body.

'Ah, the Madonna-face again,' he said. 'It drives me mad for you and you know it, don't you?'

She shook her head, not at all sure what he meant. 'It is the only face I have,' she whispered.

'Then I must kiss it.' He cupped her jaw in both palms and kissed her lips. She opened her mouth to welcome him in, parted her thighs to the pressure of his. Felt him groan. It seemed he was not the only one with power.

Then thoughts refused to form as pleasure at her core roused her to new heights of longing.

Slowly he lowered her to the cushions in front of the hearth; the velvet felt soft against her naked skin, a contrast to the brush of rough hair against her inner thigh, the hardness of his member at her hip and the firm squeeze of his hand at her breast.

Her skin became one vast plain of sensation, tingles and searing heat, heartbeats thundering in her ears and throughout her body. The kiss stole her vision of everything but the feel of his lips, his tongue, his strong male body and the need they inspired deep within.

Slowly, lingeringly, he ended the magical wooing of his mouth on hers with butterfly kisses on the tip of her nose, each eyelid, the point of her chin, while her hands explored the expanse of his shoulders, the narrow span of his waist, the rise of his buttocks. A lean body, steel covered by hot silk, so different from hers.

He slid downwards, his weight on one hand, while the other played with her breast. Delicious little arrows of pleasure speared downwards. She raised her head to see what he did. Together they watched as he rolled her dark brown nipple between thumb and finger, tugging lightly.

'Ah,' she cried at the lancing ache. A darting glance, gleaming with wickedness, met her gaze and then he bent his head, his hot wet tongue and teeth replacing his fingers. The sensation brought her hips up off the cushions.

'Oh,' she cried, stunned at the force of the pleasure, the sweet aching pain of it, and the shocking desire for more.

She didn't have to ask, he seemed to know, and the pleasure grew each time his mouth found some new way to drive her to utter distraction.

Yet no matter how high she soared, how tight her insides clenched, what she wanted seemed just beyond her reach and centred deep inside. She raised her hips, pressing against his thigh, and while the increased pressure offered a measure of satisfaction, it only added to the torture of what was happening inside her body.

When he started to go lower with his kisses, she moaned a protest.

He chuckled softly and she struck his shoulder with her fist, a demand, but for what she didn't quite know, even as the words came into her mind. *Le petit mort.* The little death. That was it. She wanted to die. To end the torture.

He half rolled on his side and cupped between her legs, pressing and moving his hand in a small circle. The tension only got worse. A thrill screamed through her blood, even as his fingers parted the folds of her most intimate place.

A breath hissed between his teeth. 'So small and so hot,' he muttered. He pulled away.

'What—'

'Hush. This will take but a moment.'

Even as the words were leaving his mouth he was lifting her hips with one hand cupped beneath her bottom and pushing another cushion beneath her.

She frowned at him, and he smiled. 'Never tried it? You'll like it, believe me.'

She gazed up at him and nodded. She had to trust him, for she had no practical knowledge. Would he be able to tell?

Would there be blood and pain as some said, or only a moment of discomfort? Since this was the most natural, if wicked, act between a man and a woman, she had to believe the latter.

She widened her legs at the push of his knee as he hung above her, her hips tilted high, like an offering. He glanced down, his eyes heavy and his expression darker and wilder than she had ever seen him as he focused on the wickedly delicious sensations caused by his hand between her thighs. Once more she felt him open her to him, and when she glanced down, she saw it was not his hand this time, but his shaft, his rod, as the other woman had laughingly called it, pressed against her opening.

She tensed, glancing up at his face. His eyes were closed, pleasure already softening the stern line of his jaw.

He thrust forwards.

Chapter Nine

Pain seared through her. She cried out. Closed her eyes against the agony gripping her flesh.

He stilled. 'Bloody hell.'

Panting, she lifted her lids to meet a face filled with regret and a sort of strained agony. 'Oh, Rose, love, what have you done?'

'I'm sorry,' she whispered.

'Are you hurt? Shall I stop?'

The pain was receding. While the feel of him inside her felt foreign, it also felt good. She moved her hips and felt the sting, but also a return of thrilling sensations. An echo of the pleasure that had held her in its thrall only a moment ago.

'No. Please. I am fine. Don't stop now.' She brought her hands up to his face. For a moment she thought he would jerk away, refuse to let her touch him, but then he groaned and let her palm his jaw. 'Please. Don't stop.'

A savage expression set his face in harsh lines and his lips twisted in a mocking smile. 'Well played, my dear.'

She stared at him blankly, not understanding this sudden change.

With infinite care he moved within her, first slowly withdrawing, until she thought he would leave her. She gripped his waist with her calves. His jaw hardened. He refused to be restrained. Before she could cry out a protest against his leaving, he eased forwards, the slide a gentle torture. Again and again, he stroked her from the inside, teasing the twist of tension inside her, and all the while he watched her face with his mocking smile. Yet she had the feeling he mocked himself, for he treated her with great gentleness.

Hanging above her, his weight on his hands each side of her head, he seemed so distant. So uninvolved, when his body was bringing her so much delight.

She ran her hands across his chest, felt the muscle around his flat nipples, tested the rough dark hair that trailed off towards his belly with her fingertips. He felt lovely.

But when she glanced up to his face, there was no pleasure, only a kind of pain, his lips drawn back from his teeth, while he moved his hips with gentle patience. A thrilling kind of torture that left her hanging on the verge of some great discovery, which for some reason he seemed determined to deny.

The longer it continued, the deeper the waiting abyss became. The nearer she came to flying over the edge, the more he seemed to hold her back.

Furious at his teasing, she tweaked his nipples as he had done to hers. He groaned and slammed himself into her body.

A sense of satisfaction filled the void. She grabbed his shoulders and lifted her hips, impaling herself, clenching her muscles to hold him fast; when she found his ear brushing against her mouth, she nipped at his earlobe.

A shudder ran through him. He thrust into her hard and fast. Her body drew bowstring tight as the brink fell away and she soared on a hot rush of light and shattered.

He cried out, a sound of shock as he shuddered deep within her body.

Panting, she collapsed, her hands too weak to hold him, her limbs heavy and languid, her body pulsing around him, before he pulled away.

He lowered his head to her shoulder. His heart beat a thunder against her ribs, his breathing ragged and tumultuous as her own. 'Oh, hell,' he whispered with what sounded like despair.

'I'm sorry,' she gasped, her heart thundering, her body trembling with shock after shock.

He raised his head and gazed down on her with such tenderness he looked almost a different man. 'Not you, darling,' he said, his breathing hard and ragged. 'Never you.' He stroked damp strands of her hair back from her temples with hands that shook. 'You were wonderful. Amazing.' He kissed the tip of her nose. 'Are you all right?'

The gentle concern in his face unfurled something in her chest. Something warm and wonderful. She knew right at that moment she'd fallen in love. She stroked his cheek. 'I'm fine,' she said smiling. 'Really.'

He smiled sweetly and drew away from her, leaving her body, immediately drawing the sheet he'd used earlier over them both and pulling her into the circle of his arms.

'Rest, sweet, and we'll talk later.' He rhythmically stroked from shoulder to hip and she felt warm and protected in his embrace.

Unable to shake the lethargy stealing over her senses, she sank into darkness.

Cocooned in blissful warmth, it was some moments before Rosa made sense of the sounds of the deep breathing nearby or the cushions beneath her and the heavy weight across her stomach. The glow of the fire answered her questions.

The kitchen at Gorham Place. Garth, sprawled naked beside her, one arm across her belly, his face turned away. He'd slipped off the cushions on to the hearth rug. She extricated herself from beneath his arm, sliding off the cushions to pull on her shift. He looked lovely in the warmth of the firelight, relaxed, his face devoid of all cynicism.

It would be dawn soon. They must leave before anyone arrived. There would be no more opportunities to search the house.

The realisation struck her hard. She had searched. She'd found nothing.

It wasn't here. There was no will. For whatever reason, Papa had not kept his promise. Something must have gone wrong. Perhaps he simply hoped Grandfather would take care of them. Or thought he would wait until he came into his inheritance, not realising that he never would. One thing she knew for certain in her heart, one truth she would not give up. He had loved his daughters. Whatever had happened, it had been a mistake.

No sense in dwelling on what might or should have been. She had carved a new path out of her difficulties. It might not be particularly honourable, but at least she wasn't crawling back to her grandfather in defeat. At heart, Garth seemed a much kinder man than her grandfather. She liked him. She just had to hope she was right to trust him.

She glanced around. There must be no evidence left of their presence here tonight. A banked fire might cause some raised brows, but could be seen as something Inchbold would do to warm the house after it had lain empty. Cushions on the floor and makeshift clothes-horses were out of the question.

Garth stirred and sighed in his sleep. He looked so peaceful, she hated to disturb him.

She flung her cloak around her shoulders and gathered the cushions. She carried them through to the library and replaced them on the sofa. An odd sense that she'd missed something nagged at her mind. But what? Was there perhaps more than one secret door in the desk? The urge to look again drove her upstairs. She discovered nothing new, but the feeling remained with her.

When she returned to the kitchen Garth was already up and buttoning his shirt.

'Is it dry?' she asked.

His dark eyes met hers and she was shocked at the anger she saw in their depths. 'Where did you go?'

Feeling very naked, she pulled her cloak around her. 'To put the cushions back. Why?'

He sat down on the hearth stool and rubbed a hand across his jaw, shaking his head. 'I thought you'd run off.'

She stared at him, surprised. 'Would you care?'

'No.' He winced. 'Yes.' He sat on the settle by the hearth, forearms resting on his thighs, his gaze intent. 'Rose, what kind of game are you playing here?'

'Game?' She stared at him blankly.

'Until a couple of hours ago, you were a virgin.'

Heat enveloped her. She hung her head. 'Oh, that.'

'Yes, dammit, that. You couldn't possibly think I wouldn't know. So I ask you again, what is your game?'

A guilty wince tightened her lips. 'No game. I didn't think you would mind.'

'Not mind?' He stared at her as if she was mad. 'Why on earth did you pretend to be a widow? How could you be so bacon-brained?'

Her hackles went up. 'Lady Keswick stipulated she wanted a widow in her advertisement. I didn't think it would matter.'

He shook his head wearily. 'You should have told me. I would never have...' He gestured at the floor, where they'd lain together.

A trembling started inside her. Fear that she'd gone from

one disaster to another. 'I thought you wanted me.' The pleading note in her voice made her cringe inside. 'I thought you
would set me up as your mistress.'

His head came up, his mouth flat. 'Is that what you
thought? Really?'

Oh, God help her, what had she done? 'Was I mistaken?'
Her voice shook.

'Just what sort of man do you take me for?'

He sounded so scornful, she wanted to hit him. She curled
her fingers inside her palms, forcing herself to speak with a
coolness she did not feel. 'A degenerate rake.'

Fury blazed in his eyes. 'Damn you, Rose Travenor. I am
both, but I am not a seducer of innocents.' He let out a laugh.
'Or was not until now.' He raked a hand though his hair. 'Is
that even your name? Clearly there is no Mr Travenor.' He
put his hands on his hips. 'Out with it. Who are you?'

He looked so furious, she couldn't look him in the eye, so
she gazed at the fireplace instead. 'I don't see why my name
matters.'

He tipped his head back as if seeking divine intervention.
'It matters on a marriage certificate.'

'What!' Her mouth dropped open. Her heart leapt with a
kind of hot joy, more powerful than their lovemaking. Never
in her wildest dreams did she imagine he would ask for her
hand.

'How proud you must be,' he said. 'You are the first
gently bred *innocent* female who has ever tricked me into
bedding her. I suppose this was all a lie, too.' He waved an
arm around. 'The searching. The sadness when you found
nothing. Your way of getting me alone.'

The joy was swept away on a blast of cold reality. Her
anger rose up, clamouring in her blood and pounding in her
ears, turning her vision crimson. 'The seducer is seduced,
in other words.' She laughed bitterly. 'I never asked you to

follow me. I didn't want you to follow me. It was all your own doing.'

He narrowed his eyes. 'And so I get to live with the consequences. Did I seduce someone in your family and this is some form of revenge? Or has Lady Keswick turned matchmaker?'

None of this was making any sense. 'I don't want to marry you, and I won't marry you. Does that make you feel any better?'

He scrubbed at the back of his neck. 'Don't be stupid. I have to marry you. You might be carrying my child.'

The wind of anger went right out of her sails. She sank on to the wooden settle. 'But…but some people are married for ages before a child comes along. It takes practice.'

He gave a pained laugh. 'Believe me, I've had lots of practice. And it can happen the first time.'

'Oh.' She frowned. 'But mistresses don't… I mean, somehow they…'

'They take precautions. But you didn't, did you?' He looked hopeful.

'No. I wasn't expecting…'

'Damn.' He sat beside her. 'Then the piper must be paid.'

'Do you want to be married?'

'Not in the least.'

The finality in his voice was like a surgeon's scalpel. It sliced a piece out of her heart and left it bleeding.

'Then don't. You don't love me, do you?' Did she have to ask him that? Did she have to give him another weapon?

His laugh was scornful. It hurt to hear it, the way a stone scratched across slate pained the ears.

'Love is a fabrication, made up by poets to get silly females falling at their feet. I'll marry you because I'm damned if any child of mine is born a bastard and that's all. Don't think you are going to change me.' His voice was hard, his face implacable.

She wrapped her arms across her stomach. 'But there might not be a child.'

'I won't take that chance. Come on, let me help you dress, we've a busy day ahead of us.'

'I—'

'I don't want to hear any more about it, Rose. The matter is settled.'

The hands that had been so gentle and caring earlier were now brisk and firm. He barely looked at her.

Cold reality scoured her heart. He was right in a way. She should have told him she was an innocent. But how was she to know he'd take it to heart, feel his honour was impugned? She didn't think rakes had any honour.

A good marriage might well have been the answer to all of her problems, but a bad one could only make things worse. If she couldn't marry for love, she wasn't going to marry at all. She had always said so.

She should never have thought she could be a mistress. Never let him change her mind. She should have stuck to her plan and opted for the opera.

The three-mile trudge along rutted lanes deep in mud in a heavy silence left Rosa exhausted. Stanford had been right, they would not have been able to accomplish the journey at night in the storm, but she wished they had tried. Life would not now be so complicated.

The river had not washed away the bridge in the village, but in the low places water lay in deep puddles across the road and the mud made walking exceedingly difficult.

They met a couple of farm labourers who were on their way to the fields. Garth tipped his hat when they stopped to stare in dull curiosity. As far as she could tell, no one else remarked their passing.

She was glad of his grim silence, because it gave her time to think and the more she thought the more she realised she would not marry a rake and a libertine who thought she'd tricked him into marriage. What kind of marriage would it be if he carried so much resentment? He was probably horrified because he knew her mother was an opera singer. She couldn't blame him for the seduction. She'd been eager for it. She'd even convinced herself she'd fallen in love. So foolish. So naïve.

Naïveté should not ruin his life or hers.

The opera really was her only choice. It always had been.

She halted as they approached The Grange's front door. 'May I crave your indulgence? Would you permit me to speak with Lady Keswick alone?'

He narrowed his eyes.

Suspicious. Always suspicious. A man who trusted no one. It was hard to blame him after what she had done. 'She has been good to me. I owe her an explanation. I will talk to her the moment she arises at eleven.'

A smile broke on his face and for a second she glimpsed that other man, the one she'd fallen for on the beach and again last night. Her heart ached. After today, she would never see him again.

'You are not such a bad lass, are you?' he said almost as if surprised. 'Very well. It will take me an hour or two to get rid of the mud. We will depart at midday.'

They entered the house as the cased clock beside the stairs chimed seven.

'I will take the backstairs, so we are not seen together.'

'What matters that now?' he said, the grim expression returning.

'It matters to me.'

He gave an impatient shake of his head, but started up the stairs. Two steps up he turned. 'At half past eleven, then. In the drawing room. Be ready to leave.'

She'd be ready to leave before then.

Up in her chamber, she changed quickly, packed a valise and carried it along to the other wing.

Lady Keswick was sitting up in bed with a lace cap covering her iron-grey hair, sipping on a steaming cup of chocolate. She always needed a little sustenance before she closed her eyes and napped until it was time to rise. 'You are up early today, Rose?'

'I'm leaving.'

The old lady stared at her. 'Stanford.' She slapped a hand on the counterpane. 'I knew it.'

Rosa winced at her employer's perspicacity. 'It has nothing to do with him. Not really. I having been thinking and decided I want to start on my career as a singer right away. I really need to earn more money. Did you hear anything from your friend?'

'Not yet. She is touring in Italy and won't be back in London until the end of the summer. Stay until then. I am sure she will be able to help.'

Once Lady Keswick realised Stanford's intentions were honourable, or at least his form of honourable, she would join forces with him. 'Would you give me a letter of recommendation?'

'Are you sure this is what you want, gel? The theatre is no easy life. Oh, to be sure you might find a patron, someone to keep you in fine style, but you just don't strike me as that sort.'

Last night had proved different. Shame washed through her, but she met the old lady's gaze calmly. 'I want to sing.' She wanted to be free of debt. She wanted to support her sisters. Give them the kind of life her father should have provided.

But she wouldn't do it by tricking a man into a marriage he didn't want.

Lady Keswick sighed. 'I can see there is no moving you, gel. Hand me my writing implements and a tablet.'

Trembling with anxiety that she might miss the stagecoach in the village if Lady Keswick didn't hurry, Rosa fetched what she needed and stood shifting from foot to foot as she watched the minutes on the mantelclock tick by.

Lady Keswick blotted her note and folded it carefully. 'I am not sure how much good it will do you, my dear. It is a long time since I walked the boards.'

'Thank you.' Rosa took the note. In a rush of tenderness she leaned forwards and gave the old woman a hug. 'Thank you. I will write and let you know how I do.'

'You do that, my dear. But I am going to give Stanford a piece of my mind.'

Hopefully, not until after eleven when the stage would be well on its way to London. Rosa tucked the note in her reticule and slipped out of the door. Now to start the next stage of her life.

No more silly mistakes. She'd made enough for a lifetime.

She pelted down the servants' staircase, valise in hand. The rest of her clothes she would send for once she found work. She wouldn't allow herself to think about what she would do if she couldn't find a position.

It was unthinkable. She had enough money left from her first month's employment to hold off Triggs for a week or two, and some left over to pay for lodging, if she was careful.

She tiptoed past the library, its door slightly ajar, though she could not imagine any of the guests being out of the bed so early. The muffled sound of someone crying stopped her steps. It wasn't her business. She took another stealthy step.

Another choked sob, then a paroxysm of crying issued from the room.

Lady Smythe. She just knew it. Perhaps she'd had bad news from her husband. She pushed open the door.

Lady Smythe looked at her, then turned her back, her shoulders hunching as if trying to make herself invisible. Rosa winced and stepped inside, dropping her valise inside the door. 'May I come in?'

Lady Smythe sniffed. 'No.'

Thank goodness. Rosa turned to leave.

'Oh, Mrs Travenor, I'm sorry, but my life is ruined.'

The rise in her voice, a most pathetic wail, brought Rosa up short. She turned back. Even with her nose pink and tears running down her cheeks, Lady Smythe looked adorable.

'Did you speak to Lady Keswick?'

'I did. Last night.' Her shoulders drooped. 'She said I was a goose. That Mark would come for me the moment he heard I was here. But it has been days and days and still no word.'

'How would he know where to find you?'

She sniffed. 'I left a note.'

Startled, Rosa sat down beside her on the sofa. 'You never mentioned a note.'

The young woman lifted her tear-stained face. 'That's not the worst of it. Bannerby came to my door last night. I wouldn't let him in. He said he knew I had Stanford in with me, and he would let the whole world know I was his paramour.'

'But Stanford...' She bit her lip. 'I mean, he wasn't with you.'

She shook her head. 'Bannerby knocked on his door and there was no answer so Bannerby took it as evidence. Oh, if only the storm hadn't stopped me from leaving last night.' Her shoulders sagged more. 'Everything is so awful. I want to go home.' She gave a little hiccup of a sob.

Rosa put an arm about her shoulder. 'Then leave today.'

'I am. The post chaise will be here at any moment.' She raised her watery gaze, her lower lip trembling. 'But I fear it is too late. When he finds out what I've done, when he hears Bannerby's lies, he will be so angry.'

'Are you afraid of your husband?'

'Oh, no, he is the dearest, kindest man imaginable. But Mama said even the nicest of men can be brought to the end of their patience. I thought he loved me.' Tears flowed down her face.

'You love him.'

'Oh, yes. It was a love match. Everyone said so.' She turned her face away. 'Or I thought so. Mama said the first thing every man does after the honeymoon is set up a mistress.'

Mama sounded like an idiot. She took the delicate hand in hers. 'Not every husband. I think you must ask him. Confront him with what you saw. Confess what you did, and tell him that nothing happened. It didn't, did it?'

'Oh, no. I couldn't. I thought I could, but I couldn't. You have been married. Do you think he will believe me?'

Dear heavens, trapped by her own lies. 'I am sure of it.'

'Will you vouch for me?'

She winced, but she supposed she could vouch for Stanford's whereabouts. She opened her mouth to say so, when the sounds of a carriage drawing up in the courtyard brought the weepy young bride to her feet. 'The post chaise. I must have my luggage brought down.' She glanced at Rosa's valise. 'Are you leaving, too? Are you going to London? Come with me.' She ran to the window to look out.

Rosa stared at her back. A feeling of recklessness entered her chest. 'Yes. I am going to London.' She could also vouch for Lady Smythe's innocence, as far as Garth was concerned, and it would be comforting to have a friend on her journey to London.

Penelope swung around, her eyes wide and round. 'What shall I do? It is not the post chaise. It is my husband.'

Oh, now the fat was in the fire along with Rosa's hope of an easy escape.

'He mustn't find me here,' the young bride said. 'I must hide.'

'Far better you face him right away,' Rosa said, hoping she was right. 'Tell him the truth. If he cares for you, he will believe you.' She crossed her fingers in her skirts. 'You look so adorably sad, all you have to do is fall into his arms and thank him for coming to your rescue. I am sure he will melt.' If he loved her he would.

Lady Smythe smoothed her skirts and patted her hair. 'Do you think so?' Her lower lip trembled. Her lovely green eyes glistened with tears. Who could resist?

'I am sure of it. Far better you greet him alone, though.'

The sound of a slamming door made them both jump. 'You don't think it would be better if you stayed with me?'

'No, but I will stay close by, in case he...in case you need my help.'

She nodded and straightened her shoulders. 'After all, he is the one in the wrong.'

Rosa wasn't sure accusing him would work, but what did she know? She picked up her valise and scurried ignominiously out of the door, saying, 'I'll wait further along the passage, just in case.'

She barely escaped being run over by a fair-haired young man with steely grey eyes and very definite chin.

'Library?' he snapped at her.

She pointed. Oh, dear, perhaps she had been wrong to desert Lady Smythe. She hesitated just beyond the door, then slipped into a niche, squeezing behind a statue of Eros artfully draped with fabric. She had no wish to be caught eavesdropping.

'Mark,' Lady Smythe said in dramatic accents. 'You came for me. What took you so long?' She burst into tears.

The deep sounds of a male voice offering comfort was followed by the sound of sobbing and explanations. Rosa could only imagine what Lady Smythe was saying, but whatever it was seemed to work because Lady Smythe said, 'Oh, Mark, I never should have come here.'

A lengthy silence ensued. Lady Smythe clearly wasn't in need of help. Rosa was working her way around the statue's plinth when she heard footsteps. She held her breath and remained perfectly still. It was probably one of the servants going about their business.

'Mark?' Stanford's voice. 'Thank God you are here.'

'Stanford? You bastard,' the other man said in a low growl.

Oh, dear, this could get ugly. Perhaps she ought to go and testify on Stanford's behalf.

The sound of a strike and then a thud made her run for the door and peep in.

Garth was measuring his length on the carpet and staring up at Lord Smythe. He was grinning. He tested his jaw. 'You always did have a punishing left.'

'Get up, you coward,' Lord Smythe growled. 'I will have satisfaction.'

Stanford looked at Lady Smythe and raised a mocking brow. 'Well, Penelope?'

A pained expression crossed the other man's face. He pulled Lady Smythe against his side.

'Mark, it isn't his fault,' Lady Smythe said.

'Whose fault is it?' he said.

She hung her head. 'Mine. I came here with Mrs Mallow. I— Stanford has done nothing but tell me to go home since he arrived. You have to believe me.'

Her husband looked from one to the other, then put out a hand and heaved Stanford to his feet. 'It seems I owe you an apology.' He still sounded dangerous, but the hostilities were apparently over. 'Perhaps one of you can explain what is going on?'

Rosa inhaled a deep breath. It seemed her help was not needed and eavesdropping was making her feel very uncomfortable. Besides, she had no wish to run into Stanford. He'd try to stop her from leaving. Oh, goodness, if she wanted to make the stagecoach leaving the village at nine, she would have to hurry. She spun around and continued on her way, letting herself out of the back door just as a yellow bounder pulled into the courtyard.

'You the young lady what ordered the chaise?' the postilion asked, swinging down from his mount.

Lady Smythe wasn't going to need her rented post chaise now her husband had come, was she? And there was no faster way to reach London. She winced. The fare would use up a good deal of money, but it was just too fortuitous an opportunity to pass up.

'Well?' the postilion said, frowning at her valise. 'Payment due in advance.'

'Yes,' she said, raking in her reticule. 'Yes.' She counted the coins into his palm until he nodded his satisfaction. 'Let us be off at once.'

She climbed aboard and settled back against the seats. As the coach pulled away, a heavy lump settled in the depths of her stomach. Stanford would not be pleased she'd gone off without a word. She pressed her hand to her suddenly hot cheeks. He'd actually asked her to marry him. For an instant of madness she had let herself dream they could have a future. He'd managed to steal a piece of her heart when she wasn't looking. But it would be wrong to marry a man who saw her as an unwanted responsibility. It was no way to begin a marriage. No matter how hard she wished it wasn't so, once she was gone, he would no doubt heave a sigh of relief and thank heavens for a lucky escape.

Her chest tightened and she pressed a hand to it to ward off the pain. It was no good wishing. She must put the whole thing down to experience and move on with her plans. With Lady Keswick's letter of introduction, she was sure to find a good role with an opera company and put Stanford's allure behind her.

Her hands went to her belly. What if she was carrying his child? She pushed the thought aside.

She could only deal with one problem at a time.

Chapter Ten

'Mrs Mallow lured her here,' Garth said. 'Your wife never let me or anyone else near her.'

Penelope's innocent green eyes widened. Her rosebud lips formed a small O of surprise. No doubt she thought he was going to tell tales on her for flirting with Bannerby. Well, she'd have to own up for herself.

And if Mark wanted a brawl, he would give a good accounting of himself, because he wasn't the guilty party.

Mark raked his fingers through his normally neat fair locks. 'Why the hell didn't you just put her on a coach and send her home?'

He shook his head. 'If there's one thing I've learned over the years, old chap, it's never get between a man and his wife.'

Mark leaned close. 'You really are a bastard sometimes.'

'All the time,' he said coolly.

'Dammit, Garth. You know I didn't mean it that way. I'm just too angry to choose my words carefully.'

Mark was one of two people who knew his secret. Him and Kit, his brother, apart from his dear mother, of course. 'I'm glad you finally arrived.'

'I found Penelope's note.'

Penelope stared at him. 'I thought you would be home days ago.'

Mark's face turned grim. 'I was delayed.'

Penelope froze, then shrugged. 'I had decided to leave anyway. It's all been perfectly horrid.'

He smiled down at his wife. 'Then I am glad I am in time to escort you.' He pulled her close. 'We'll talk more when we get home.'

Nauseated by the expression on his friend's face, Garth turned away. Heaven forefend he would ever look so besotted. 'Well, this is all very nice, but if you will excuse me, I am meeting Mrs Travenor in an hour or so. I just came in here for a newspaper to pass the time while I wait.'

Penelope gasped, then tried to cover it up with a cough.

'What?' Garth asked.

She shook her head, her cheeks flaming red, guilt writ large on her face.

'Blast it, Penelope, tell me.'

'Steady,' Mark said, moving to shield his wife with his body.

'Tell her to tell me, Mark,' Garth said, clenching his fists.

Mark stared at him, then a grin broke out on his face. 'Oh, not you, too.'

'What on earth are you talking about? I just want to hear what she has to say about Mrs Travenor.'

'Tell him, Penelope. He won't let it go until you do.'

'She left,' Penelope said.

'Left?' Garth felt as if he'd been kicked in the gut by a horse. A bloody big one. 'Left when?'

'I mean, I think she left. She was carrying a valise. She said she was going to London.'

'How long ago?'

'If she was the dark beauty I met in the corridor when I arrived, it was not more than a few minutes ago,' Mark said.

Penelope looked at him. 'Beauty?'

He shrugged.

'That was her, all right,' Garth said, his stomach tightening, quickly followed by a hot buzz of anger. So Rose had lied to him again. What else had she lied about? Was there no end to her deceit? Perhaps she really had found what she was looking for in that house while he was sleeping.

It seemed where *Miss* Travenor was concerned he was a fool, but if she thought to escape him, she was in for a surprise. He wasn't going to take the chance of her carrying his child, though God help him, if it was a boy, it meant he would never be able to put things right for his brother.

Well, he had one advantage on his side. He knew she was headed for London and the only way to get there from here was by stagecoach. And even if he missed her in the village, he'd soon catch up to her on the road.

He bowed. 'If you will excuse me. You two have lots to discuss.'

'Your absence will not be remarked upon,' Mark said.

Garth wanted to knock the smile off his friend's face. Being caught in the parson's mousetrap was a fate worse than death, at least to him. His friend had seemed very happy about being leg-shackled. He hoped, for both their sakes, the events of the past few days wouldn't change his mind.

Right now he had a more important matter on his mind. Rose.

'Let's hear you, then.'

Rosa stared out into the theatre, at the fussy little assistant manager's assistant, with his springy blond hair and Lady Keswick's letter in his hand. He squinted at Rosa over his spectacles from the front of the pit.

Nerves always tied her stomach in knots when she began
to sing, but it was far worse this time. The theatre was cav-
ernous. Unfriendly. It was so important that she do well and
the aria he'd given her was pitched far too high for her voice.

She took a deep breath.

'I haven't got all day,' the little man said. He pointed to
the sheet of music in her hand. 'Sing.'

Settle down. Just sing. She took another breath. Her heart
was sitting too high in her throat. She swallowed it down.
The first notes came out a croak.

'Stop!' the little man shrieked. He put his hands to his
ears. 'No more.'

'No. I can do it. Just let me—'

'I'm not looking for frogs. Can you dance? We need danc-
ers.'

No. This was all going wrong. Why wouldn't he listen?
'If I could just try again? Please.'

'Next,' he yelled

Another girl, with carrot-red hair, stepped on stage from
the wings.

She couldn't let this happen. 'I can dance,' Rosa cried out
to catch his attention. 'I know all the country dances.'

He rolled his eyes. 'Saints preserve me from bloody ama-
teurs. I meant *pas de chats* and *pirouettes*, not the flippin'
Roger de Coverly. Next.'

The words pushed through her panic. Mama had shown
her some of the dances required for performances. It had been
so long ago, she'd all but forgotten. Rosa went up on her right
toe and twirled, landing off centre. 'You mean this?'

Another woman walked on stage from the opposite side,
a large-bosomed woman in a sumptuous red silk gown and
flashing jewels.

'Gif her a chance, *mein Herr*.' The woman gracefully
twirled her wrist in the direction of the seats. 'At least she
appeals to the gentlemen more than the herd of cows you haf

now. Look at that bosom, those legs.' She grabbed Rosa's skirt at the knee and hiked it up.

The harried little man stopped fussing with his papers and leaned forwards.

'Hold up your skirts and tvirl once more,' the woman said.

Blushing, Rosa did as she was bid. This time she landed on balance and placed her heels neatly together and turned out her toes.

The woman laughed, waved an airy hand. 'See, she dances. But, Frederick, you must do vot you please. Just tell me my gown for tonight is ready.'

'It's ready,' a woman sitting at the back of the theatre called out, holding up swaths of fabric.

'Gut. Ver gut.' The woman, who had to be Fräulein Helga Von Geldhardt, the soprano and leading lady, wandered back into the wings. 'Take her, Freddy,' she called over her shoulder. 'She's the best you've seen today.'

'Which is not saying anything,' the little man screeched, pulling at his frizzy blond curls.

'Do you want me now?' the girl halfway out of the wings said in the nasal tones of London.

'You—' the assistant pointed at Rosa '—go and find Señor Paloma and tell him you are in the chorus. Be ready for rehearsal at six tomorrow morning. You—' He glared at the girl hovering half on and half off the stage. 'Can you dance?'

'I'm a singer.'

'No,' Frederick screamed.

Rosa fled before he changed his mind about her.

Walking around the back of the stage in search of the dancemaster, she decided the position of chorus dancer was better than nothing. She had a foot firmly over the threshold. All she had to do was let them hear her sing and they'd realise they'd made a mistake.

And if Fräulein Von Geldhardt was right and the gentlemen did love her, then she might find a rich protector, because a dancer in the chorus did not get paid nearly as well as a soloist. And a protector would have influence and be able to get her a starring role.

A flutter of disquiet ran through her stomach. Her mother would have been so disappointed to find she'd been forced to sink so low. If only they would give her a chance to sing. Let her nerves settle. But it was better than the loveless marriage proposed by Stanford where she had no guarantees he would help her sisters. This way, her earnings were her own to do with as she willed.

If he'd wanted to make her his mistress, it might have been easier to agree to stay. Her parents' marriage had worked because they'd loved each other. Stanford didn't love her any more than she loved him. That feeling she'd felt for him had been infatuation. It had to be. She could not fall in love with a rake who had no intention of changing his ways.

It wasn't possible life would be so cruel.

Enough whining. She had a position in the opera. She would send the rest of her earnings from Lady Keswick's to Meg for the moneylender and find a way to get another audition.

As soon as they heard her, they would give her a better role. She drew in a deep breath. She could do this.

In the green room she found a collection of young women standing around a rotund man with curling black moustaches and thinning black hair. 'Is he Señor Paloma?' she asked.

One of the girls nodded.

A pair of beady black eyes swivelled in Rosa's direction. 'Who are you, *señorita*?'

'I'm to join the chorus,' she said, feeling every eye in the room focusing on her.

The man waved his fat hands in the air. 'Now he sends me a *spilungona*? First I get all these pale little English midgets, now I get a giant. Where I put you?'

'At the back?'

His eyes widened. Then he laughed, and every part of him jiggled: his cheeks, his belly, even his thighs in their tight-fitting buff pantaloons.

He stopped as suddenly as he'd started. 'No amusing.'

The little redhead who'd been waiting while Rosa was on stage crept in. He glared at her. 'You are the last?'

She nodded.

'Bellissimo.' He clapped his hands. 'All of you. Be here at six in the morning.'

Rosa followed the rest of the girls along a passage and out of the back door of the theatre into the depths of Covent Garden.

'Where do you live?' the little redhead asked.

'I have yet to find a room.'

'You can stay with me,' the girl offered with a hesitant smile. 'I'm Bess. The room ain't much, but I've a bed big enough for two and I need help with the rent.'

Rosa stuck out her hand. 'Rosa. Rosabella di Camisa.' She decided to use one of her mother's names. It sounded more operatic and Grandfather would never recognise it. 'I would love to help with the rent.'

Bess grinned. 'What about a kipper at the chop shop, then, afore we go home?'

'Sounds wonderful.' Rosa's stomach growled agreement. It would be the first food she'd eaten since yesterday. She'd stayed at a nearby inn and hadn't dared pay for a meal, too.

Finally, she thought, things seemed to be going as planned. Well, almost. Everything would be perfect when they let her audition for a singing role.

The next few days had flashed by in a blur of long rehearsals and short nights spent in exhausted sleep. Today was dress rehearsal.

'Oh, no.' Rosa regarded her costume with dismay. It was even worse than she'd imagined, when her brain had any energy left for such pursuits. 'I can't wear these.'

She held up the breeches and stockings. She didn't need to try them on to know they would hug her legs.

Señor Paloma had solved his problem of what to do with his giant after an hour of their first rehearsal. She would play a trouser role. A silent trouser role. While the girls occasionally sang, all she got to do was lift them and carry them about the stage. They might just as well have employed a horse.

'Never mind,' Bess said, twirling around in a bit of gauze that barely covered her knees. 'Remember Mrs Robinson.'

Mrs Robinson had snared the Prince of Wales in seventy-two. Since then every actress had hoped for the same.

'It didn't do her a bit of good,' Rosa grumbled. 'And besides, in these, who is even going to know I'm a girl?'

Was that really so bad? Even though she slept the sleep of the dead every night, she kept having the same dream. Stanford arriving to cart her back to Grandfather's house. Not that he had a clue she even had a grandfather. He knew nothing about her and would never find her here. Not that he'd want to, she assured herself, remembering the look on his face when he'd realised she'd never been married. The hunted look. It still made her feel hot and cold by turns.

But she couldn't stop thinking about him.

She slipped on the breeches and shirt. 'What do you think?'

Bess laughed. 'With that bum and that bosom, they'll have no trouble guessing you're a girl.'

Should she try to be more realistic? She frowned. 'Perhaps I should try to disguise them.'

'Don't you want to be whisked off to the prince's bed?'

There was only one bed she wanted to be whisked into, but she'd had the strong sense that once the passion was over, his bed would grow cold. And that she could not bear. He'd certainly acted with chilly reserve after only one night. 'You heard Señor Paloma. I'm a giant. What man would want me anyway?'

Bess tilted her head full of red curls and pursed her lips. 'You could bind your jugs. And perhaps if you gave yourself a nice little package in front, no one would notice the hips.'

'Package?'

'You know, sausage and spuds—in the front of your breeches.' She pointed at Rosa's smooth placket.

'Oh. I see what you mean. And if I put padding around my waist, my bum won't look so out of proportion.'

'That's the ticket.'

And thinking about it, she wouldn't garner any more unwanted male attention.

Unwanted? If she didn't garner male attention, how would she possibly gain a rich protector?

If only they would let her sing. She could make a lot more money as a solo performer, and have the pick of the gentlemen. The men who came around the stage door for the members of the chorus didn't look at all rich or in the least bit gentlemanly.

It might be better pretending to be a boy for a while, until she had a better role.

'Do we have any bindings or padding?'

'Mrs Ellis is sure to have something, if that's what you want.'

'It will make me true to my character.' Something Mama once said was the secret to her long-ago success.

Rosa huddled in her usual dark corner of the green room after the performance. The final performance of the week. And tomorrow the company left for Birmingham.

Fräulein Von Geldhardt had been a huge success and the

chorus had come in for its share of praise and attendant gentlemen, all of whom were milling about with their dancer of
choice, including little Bess, who sat on the lap of her special
gentleman with tears in her eyes and a guinea or two in her
pocket.

Bess had tried to convince her to drop her costume at
the end of the performance and take part in the fun. The
gentlemen, she said, loved a woman who played breeches
parts, because they loved to look at their legs. Rosa had been
tempted. Some of the young men who came back after each
performance were lots of fun, but most of them had wandering hands and no money.

She glared at Freddy. Every time she asked him for an
audition, he said 'later' and dashed off on some errand for
the *prima donna*. She couldn't blame him. The *fräulein* was
a star, the one the audience came to see.

A stir at the green-room door caught her attention. Several
gentlemen she hadn't seen before entered. Rich men from
their clothing. Excitement rippled through the girls.

'It's Forever,' Annie squealed. She'd been dancing for one
company or another for years. She wouldn't be joining them
on the tour of the north. She'd been hired on at the Haymarket
Theatre.

She flung herself at the man who entered last.

Rosa almost swallowed her tongue.

Stanford. He sauntered in, looking around with slitted
eyes, his sensual mouth sullen, his eyes mocking. He looked
darker and more dangerous than ever.

Surely he wasn't seeking her. She wasn't quite sure how
she felt about that. Or her head wasn't. Her heart seemed
to be doing something like *pirouettes* in her chest. Painful
prickles ran across her shoulders.

Shocked at the power of her reaction, she drew deeper
into her corner.

He tucked Annie under his arm, opened his other arm and two more girls rushed to join him, petting the front of his coat as he kissed each one on the cheek, while all the time he managed to keep the cigar held loosely in his fingers from setting fire to their hair or their clothing.

'Trust Stanford to bag the best of the bunch,' Fitzwilliam, who accompanied him, complained, but he grinned as another member of the chorus sidled up to him.

Hiding deep in the shadows, Rosa couldn't take her gaze from Garth. He looked nothing like the man she'd played cricket with on the beach, or the seductive nobleman who had made love to her one night in an empty house. His cravat dangled about his neck. His coat hung open, revealing a crumpled waistcoat. And he didn't look happy. The devilish sparkle in his eye was missing. The sullen cast to his beautiful mouth and his dark expression made him look thoroughly jaded. And lonely.

As if... Oh, how could she even think he might be missing her? Loaded down with three girls, he staggered to an armchair in the middle of the room. He clamped the lit cigar between his teeth and scanned the room from beneath lowered brows.

An air of dissipation hung around him. A wild young buck for whom the world held no surprises. A wickedly handsome rake. Even dissipated and probably inebriated, his knee looked inviting.

He whispered something in Annie's ear. Making love to her, no doubt. Rosa clenched her fists on her thighs, longing to push the girls off his lap. She looked away, trying not to notice. He wasn't her concern. She'd rejected him roundly.

'Did you bring presents?' one of the girls squealed, searching his pockets in a way that said she'd done it before.

His lip curled sardonically as he blew a stream of smoke at the ceiling. He would set fire to the place if he wasn't careful. But no one said a word. He was nobility. They were a rule unto themselves as long as they had money to spend.

He grabbed the guinea from the girl's hand and held it up, saying something to which all three of them shook their heads and pouted.

What on earth could he be asking them to do?

Bess joined her on the bench. 'We'll be lucky if those girls are ready to set out in the morning after a night with Forever.'

'Forever?'

'Stanford. Before he came into the title he was Evernden. One of the girls said he could make a quickie behind the stage last forever. The nickname stuck.'

Rosa went hot, then cold, knowing exactly what the words meant. Remembering his touch. The wild sensations. The way she'd thought she'd lost her heart. She couldn't stop herself from looking his way again, torturing herself with the thought of him making love to those other girls.

Except he wasn't making love to them. He was sprawled in the chair as they petted and pawed him, while he looked thoroughly bored. His weary gaze swept the room as if he half hoped to find something better, someone more interesting.

Her mouth dried. He couldn't be looking for her. She touched the straggling beard on her chin, the bit of moustache on her upper lip. Not even her sisters would recognise her, especially in the short blond wig.

Freddy rushed past, stopped and glared at her feet. 'Shoes, missy.' He held out his wicker basket.

While they allowed her to take her costume home every night, shoes were expensive and players were not permitted to wear them home. In case they sold them for gin, Bess said, or the price of a night's lodging.

Rosa unlaced the soft-soled boots and held them towards the waiting basket. 'I'll give you the shoes, if you'll let me audition to sing when we get to Birmingham.'

His yellow curls seemed to spring higher off his head. 'No. Shoes. Now.'

Rosa sighed and tossed them in. One of these days he was going to say yes. She rubbed at the sore spot on her foot from the ill-fitting footwear.

The back of her neck prickled oddly. She looked up to find Stanford staring at her feet. He'd paid attention to her feet before, but surely he wouldn't recognise her by her toes.

He stood up, the two girls on his lap sliding off his knee. Startled, as if he'd forgotten their presence, he grabbed them before they hit the floor, soothing their ruffled feathers with a quick stroke.

Sure he was coming her way, Rosa slipped her feet in her slippers. 'I'll see you there, Bess.' She ignored the sounds of a commotion behind her and fled. She'd meet the players at the chop house where they always went for a meal after the performance. Tonight would be a farewell to those who were remaining in London, a celebration of their success and a toast to the future.

Best of all would be the payment of her wages. Money she could send to her sisters.

The last letter from Meg had been terrifying. Yes, the moneylender would wait, but the money they owed was growing by leaps and bounds. There was nothing left over to pay more school fees. The girls were already looking for work, so she did not have to bear the burden alone. Sam was coughing and Meg feared she might have to call for the doctor again.

It didn't seem to matter what Rosa did, things just kept getting worse.

She ran down the alley.

Garth gazed over the heads of the girls hanging around his neck. They'd denied any knowledge of a girl called Rose. He stared into the dark corner beside the exit. Only one girl there now. A redhead. There had been two people there a moment ago, the redheaded girl tying her shoe and a...a blond-haired boy. It was a pair of feet he'd noticed. The redhead wriggled the toes of her bare foot. Hers were definitely not the feet that had caught his attention. Or perhaps he'd imagined them.

He squeezed his eyes shut and opened them again. Why would he imagine Rose's feet on a boy? Lady Keswick's assertion of Rose's ambition to join an opera company had made him wonder if the old girl was losing her faculties. On the other hand, she had no reason to lie. Rosa hadn't been singing here tonight, or at any of the other places he had visited this past week. He would know her voice anywhere.

Why wasn't he just letting this go? She clearly didn't fancy him. He would have, he assured himself, if there wasn't a chance of her carrying his bastard. But for that he'd have abandoned the quest days ago.

The twisting in his gut was simply concern about an unwanted child. He would act the same with any woman. Wouldn't he?

Of course he would. He didn't want a wife. He didn't want a child. But he'd be damned if he'd let any child of his bear such a stigma. The thought of it made him feel ill.

All these years, he'd been so damned careful, so sure he could present his brother with what was rightfully his. The title. It would atone for the guilt he'd felt when he'd realised he wasn't Evernden's son.

It would make it all up to the man who'd given him a name and place in society because he'd been given no choice by the woman he'd married.

The cold place in his chest seemed to grow. He'd messed his chance of redemption up royally, especially if Rose was brought to bed with a son. Damnation.

The redhead worked on the second slipper. Acting on instinct, he turned to the girl hanging on his arm. 'Let go.'

She swore and flounced off. For some reason none of
the ladybirds he'd tried to sample these past two weeks had
aroused his interest. None of them looked like a seductive
nun, not even when they dressed up for him.

He thought about asking about the...the boy? Good God,
had he grown so dissipated?

He headed for the girl still sitting on the bench beside the
door.

'Where did she go?'

She popped to her feet with a cheerful grin. 'Who?'

'The girl sitting beside you.'

She eyed him warily. 'Why do you want to know?'

'So it was a girl.'

She shrugged. He caught her arm. 'Where did she go?'

'Get off me.'

Fitzwilliam caught him around the shoulders. 'Great news.
We've been invited to the party at the chop house. I promised
we'd give some of the girls a ride in your carriage.'

Garth shook him off. The redhead was gone.

'Come on, we will miss the champagne.' Fitz slapped him
on the back.

If *all* the players were going to the chop house, then so
was he, and champagne sounded like a very good idea.

Jammed between Bess on one side and old Jack on the
other, Rosa nursed her gin. After a week of being with the
company, she'd learned to order herself a mug of the dreadful
stuff and pretend to drink it. The alternative was for someone
to see she wasn't drinking, buy her one and then expect one
in return. It didn't take long to spend more than you had.

She raised the mug to her lips and tried not to inhale the
fumes or get her moustache wet. It tended to fall off. Bess
took a swig of hers.

'Lawks,' she said, looking over at the door. 'They brought the gents with them.'

'What? I thought only the cast were allowed.'

'On closing night anything goes.'

Neither of the two men who entered were Garth. Rosa relaxed.

Bess gave her a saucy grin. 'Once those girls have their hooks in a couple of rich nobs do you think they'll let them loose? They'll squeeze 'em dry.'

Blast. If she had known, she wouldn't have come here. She could have got her pay the following day.

Except she'd wanted to write to her sisters and send some money off first thing in the morning. Before the moneylender pressured them again.

Bess groaned. 'It's Forever.'

Anger at the horrid nickname roared in her blood, not at the name itself, but what it meant, quickly followed by a shiver of fear. Back there in the green room, she'd half thought he'd recognised her, but he'd been too busy cuddling his girls.

'He was asking after you, before I left,' Bess said. 'I told you the gents like a girl in a trouser role.'

Breath left Rosa's body in a huge rush. 'What?'

Bess nodded. 'He came over to me after you went.'

Her heart drummed in her chest. Her throat dried. 'Why on earth didn't you tell me before?'

'I forgot.' Bess took another swig of her gin.

He couldn't possibly have recognised her. 'What did he say? Exactly what words?'

'He asked after the girl sitting beside me.'

'He can't have meant me.'

Bess frowned. 'No one else was sitting beside me.' She shrugged. 'Beats me, it do.'

Her hands started shaking. Even if he was asking about

someone else, she didn't want to have to face him. To watch him with the other girls. 'I'm leaving.' She pushed at old Jack's arm.

The burly scene-changer gave her a toothless grin. 'Leavin' without yer pay?'

'Bess will collect it.'

'Be careful going home by yourself,' Bess said.

'Don't worry about me. Everyone thinks I'm a boy.'

The old man grumbled to his bandy legs and she squeezed past him and out of the door into the courtyard, exchanging the smell of stale beer and gin mixed with pipe smoke for the scent of horse dung and rotting garbage.

A hand grabbed her arm.

'One moment, if you don't mind.'

The smooth richness of the voice sent a shiver down her back. She had no trouble recognising its owner.

'Get off me,' she said much as Bess would.

'Not on you. Yet.' He laughed darkly.

'Filthy beast.' She pulled at her arm, but his grip only tightened. 'Let me go, or I'll yell bloody murder.'

'Do that. And when the watch or the constable comes to see what's to do, I'll tell him about your little trips into other people's houses in the middle of the night.'

She stilled. It wasn't other people's houses. It was her grandfather's house, the house she'd been sure her father would leave to her and her sisters. But he hadn't. The pain of it struck her anew. Her shoulders sagged.

'That's better.' He dragged her to a wooden bench against the courtyard wall beneath the lantern by the door. 'Sit.'

She sat. The man was drunk. All she had to do was wait until his attention waned and run.

She snatched her arm clear of his grasp and folded her arms across her chest. 'All right, so I'm sitting. What do you want?'

In the flickering light he gazed down at her. He didn't look angry, he looked confused and something else. Hurt? Surely not?

'Why did you run away?'

She stuck with her role. Perhaps she could confuse him into thinking he'd made a mistake. 'I don't know what you are talking about, mate.'

'Rose,' he breathed and shook his head. 'You can't fool me. I'd know you anywhere. Why did you run?'

Caressed by the gentleness in his voice, she wanted to weep. What did she do now? Talk about disappointed love to a man who had scoffed at the very notion? Never. 'I thought you were going to hand me over to the magistrate.'

He stared down at her. 'I half wish I bloody well had. I've been searching London for you.'

She shrugged. 'What I do and where I go is none of your business. I never stole anything from that house.'

'Why do I think you are lying?' He frowned at her.

'I'm not. Remember, you just think every woman lies.'

He curled his lip. 'But not you?'

She winced. She'd done nothing but tell him lies. 'I did not steal anything.' At least that was the truth. 'If I had found some sort of treasure, do you think I would be working as a boy in the chorus?'

'A question answered with a question. It means you have something to hide. What is it, Rose? What are you afraid of? You knew I'd come after you. We have unfinished business. The small matter of a wedding.'

She leaned back against the wall, tried to appear relaxed, resigned to being caught. 'How did you recognise me?'

'Your feet.' He grinned and her heart tumbled over at the sight of his smile. 'Other people never forget a face. I never forget a pair of feet. At least,' he mused, sounding irritatingly smug, 'not a pair I like.'

'How peculiar.'

'Mmm. One could almost call it a fetish,' he purred. He slouched back against the wall and stretched out his legs.

'What now?' she asked, measuring the distance to the archway that led out into the alley.

His hand moved to curl around her thigh. A thigh clad in cheap velveteen breeches. Her insides clenched in a most inappropriate way. 'I think I will take you home and seduce the truth out of you.'

His eyelids drooped as if he was imagining what he would do to her. Her insides fluttered in anticipation. Yearning.

Damn him.

'No doubt it will take *forever*.' She knocked his hand away and winced when his eyes opened and observed her with a keenness she hadn't expected.

'Oh, so you have been asking about me, have you?'

She should have pretended to go along with his game, pretended she liked the idea of a seduction. Only she feared if his fingers had travelled one more inch up her leg she would have melted at his feet and given up all thoughts of running.

'Why would I ask about you?'

He acknowledged the cut with a slight incline of his head. 'Why indeed? But you see, I have been asking about you.'

She straightened.

'I thought it wise, d'you see,' he drawled, his voice lazy, his mouth hard. 'In the wake of your deceit.'

'You asked Lady Keswick?' The old woman knew nothing except what was in her letter of application.

He shook his head. 'I asked the owner of the neighbouring house. I asked him about previous tenants, about a man with three daughters.' He smiled then, and it was hard and mean. 'And he told me there was never any such tenant.' He let his head fall back against the wall. 'You are a thief.'

She leapt from the seat and ran.

She didn't make it to the arch.

His arm snaked around her waist. She opened her mouth to yell. He clamped his hand over her mouth. 'Scream and you'll have the law upon us. When I told Pelham of the woman searching his house, he asked for your name so he could swear out a warrant for your arrest.'

Her grandfather was going to have her arrested. Her mind whirled with the pain of it. Her knees trembled. Nausea rose in her throat. The fight went out of her, leaving her limp.

'It's all right,' he said, releasing his hand. 'You are all right.' His voice was surprisingly gentle. He carried her back to the bench and sat her down. 'Put your head between your knees if you feel faint.'

She did as he bid. After a few moments of taking deep breaths, she was able to sit up. 'He's lying. We did live there.'

Garth shrugged.

'Are you going to hand me over to the magistrate?'

'I could.'

Her heart lifted. 'But you won't.'

His lips twisted in a bitter line. 'Not unless you try to run off again.'

'Pelham lied.' For some reason she wanted him to believe her. Desperately.

'Then you will come home with me and tell me the real story and everything will be fine.'

'But...'

'Hush.' He pressed a finger against her lips, brushing them lightly, reminding her of the way his mouth felt against hers. 'My carriage is waiting. I am waiting. For you.' His voice purred deep and low. Utterly seductive.

Desire flooded through her. Longing. She glanced at the back door of the chop house in one last desperate attempt to break free of his sensual pull. 'I can't. Bess will wonder what has happened to me. I am supposed to go to Birmingham tomorrow with the company.'

A roguish smile lit his face and a shiver went down her spine. 'Then we will send Bess a note in the morning and tell her you have changed your mind.'

He made everything sound so seductively easy. And perhaps it was. She could ask him to lend her the money to pay off the debts and find her a good singing role so she could pay him back. It was a fair bargain. Her stomach fluttered. He'd probably want more than his money back. Would it be so bad?

Unable to see a way to break free, she let him lead her to his carriage.

Chapter Eleven

Standing in the middle of his study, Garth stared into the brandy he'd poured and tried not to think about the woman upstairs taking her bath. Tried not to think about long slender limbs, a curvaceous body and the delicate arches of her feet.

His body hardened. He brought it back under control. This wasn't about attraction, or lust. It was about regaining control of the situation.

The fabled control that had eluded him when they'd made love. It had never happened before and would not happen again.

He also wanted the truth, and would have it, if it took him all night. And all of tomorrow.

Pleasure at the thought shuddered deep in his bones.

She'd heard of his reputation; now she would learn what it meant. And he would learn all of her secrets.

A glance at the clock told him an hour had passed since she went upstairs. It was time.

A sense of urgency shortened his breath. His loins quickened in anticipation. He set down his untasted brandy with deliberate care. Strolled out of the room, breathing deeply and clearing his mind.

No need to rush. He had tonight and many nights thereafter. Because no matter what she thought or what she wanted, she was now playing by his rules.

There was no doubt in his mind that Rose was a thief and a liar. Clearly she'd fallen on hard times and had done what she needed to survive. He would get to the bottom of why and exactly what it was she had done.

No matter who or what she was, she would learn he did not litter the English countryside with illegitimate children. Nor did he seduce innocents and leave them to rot on the streets. She'd tricked him, he thought darkly, and for that she would pay, most pleasurably.

He opened the door without knocking. A maid was brushing the long raven hair hanging past Rose's waist. The maid took one look at his face and scurried into the dressing room where she would leave by way of a hidden door to the narrow stairs at the back of the house.

Gold-flecked brown eyes stared back at him in the mirror. The light from the candelabra on the dressing table gilded her skin, deepening the rose of her generous mouth. His face remained in shadow over her shoulder.

Slowly he prowled towards her. As if she sensed a threat, her chin came up, her nostrils flared and she inhaled a deep breath. Her breasts beneath the fine lawn nightgown with its edges of finest lace rose up as if offering their bounty. Yet beneath the warm lovely skin he saw the throb of her heart, a beat of panic and warning.

A smile touched her lips. A lie, of course. Bravado he could not help but admire.

He picked up the brush and continued where the maid had left off, long slow strokes down the shimmering midnight-black tresses. He raised a hank to his nose and inhaled the subtle scent of soap and woman.

His blood grew thick and heavy, its beat a solid pulse in his shaft. He continued his brushing, long slow strokes, and watched her face in the mirror, the lowering of her lids over eyes gone smoky, the speeding up of her breath, the rapid pulse beat at the base of her throat. Heat wafted up from her body.

'Enjoy your bath?' he murmured in her ear.

Goose-flesh rose on her shoulders and her arms. A little shiver vibrated the warm air against his face. The primal urge to toss aside the brush and throw her on the bed, to force her to his will, was close to overpowering.

'Thank you, I enjoyed it very much,' she said in her low throaty voice that was like a rough stroke of firm fingers on his shaft.

'I'm glad.'

She looked up at him in the mirror, the gold burst around her large pupils glittering. 'I have a proposition.'

He almost laughed. How like this woman to go on the attack when already she'd been defeated.

Not too many men would try to bargain from a position of weakness, something his brother, Kit, had told him over and over again in their business dealings.

Garth liked her spirit. There was a great deal about this woman he liked. A surprising amount. He rarely liked them at all.

He ran the back of his hand down her jaw, watching the skin flicker beneath his touch, feeling the silky texture of her skin and the delicate contours of bone.

He set the brush down, silver side up, and clasped her elbows in his palms, slowly lifting her to stand with her back to him, the stool at his knees the flimsiest of barriers, her nape exposed and vulnerable. Her gaze met his in the glass, and in that brief clash, her eyes looked completely honest, open, trusting.

The notion that she fooled him so easily gripped his gut in an iron fist. The only place a woman was ever honest was in bed, beneath his touch. There his skill was so honed, so refined, he could expose them utterly.

Gentle pressure on her arm turned her to face him. He tipped her face with his thumb and forefinger, brushing her full lying mouth with his thumb.

Her eyes widened, not in fear, but desire.

'A proposition,' he purred against the soft flesh of her neck. 'Do enlighten me.'

A quick deep breath lifted the swell of her breasts within a whisker of his chest. He waited for whatever would come out of her mouth with anticipation. A sense of excitement at the challenges she would present, before she revealed her secrets.

'If I…if we do this now…' Her voice was low and breathless and his loins responded to the sound instantly. 'Will you help me with an audition at the Haymarket?'

He tipped his head.

'It is all I will ask of you. A chance to be heard. I have debts I must pay. A singing role would help pay them.'

Her gaze met his full on.

Truth. This was the truth.

After so many deceits it was merely the start. And besides, the idea that she thought she could walk away after one night had his blood running hot with anger.

'A proposition indeed.' He bent his head and took her lips in a brief brush of a kiss. She tipped her head to grant him better access, slid her arms around his neck the better to woo him to her will. She'd forgotten he was a past master at the game of love and she was still a novitiate.

The image pleased him.

He broke away and cupped her cheek. 'Let us talk about it later.'

Her shoulders stiffened. 'No. We will talk about it now. These are my terms—'

'Your terms?' He mocked. 'The terms were set the night you gave up your maidenhead.'

Eyes huge, she shook her head. 'Why? It is done. What can it matter now?'

The desperate note in her voice gave him pause. She didn't believe what she was saying, but she believed she had a say in her destiny. She didn't realise it yet, but she would bend to his will.

'I won't offer something not in my power to give. It would be a lie.'

She frowned. 'But you could try?'

He shrugged. 'I could.' But he wouldn't.

Her smile warmed him, even as he cynically knew she did not see the escape in his words, or didn't want to. Not as clever as she thought, his little nun.

He walked her around the stool. She came willingly, if hesitantly, and the willingness pleased him. As did the spark of heat dancing between them. Embers that carefully nurtured would leap into flame. The flame had seared him the last time they came together. The flame for which he hungered. The flame he would ignite again and again, for as long as it lasted.

He dropped her hand and placed his hands in the dip of her waist. The nightgown disguised nothing of her shape, the ribcage above, the gentle curve of hip below, the waist he could fully encircle with his hands, should he try.

This time, when he took her lips, he lingered, tasting her, renewing his acquaintance with the feel of her velvety mouth, the taste of her tongue, the way her eyes drifted closed and her dark lashes formed mysterious crescents against the warm tone of her skin. Her body melded to his, not yielding, not bending, but expressing its own hunger.

Delicious. Sweeter than honey, more potent than brandy. Intoxicating. He devoured her mouth, explored every inch of her back with eager hands. The span of her shoulders, while not broad, had unexpected strength, backbone, determination; her back narrowed at her waist, then flared to the softest sweetest buttocks it had ever been his pleasure to stroke and caress. They filled his palms like delectable fruit. She arched her back, pressing into his hips, unconsciously, innocently, arousing him to greater heights of lust.

Only with effort did he break free. She stared up at him, her lips red from his kiss, her cheeks scraped by his scruff of beard. He winced and rubbed his jaw. He should have shaved.

She followed the movement. 'I like it,' she whispered. 'It makes you look like a pirate.'

A thief like her.

But the treasure he planned to steal was not wrought of gold or precious jewels. In a woman it was quicksilver and hard to hold. The truth.

He smiled and held out a hand. Unhesitating, she took it. Bold. Brave. No outward sign of trepidation, but it was there, in the too-fast inhale and exhale of breath, in the tremble of her hand in his. She sensed danger. But she hadn't yet learned where it lay.

He led her to his bed.

He grinned. 'Shall I lift you up?'

With one hand, she swept the hair back from her breasts and over her shoulders. 'I can manage a few steps.' She hopped up and leaned back against the pile of pillows and gave him a sultry look from beneath half-lowered lids.

More bravado. A strangely soft feeling in his chest caught

him off guard. He almost opened his mouth to set her free. What, had he turned into some chivalrous knight? Hardly.

No woman walked away from his web of seduction until he was ready.

'Comfortable?' he asked, slipping out of his waistcoat and pulling his shirt free of his pantaloons.

'Very,' she said in that low voice that drove him wild. About to pull his shirt over his head, he glanced at her and caught the swipe of her tongue over her lips.

When she saw him looking, she smiled.

He ripped the shirt off and discarded shoes and stockings.

Putting one knee up on the bed, he stole a brief kiss. 'Wicked minx.'

She laughed. 'No more wicked than you.'

He grinned ruefully. 'I know.' He pulled at the white satin bow nestled in the valley between her breasts. The ribbon slithered undone. Gently he pushed aside the froth of lace on one side, revealing the full rise of an impertinent breast, the furled nipple clearly visible through the lace. The crescent of dark areola peeked at him over the skimming fabric beckoning, his tongue. He obliged with a swift lick.

She gasped and shuddered.

His shaft jerked in reply, demanding its place in the proceedings. Not yet, lad. There was much to accomplish before he took his own pleasure.

Although words were the last thing forming on his tongue when such delights nestled close by.

Her fingers raked through his hair, encouraging him to greater efforts. He pulled the bodice down, exposing one lovely globe of soft tender flesh. He stroked the peak with his tongue, over and around, tasting and savouring the softness and the contrasting hard little nub at the peak.

She squirmed and gave a moan of pleasure.

He smiled at that sound and stretched alongside her on

the bed, taking in the softness in her expression, the haze of heat in her gaze, the desire.

He rolled the budding nipple between thumb and forefinger and watched her melt. 'Where did you go, that night, when you left me sleeping beside the hearth?'

Eyes blank, she stared at him. He swept his tongue across the rise of her breast, then blew gently.

She shivered and moaned.

'Where, Rose? Where did you go, all wrapped up in your cloak?'

'To return the cushions and then to the bedroom,' she said, her breath coming hard when he turned his attention to the other breast. 'I looked in the desk.'

Truth.

He licked and nipped at each hardened peak in turn, caressing them, worshipping them with hands and mouth until she cried out each time he lifted his head to move from one to the other.

He raised himself up on one elbow, ignoring her cry of protest, and dropped a kiss on the point of her stubborn chin. 'And did you find anything?'

'I... No,' she whispered her voice low and hoarse. 'I found nothing. Oh, please, don't stop.'

Her eyes were guileless. The heartbreak buried in her voice beneath the urgency of the desires he'd roused rang true.

A sense of relief flooded through him because she'd been telling the truth all along. About that, he forced himself to remember. Only about that. 'And your real name?'

'Rosabella.'

Truth. She spoke it too naturally for it to be anything else. Rosabella. He liked the way it sounded. He rewarded her by returning his mouth to her breasts and pressing one leg between her open thighs. She welcomed his intrusion with a lift of her hips, seeking the pleasure she'd learned at his hands.

He suckled.

She cried out. Her back arched. Her hands clutched at his shoulders, nails digging, as she uttered guttural cries of encouragement. In her need, her body sought to join with his, her hips rubbing against his erection inside his falls. If he had been hard before, he was more rigid than iron now.

The desire to be inside her, to fill her, to prove she was his, was unlike anything he'd ever experienced. It shredded his reason. He hung on by a thread. In that moment he knew no matter what happened, no matter who she was, or what she wanted, he would want her for a very long time.

And after that, she'd have marriage as her reward.

He lifted his head and gazed into her face, at the almond shape of her eyes, the taut skin over finely cast cheek-bones. 'You really are beautiful.'

He broke from the mesmerising depths of her lovely eyes and kissed each nipple in turn; a light brush of his lips and each peak instantly puckered. He trailed kisses down between their shallow valley, through the filmy fabric, down her breastbone to the dark shadow of her navel, swirling his tongue while her hands wandered across his back as if they weren't quite sure what to do. But when he kissed lower down, nuzzling into her curls through the fine lawn of the gown, she gasped and tried to push him away.

'You can't,' she said breathless.

'Can't I not?' he said, trying not to smile at her innocent shock.

He worked his way down the bed until he was sitting on his heels between her feet. He lifted her right leg, bending it at the knee, and wrapped his hand around her heel. She tensed and he smiled at her. She smiled back and relaxed.

Hers were not small feet, but slender and elegant, high

arched and beautifully formed. 'The winged Goddess of Victory never had such beautiful feet,' he said, raising her foot to his mouth, kissing the arch, massaging the ball. She spread her toes like a cat stretching its claws.

'Mmm,' she said. 'That feels good.'

He leaned forwards and opened the drawer beside the bed. Retrieved the scented oil he kept there for just such occasions. He put a small drop in his hand and rubbed his palms together to warm the oil and release its perfume.

She watched him wide-eyed.

'I promise you will like it.'

She smiled hesitantly.

First, he worked the pad of his thumb along the arch, in slow firm strokes, and she relaxed into the pillows. The weight of her leg rested in his palm where he cupped her heel. He slid his palm up her smooth rounded calf and raised her leg, the glimpse of shadow between her thighs begging for his attention. He ignored its call and massaged her delicious sole and the plump little heel with both thumbs.

She sighed with pleasure.

Gently he lowered her leg to the sheets, angling it wide, and picked up her other foot. No resistance this time—indeed, she was eager to place her foot in his hands. He poured more scented oil in his palm and massaged it in. He frowned at the red mark on the smallest toe. 'What happened here?'

'The shoes. The ones I wear on stage, they pinch.'

He frowned, but said nothing. She would not be wearing those shoes again. He kissed the tiny blemish and she chuckled softly. 'Kissing it won't make it go away.'

'But it can make things feel better,' he said, flashing her a grin, then returned that foot to the bed, her legs spread wide as he smoothed his hands up her shins, pushing the hem of her nightdress higher to expose her knees.

Lovely long limbs, skin kissed golden by a sun it had

never seen, yet somehow remembered. Reverently he kissed the rounded bone and grazed his fingertips along the delicate flesh of the small indent behind. A little gasp rewarded his efforts and encouraged him on. Both hands slid up the inside of her parted thighs, the skin velvety soft beneath his palm, the muscle tender, yet lithe. A feast for the senses. He couldn't recall another woman whose feet and legs were so utterly beautiful.

He cast her a smile designed to seduce, and she smiled back with all the mystery of a woman whose passion lay just below the surface, waiting for one man to release its power. What he had experienced so far was only a fraction of what burned inside her. He would have the key to the rest.

He explored her thighs, the places that made her legs fall further apart, the spots that tickled and made her flesh jump and brought forth her low throaty chuckle.

Lust rode him hard. The urge to sink into her depths, to drive home to the hilt and make her cry out, had him grinding his teeth as he fought for control.

He eased her nightdress up to her waist and exposed the delights of her feminine flesh nestled within the dark bush of midnight-black curls slick with the evidence of her desire. He parted the folds of tender flesh and found the centre of her pleasure, the secret source of bliss.

She drew in a sharp hiss of breath as he caressed that tender nub. The small sound played havoc with his iron control, sucking the air from his chest and firing his belly as if he was the forge and she the air fanning his flames.

'And your last name?' he asked softly.

Chapter Twelve

On the brink of flying apart, at the edge of shattering, he was asking her something. For a moment, Rosa couldn't make sense of his words.

He leaned forwards and licked and then sucked the place where his fingers were moments ago. She almost died from the spiralling pleasure. She wanted to die, to soar free of her body. But somehow he kept her tethered to him, enslaved to his tongue and the rough edge of his beard against her thighs.

A soft warm breath drifted across her heated flesh, bringing no relief, but a promise. 'Tell me your family name, Rosabella.'

'Pelham,' she gasped, willing to do anything to be sure he wouldn't stop now. Not when the end was so near.

He circled his tongue and she wanted to scream as he nudged her so close to the edge, then stopped.

'The truth, Rosabella.'

'Cavendish of Pelham,' she surrendered. 'I swear.'

He stilled, raised his head. Something hot flared in his eyes. Fury. 'Earl Pelham is your father.' He said it flatly as if the answer was moot and she had admitted to some dreadful crime.

She moaned and grabbed at his shoulders, trying to draw him against her fevered body. 'He is my grandfather.'

His lips drew back in a grimace. 'God help me. That I did not expect.'

The bitterness in his voice chilled her. 'What do you mean?'

'It means the matter is closed, child or not. The shackles are fastened.'

Before she could question him further, he had renewed his efforts with his tongue and her mind emptied of all but the need for fulfilment. He sucked at the hot swollen bud between her thighs.

She fell apart. Wave after wave of delicious pleasure washed through her.

Her reward for the truth.

Yet why did she have the sense it was also a punishment? Perhaps it was the hard set to his jaw as he drew her night-dress over her head and looked down at her nakedness. Or the way he roughly settled in the cradle of her hips and brought his hard flesh into her body, filling her deliciously. He drove deeper, and the ache he'd assuaged a few moments before, began again. If anything it was more intense. Slowly he withdrew, and she moaned at the thought he would leave her, fastening her legs around his hips, twining her arms around his neck to hold him close. He made a sound in his throat like a groan of defeat and thrust into her, deeper, harder, over and over. It was like riding the back of the wind in a storm, caught up in a vortex and circling higher and higher. All she could do was hang on tight and let whatever drove him carry her along.

He knew her name, had stripped her bare of her secrets, and now she was completely in his power.

She surrendered to his strength.

Lost herself in the pleasure he visited upon her.

Triumph filled his eyes along with regret.

A nerve jangled. She wasn't a leaf to be picked up by a gale and tossed hither and yon where it willed. Passive was not in her nature. Nor was surrender.

He must suffer the consequences of the fire he had lit. Arms wound around his neck, she pulled herself up against a broad chest damp with sweat. The heat of him against her breasts spurred her on. She swirled her tongue in his ear, and his grunt of pleasure tugged at her core, even as she tilted her hips to meet his next driving thrust. Waves of pleasure once more caught her up. She nipped at his earlobe and, recalling the pleasure of his mouth on her skin, licked the salty skin, his corded neck and the soft part of his throat. She no longer received his driving force deep within her centre; she set the pace with the lift of her hips.

The rough sound of his breath against her shoulder increased in tempo. He sounded in pain. She ran one hand down his back, found the rise of his buttocks and the hard bone of his hip. As he withdrew to pound into her again, she slipped her hand between their bodies and found the base of his shaft and cupped the softness beneath, caressing there as he had played with her breasts.

'Holy hell,' he said in her ear. 'You'll make me…' He caught her hand and pulled it free, returning to stroke and press her sensitive flesh at their joining.

Her body flew apart in pleasure. Her mind darkened, leaving only intense flashes of white heat in her veins.

Breathing hard, Garth pulled away, groaning as if it pained him to leave her, his body convulsing and heavy on her body, his forehead pressed against her shoulder. He rolled off to one side and a moment later she felt him rubbing her at her stomach with the sheet. She glanced down. 'What is it?'

He shook his head wearily. 'It is nothing. A bit of a mess.' He looked…stunned.

He rolled on to his back and pulled her against his shoulder. 'Rest. And don't think for a moment about running off.'

The man really did like to issue orders. 'Am I your prisoner, then?'

He gave a soft rueful laugh. 'If you are, then I am also yours.'

An odd thing to say. She was too tired to question him further, but as her breathing slowed and her skin cooled, she shivered.

He reached down and pulled up the quilt, covering them both.

'Do you want me to ask Pelham for the miniature?'

Oh, dear, now he finally believed her. Guilt racked her. She shook her head. 'It isn't there. It was a fool's errand.'

By never saying the words out loud to another person, she'd somehow clung to the hope that Grandfather was wrong. That Father hadn't thought his daughters unimportant.

The hot burn of tears welled up and, furious, she brushed them away. She would not believe it. Could not. Something had prevented him from keeping his promise. Something beyond his control.

It was just too cruel otherwise.

'Why so many damned lies?' Garth murmured on a long release of breath.

She frowned. 'I wasn't lying.' Not all the time.

'You lied about who you were. What you were.'

'If you had let me alone, everything would have been fine.'

A scornful growl issued from his throat. 'Would it? Or was it all part of a very clever plot?'

'If it was a plot, it did not involve you.'

'Really. Did you not pretend to be a widow? Did you not lure me to a deserted house and get yourself ruined? The consequences are obvious.'

'Lure you?' She almost choked on her anger. 'You followed me. Next I suppose you will be blaming me for the rainstorm and the kisses. You are the seducer. And besides, it isn't possible to ruin an opera singer.'

'But you are not an opera singer. You are the granddaughter of Earl Pelham, the owner of the house you supposedly broke into.'

'We are estranged. He refused me permission to search.'

He let go a huff of breath. 'You can be sure he won't be estranged when he learns I have you in my bed. He'll insist that we wed.'

Why did he sound so smug? It wasn't as if he wanted this marriage.

'Believe me, Grandfather won't care one iota what happens to me.'

'The *ton* will care. It was bad enough I seduced an innocent, but an innocent noblewoman... I'm sorry, there is no other choice. Not to mention you might be carrying my child.' He said the last with an edge of bitterness.

A child. The idea of her own children had always been something she had treasured. He made it sound like a terrible burden. Something to be grimly shouldered. She shivered more violently.

He pulled the quilt higher up her shoulders. 'Shall I ring for a fire?'

Her shivers had nothing to do with the temperature in the room. It was in her heart she felt cold, in her bones. 'You don't want to marry me any more than I want to wed you—why not wait until we are certain there is a child? If there is not, we can go our separate ways.'

An odd expression passed across his face—not anger, it was too hard and cold for that. His lip twisted a fraction, but she had the feeling his scorn was not aimed at her, but rather at himself, as if she'd touched a sensitive spot. 'You were willing to be my mistress. Why not my wife? You will not find me ungenerous. You will have whatever you want. Jewels. Money. Whatever your heart desires, within reason.'

Within reason. What fell within the realm of 'within reason'? 'I have debts. Responsibilities. More than you know.'

'I see,' he said in a chilly voice.

'You don't see. My sister was ill. I borrowed from a moneylender to pay the doctor and their school fees. I needed a singing role to pay him back.'

'As your husband, your debts become my debts. Your responsibilities become mine.'

'It would be a marriage of convenience.'

'Yes.' He seemed not to see anything wrong with it.

'I wanted a love match.' Spoken in relation to this man it sounded ridiculous. She stared at him defiantly and, heaven help her, secretly hoping.

'There you go again.' He shook his head with a grimace of distaste. 'All women spout about is love, when all they need is a man who will provide the necessities of life.'

'By necessities I assume you mean food and heat and a roof. What about a man who will be faithful and true? A man who will share joys and sorrows? A helpmeet?'

He shifted as if the very idea made him uncomfortable. 'Without food and heat and a roof, a person cannot survive. Especially not a child.'

'A child cannot survive without love.'

At that he laughed outright. It had an ugly ring to it. 'I don't know who filled your head with such tales, but children survive all the time without love. Use your head. Look around you. Men only care about satisfying their lust and getting an heir. If they could do the last without getting married, they would.'

'It broke my father's heart when my mother died. He loved her and he loved his children.'

'Then why make no provision for you?'

Silent, she stared at him.

'He should have,' he said. 'But not out of love. Out of duty and honour. Love is merely a figment of overwrought female imagination.'

'You are awful,' she whispered, but the cold feeling spreading into her stomach was the fear he was right. Fear that the love she remembered, clung to, held on to like a child clinging to its mother, was all her own creation.

A myth.

'I simply tell the truth,' he said.

She would not let him destroy her beliefs. 'You are wrong.'

Another twist of his lips. 'All right, then, name your price for this marriage. Anything in my power to give.'

What she wanted most in the world was to know her sisters would have a future. Have the chance to choose a man for love, not out of desperation. For Sam to see a doctor without fear of the debtors' prison looming over their shoulders. Could she give up their futures while she searched for the perfect man? A man who would love her back, when she had so much love inside her to give.

It wouldn't be fair to them, when she could solve everything right now.

And for her there would be physical passion with this man. Nights like tonight. She'd been attracted to him from the first, and if what she'd thought was love was merely infatuation, if she never let it become more than that, wouldn't it be more than bearable? Wouldn't it be more than many women of her class experienced?

He must have seen the weakening of her resolve, her acceptance, because he stroked her shoulder, a sort of solace because he knew she'd give in.

He looked just too smug about her succumbing to his superior male logic. A hot buzz built up in her veins. Anger. The same anger that had driven her to the moneylender, so she would not have to listen to the doctor lecture her about the money she owed.

An anger tainted with the desire to salvage what little pride she had left.

'You spoke of giving me whatever I wanted in exchange for this marriage. These are my terms, then. Pay my debts. They are considerable. Pay for a come-out for each of my sisters and provide them with a reasonable marriage settlement and I will agree to be your wife. But if there is to be no faithfulness on your side, then there is no need for any of this.' She gestured vaguely at the bed.

As he stared at her, the gleam in his eyes an acknowledgement that he'd won, a slow seductive smile curved his beautiful mouth. Her insides clenched, unable to resist his allure.

'I will agree to all but the last,' he murmured. 'As my wife, I expect you in my bed.' The smile broadened, became wicked. 'I promise I won't force myself upon you, but I defy you to resist me.'

Her unruly stomach tumbled over. Resisting him seemed to have been out of the question from the moment she saw him on Lady Keswick's terrace. But she would not submit without a fight. 'Nothing you can do could induce me into your bed.'

'Are you so sure?' He bent his head and brushed her lips with his. Softly. Sweetly. Her heart tumbled with longing.

Longing for more than physical attraction.

It was not to be. And for the sake of her sisters, she must endure.

She turned her face away. 'Very well. If that is part of the price, I will agree. But I want our agreement in writing.'

He laughed. 'Good for you. It seems you have learned something after all.'

Instead of learning about love, she had learned the art of striking a bargain, if she dared trust him to keep his word. Her father hadn't kept his word and she'd trusted him. A bitter taste filled her mouth. 'Then once the contract is signed the matter is settled.'

Cold enveloped her.

Garth really couldn't blame her for her misgivings or her wariness. He'd done his best over the years to ensure that even the most desperate of matchmaking mothers wouldn't accept him, even if he crawled on his belly.

Fortunately, she'd shown him the cards in her hand and he'd played to them. Debts.

Large enough to make her desperate.

Even so, she'd bravely held her ground for longer than he had expected. Was there something behind her reluctance? Had Penelope revealed the circumstances of his birth? Mark knew. Had he told his wife? His back teeth ground together. Dammit, he didn't care if she knew or not. The agreement was set.

She could think what she liked of him. He'd had his unworthiness drummed into him since he was a child. No woman had the power to hurt him, because he didn't allow himself to feel. And if he produced a son as a result of his carelessness, then he'd find another way to make it up to Kit. He might be able to break the entail. It wasn't as if his brother was relying on the title or the land, it had just seemed the right thing to do. A way of making up for stealing his brother's birthright.

He glanced down at his wife to be. She looked none too happy. Might as well deliver all the bad news. If they were going to do this, they were going to do it right. 'About the singing.'

She looked hopeful.

'If you want your sisters to make good marriages, it is out of the question.'

Her face fell. The urge to comfort her took him by surprise.

'There are lots of hostesses who have musical evenings. Once they hear your voice, I am sure you will be invited to sing, not for money admittedly, but people will want to hear you nonetheless.'

He hoped. Most of the *ton*'s hostesses shunned him as if he carried a disease. His own fault. Once he'd learned the truth about his birth, he'd shunned them and their trumped-up mores.

He would have to tell Rosabella that he wasn't exactly considered good *ton*, but not until after the wedding. He wouldn't give her an excuse to refuse him. Which was madness, since he should be glad she didn't want to wed him. No. Not madness. No child of his would suffer what he had gone through.

'Or we could have our own,' she said more cheerfully. 'You could invite your friends.'

His friends, most of them, were not the sort of men he wanted meeting his wife. He would have to enlist Mark's help.

Or he could ask his mother.

He'd sooner be roasted on a spit over a slow fire than ask his dear mother for anything.

Too bad Kit had left England. He was probably the one person who would be happy to help, even if he was the person who should resent Garth the most. But Kit was abroad, so Mark it was. He hated asking his friend for help, when it seemed he had troubles of his own.

'If you are having second thoughts,' she said, pulling her

nightgown on over her head, 'I really would be quite happy to rejoin the opera company.'

Could she read his mind? He gritted his teeth. 'I am not having second thoughts. I am just thinking about the best way to go about this.'

She leaned down and picked her discarded dressing gown from the floor. She turned her back and put it on, effectively distancing herself. He pretended not to notice, but rose naked from the bed and picked up his robe from the chair. He shrugged into it.

'First thing in the morning, I will visit your grandfather and request his permission to wed you.'

'Why? He cares nothing for what I do.'

'Because it is expected and right. And it will help stem malicious gossip. I assume he has guardianship of your sisters until they are of age?'

'No. He wanted nothing to do with us when my father died. I am their guardian.'

The whole thing was odd. To leave a young woman with so much responsibility and no wherewithal to carry it out. No wonder she had debts. 'How old are you?'

'Three and twenty.'

She said it as if that made her a woman of the world. 'You are little more than a child.'

She shot him a glare and he wanted to laugh, but decided against it. He had her where he wanted her and women were unpredictable when their tempers were aroused. They threw things or cried. He hated tears. 'Then we'll ask for his blessing, if not his permission. He'll give it, because he won't want his name bandied around as the man who let his granddaughter be ruined.'

Suspicion filled her expression. 'Do you have enough money to make good on your promises right away? My sisters' need is urgent.'

'I do. Give me a list of your debts first thing in the morning and my man of business will see to them immediately.' Kit hadn't kept his financial brilliance to himself and his generosity had filled Garth's coffers very nicely, despite an expensive and dissolute lifestyle. He'd made sure of it for Kit's sake.

'Thank you.' The words sounded heartfelt and full of relief. A considering expression crossed her face. 'There is one other thing you could ask of my grandfather.'

Ah, here it came. The real reason for her sneaking around in Gorham Place. 'What?'

'My mother's chest and my father's writing desk. I'd like to have them as mementos.'

Surprised, he stared at her. Why would she want old furniture? Mementos of parents who had abandoned her? He shrugged. 'I'll ask.'

She glanced around his room. 'Am I to stay at your house until we are married? It would probably be better if no one knows I am here. Unless you think it won't matter?'

He hadn't thought. And it did matter. She would have enough trouble with the high sticklers, without throwing their odd arrangement in their faces. 'You are right. We will have to keep your presence here a secret. You won't be able to be seen in public until we are wed, I'm afraid.'

'Won't your servants gossip?'

'You will find them very discreet.'

'I suppose they have to be.'

A niftily placed barb. He gritted his teeth. 'Indeed.' He glanced down at the pile of rags on the floor. The breeches and shirt she'd worn from the theatre. 'Where are the rest of your clothes?'

'I only brought one gown with me from Lady Keswick's house. It is at my lodgings in St Giles, with my valise.'

'I'll collect it in the morning.'

She nodded. 'Thank you.'

He put an arm around her shoulders. 'Now, sweet betrothed of mine, let us go back to bed.'

She shook her head. 'Not until after our contract is signed.'

The hackles on the nape of his neck rose. 'Are you afraid I won't keep my part of the bargain?'

'Is it likely?'

She didn't trust him and he didn't blame her one bit. 'No. Not likely, until I am tired of teaching you the art of love-making. That isn't going to happen for a very long time.' He brushed her mouth with his, then nipped her lip.

For all that she was trying to hide her desire, her eyes grew slumberous.

His body sprang to life. Impossible as it seemed, he was more than glad he was marrying this woman, even if it did ruin his plans.

All he had to do was make sure he didn't take any chances. Keep firm control and spend outside of her body so if it turned out she wasn't with child, everything would be perfect. He could have what he wanted and still keep to the promise he'd made to himself the night Christopher left England.

He gazed at her lovely face. She looked weary, as if she hadn't slept well for many nights.

He reached out and took her hand and led her to the bed. 'Lie in my arms and sleep. Tomorrow we will begin our explorations anew.'

He felt exceedingly pleased when she smiled and let him help her on to the bed. He wasn't a boy without control; he could lay with her, enjoy the feel of her, without touching.

In time, she would come to trust him.

* * *

Garth awoke with a start to the sound of a clock chiming six somewhere below. His usual time to awake no matter what his activities the night before. He generally went riding in Hyde Park before it became crowded with people wanting to talk.

He rolled on his side to watch Rosabella curled up facing him, her cheek pillowed on her hand, breathing deep and untroubled. She looked like a child. Twenty-three. Viewed from his years of profligacy, she was terribly innocent, yet seemed much older, more self-assured than most of the débutantes he'd carefully avoided all these years.

A smile tugged at his lips. Clever enough to catch him in her web of lies and deceit. Why didn't he care? Not that he'd let her deceive him again.

In winning her over, he'd made some promises that would not be easy to keep. No riding today. First he'd visit Mark and, depending on the outcome, would move on from there.

He hopped out of bed and went to his dressing room, where his valet was already waiting.

'Good morning, my lord,' Callen said.

'Good morning, Callen. The lady in my bed is to be treated with the utmost respect since she will soon be your mistress and my wife.'

Callen's jaw dropped. 'Y-yes, my lord.'

'I will inform the other servants on my way out.'

Callen bowed and began stropping the razor. 'May I offer my congratulations, my lord?'

Garth looked at him for a minute. Tested whatever it was unfurling in his chest. The pleasant knowledge of sharing his life, his hopes and ambitions, as well as his bed. Waking up beside Rosabella had apparently filled a void he hadn't known existed.

Surprised, he sat down in the chair in front of the mirror. 'Yes, Callen. I believe congratulations are indeed in order.'

After a visit with his man of business to ensure he had enough ready funds on hand to pay off Rosabella's debts when he received her accounting, Garth found himself at Mark's front door in Golden Square, confronting his friend's cheery butler. 'His lordship isn't available to callers.'

Garth forked over a crown. 'Nonsense, Steed. He'll see me.' He pushed inside the door.

'Wait here,' the butler said, pointing to a carved wooden chair against the wall. 'I'll enquire if he is up.'

Garth followed the man down the hall, practically stepping on his heels, and was through the dining-room door before the man could speak.

Mark was eating breakfast, dressed and ready for the day. 'Off to the Home Office?' Garth asked, sitting down and helping himself to a piece of toast.

Mark glared at him, then nodded at the butler. 'That will be all, Steed.'

The man withdrew and closed the door.

'How's the chin?' Mark growled, setting his paper aside.

Garth touched his jaw. 'Never better.' He reached for the coffee pot.

'Why the hell didn't you bring my wife home when you found her?'

Still brooding about that. Still suspicious. Garth leaned back against the chair and grinned at the surly face of his friend. Mark had grown possessive since his marriage and Garth couldn't resist the urge to needle him. 'You mean you wanted me to manhandle your wife kicking and screaming into my carriage? Or perhaps you wanted me to seduce her into coming back to London with me?'

Mark straightened. 'You put one finger on my wife—'

'I was more concerned about not allowing anyone else to put their fingers on her. Not that she showed any interest,' he added hastily as Mark started to rise. He had no wish to drop Penelope in the soup. He didn't care a fig about the girl. She was a stupid little chit who didn't recognise a good man when she found one. They never did from his observation over the years. But he didn't want to see his friend hurt so he kept his own counsel about Bannerby.

Mark sank back on to his seat. 'It's a bloody mess. She refuses to say why she went there in the first place. Or who she was meeting.'

'I don't think she was meeting anyone. She turned up with Maria Mallow. You know what a troublemaker she is. Where were you?'

'On a mission for the Home Office. I had to escort a woman to Yorkshire. She had information about these troublemakers at the mills. I had to talk to some people she knows.'

'A woman?'

Mark absently rearranged the cutlery set out before him. 'Yes, a woman. Damned if I like the idea, but she's well placed with the ringleaders.'

'You don't think Penelope saw you with this woman?'

Mark's head shot up. 'Of course not. Do you think I'm an idiot? I took every precaution to ensure the mission was secret.'

'Maybe she doesn't like you keeping secrets. After all, aren't you two supposed to be in love?'

What the hell was he doing, asking that sort of question? He didn't believe in love. Damn Rosabella and her sentimental talk. He put up a hand when Mark opened his mouth to reply. 'It's none of my business. I came to ask for help.'

The door opened. 'Mark? Oh!' The lady of the house gasped. 'I didn't know you had company.'

Penelope looked from Mark to Garth and he was surprised to see the shadows in her pretty green eyes. And there were circles beneath, like bruises. All was not well. No wonder Mark looked so morose.

'It's only Garth,' Mark said. 'Come to ask a favour. I was about to tell him to go to hell.'

'Didn't you tell me once you owed Garth a great deal?' she said quietly. 'Wasn't that the reason you insisted I accept him as your friend when we married?'

Good Lord, was she supporting him against her husband? Now there was trouble in the making. Garth shot to his feet. 'Consider all debts paid in full.'

'Wait,' Penelope said. 'There is something I have been wanting to tell you, Mark.'

Her husband shook his head, his mouth in a grim flat line. He was clearly dreading what she would say next.

'If it wasn't for Garth being his usual horrid self, I might have made a very serious mistake in Sussex. He didn't just try to convince me to go home, he stood between me and another man.' She twisted her hands together. 'I was angry at you leaving me alone, Mark, and I might have done something I regretted for the rest of my life, but I didn't, because of Garth.'

The tension in Mark's shoulders eased. 'What man?'

'Nothing happened, Mark. It is over.'

Bloody hell, his friend had actually thought…despite his truthful denial. His word of honour. 'I ought to put out your daylights,' Garth said.

'I won't try to stop you,' Mark said. 'I'm sorry for thinking the worst.'

Wasn't the worst what everyone thought? Even Rosabella, when he was trying to do the right thing. The fault of the reputation he'd carefully cultivated all these years. 'No harm done.' He stuck out a hand and they shook.

'Did you find Mrs Travenor?' Penelope asked. 'I liked her, she was very kind. She has a wonderful voice, Mark. I couldn't think why she dashed off to London that way, but I do hope she is all right.' She looked at Garth expectantly.

Surprised, Garth stared back. He hadn't expected her to care about anyone but herself. 'She is why I am here. We are going to be married.'

If he had fired a pistol in the room, there wouldn't have been as much shock on their faces.

'Damn it, Garth,' Mark said finally. 'You certainly know how to surprise a fellow. Who is this woman?'

'Where is she?' Penelope asked at the same moment.

'With me,' Garth said. 'To cut a long story short, she is not a widow, has never been married, and she's a Cavendish. Pelham's granddaughter. Not knowing any of that, I... Well, things got out of hand.'

'You ruined her,' Mark said bluntly.

Garth gazed at the fresco around the ceiling. 'It is more complicated than that, but in the eyes of the world, yes.'

'Oh, dear,' Penelope said.

Garth paced around the breakfast table. 'The thing is, if any word of this gets out, she will never be accepted in society. It will be bad enough that she is married to me.'

Mark raised his brows in tacit agreement.

'She will need a respectable sponsor.' He winced. 'And I need somewhere for us to be married in a hurry.'

'Why not ask her grandfather?'

'He is not amenable to such an arrangement.'

Mark nodded. 'Irascible old gentleman, Pelham. I've seen him in action in the House.'

'Rosabella has two sisters and eventually she wants them to make a splash in society. I said I would help, but honestly, without some respectable female taking her under her wing, she doesn't stand a chance. None of the old biddies will so much as glance at her if she is my wife.'

'I'll do it,' Penelope said.

Mark looked at her askance.

'Please, Mark. We both owe Stanford our gratitude.'

'Where is she now? Blackheath?'

Garth's discreet little town house, recently vacant. 'Not the kind of place one takes a prospective wife,' he said, recalling what had happened when Kit took Sylvia there. 'She is here in town.'

'With your mother?'

'God, no.'

'Perhaps you could enlist Lady Stanford's help?' Mark said. 'She is well in with all the old biddies.'

Garth wouldn't ask her for a bandage if his life's blood was draining out on the floor. He shook his head. 'She would never agree.'

Penelope said nothing, she just gazed at her husband with those big green eyes of hers, eyes that seemed to melt her husband, but left Garth feeling cold.

He wasn't going to force his friend into helping him. 'I'll leave you to finish your breakfast in peace.'

'No. Wait,' Mark said. 'We can help. Lord knows, I owe you. Again. But whatever we do, I will not have a breath of scandal attached to my wife.'

'More scandal,' she said with a tired little smile, but she lifted her chin and squared her shoulders.

Garth wondered if there wasn't more to the green-eyed miss than he'd first thought. 'There is one slight problem.'

They both looked at him. 'The people at Lady Keswick's house party are going to recognise her.'

Mark looked grim. 'Wonderful. The same people who saw Penelope there. All we can do is brazen it out.'

While he sensed disharmony between this newly married pair, they seemed to have come to some sort of truce and were prepared to come to his aid. For Rosabella's sake, he wasn't going to delve any deeper. 'I am in your debt. Here is what I need.'

Chapter Thirteen

Rosa sat in the small drawing room upstairs, reading while she waited for Garth to return. A knock on the door to the street made her lift her head, listening for the sound of his voice, but he'd said he wouldn't be back until dinner time. It must be a caller. A visitor for Garth. The butler would send them away. A few moments later, the butler arrived at the door. 'Lady Smythe to see you, my lady.'

'Me?' Rosa glanced down at her one and only shabby gown collected from her old lodgings by a footman. 'Please tell her I am not at home.'

'Oh, dear,' said a gentle voice behind the butler. 'Didn't Stanford tell you he'd asked me to call?' She glanced at the butler, who swiftly withdrew. 'He asked me to come and talk to you about the wedding arrangements.'

The heat of embarrassment scorched her cheeks. She laughed, albeit uncomfortably. 'He left before I awoke this morning. I had no idea he planned to discuss my circumstances with you.'

'Oh, I see.'

'Please sit down. Would you like tea?'

'No, thank you. I cannot stay long. I have several more calls to make this afternoon. He plans for you to be married at my house. Do you have a date?'

'Not as yet. It is extraordinarily generous of you to take such a personal interest in my predicament.'

'Not at all. Stanford is my husband's best friend.'

'The last time I saw Stanford and your husband they were at daggers drawn. Or rather, fists raised?'

A brief smile tilted Penelope's lips. 'I gather it is what male best friends do. I hope we will also become friends and behave with far more civility.'

An offer of friendship? Rosa could barely believe her ears. She smiled. 'You are too kind.'

'Not at all. I would count it an honour to befriend the woman who captured Lord Stanford.'

Captured. Almost as bad as tricked. 'It was a mistake.'

'I wasn't criticising. It was more…admiration.' She smiled her sweet smile. 'About the wedding. Are there family members you wish to invite?'

She would love to invite her sisters, but the headmistress would not allow them to leave until all the debts were settled and that would take a few days. Garth wanted the ceremony to take place right away.

Also, her sisters were still hoping she would find the will. She didn't yet have the heart to tell them that it didn't exist and she had married instead. She shook her head. 'No one.'

'Who will give you away? Stanford said your grandfather is in town.'

Rosa lifted her chin, the old anger at her only living relative swiftly heating her blood. It was partly Grandfather's fault she was in this predicament. 'No.'

'Then leave it to Mark.' She beamed. 'Another of Stanford's friends can serve as groomsman.'

'Won't it all seem terribly odd to the *ton*?'

Penelope waved an airy hand. 'We'll pass it off as a great romance. My husband is very well thought of in political circles and in society. If he approves of the match, many others will follow. Perhaps not those with the highest of insteps. It may be some time before you receive tickets to Almack's, if ever, but you will hardly care about that once you have a husband.'

'I will be seeking husbands for my sisters.'

'Yes, of course.' She seemed a little nonplussed, then tipped her head and tapped her bottom lip. 'But not this year, I think. The Season is almost over. You will have lots of time to prove you are the very best of *ton* over the next few months. You must do exactly as I tell you and we can bring it off. Stanford, too.'

Did Garth account for the note of doubt in her voice? 'I will do everything I can to live up to your expectations. I am very grateful.'

Penelope took her hand. 'You were kind to me at Lady Keswick's house. I am more than happy to return the favour. I really do hope we will become the best of friends.'

'Me, too.' For the first time in a long time, Rosa felt as if her feet were on solid ground, no more threats of prison hanging over her, the prospect of a good future for her sisters and now a friend. 'I will never be able to thank you and Lord Smythe enough.'

Penelope hesitated. 'There is one more thing I want to say. I am not quite sure how to put it.'

Rosa felt a prickle of wariness across her shoulders. 'If we are to be friends, I would like you to feel free to speak your mind.'

'Stanford is not the steadiest of men. No one was more surprised than my husband at his intention to marry.'

Rosa's spine stiffened.

'Not that you aren't lovely enough to turn any man's head,'

the other woman said. 'Oh, dear, I am making a pickle of this. What I mean is, you should not have to marry out of necessity, if you do not like to do so.'

Rosa stared at her. 'You think I shouldn't marry him?'

Penelope took a quick breath. 'Stanford is a hard man to know. He has rarely stayed with the same woman more than a month or two and has very few good friends. He lets no one close. Even my husband agrees he is not good marriage material. If you want to change your mind, I will help you find an alternative.'

The words confirmed her fears. But marriage to Garth truly was her best hope for her sisters. She'd learned work in the theatre was sporadic. Only the principals made a good living. Everyone else scraped by. It was too late for second thoughts. Another payment to the moneylender was due at the end of the week and Stanford would help her only if they were married.

It wasn't a love match. She'd given up on those dreams, but she did have hope they could make a go of it.

'I appreciate your offer,' she said. 'But I think this is best.'

The other woman took her hand. 'I hope so. I married my husband for love and it has been a rocky road. Perhaps your way is better.'

She looked so sad, Rosa couldn't help herself and put an arm around her shoulders. 'Do you want to talk about it?'

Penelope sniffed. 'Things are better. I should not have spoken of what I saw. A wife should turn a blind eye to such things or risk looking a fool. I am sure everything is going to be fine. I just wish he would be honest with me, so I know where I stand.'

'If ever you need someone to talk to, I am here.'

With a brave smile, Penelope rose. 'You see, already we are friends. I will take my leave now and look forward to seeing you on your wedding day. Have Stanford let me know the moment he has a date arranged.'

'I will.'

She escorted her new friend to the front door and watched her climb into her carriage, feeling more than a little breathless. She really was going to be married. To a man she hardly knew, and of whom no one, not even his friends, had a good opinion.

Could she accept his intention to do as he pleased after the wedding? She didn't feel very accepting.

She went back up to the drawing room. She read a few more lines of her book when another knock sounded on the street door.

'Not more callers,' Rosabella muttered. She ran to the window, peeped out just in time to see a footman loaded down with packages entering the house.

Voices echoed in the hall below and a second or so later Garth strolled in with a smile, his gaze seeking her out. 'I went shopping.'

The footman followed him in, deposited the packages on the floor and left. Rosa eyed the parcels. 'What did you buy?'

'Bride clothes. Er…items you will need until your trunk arrives from Lady Keswick's. I persuaded your grandfather to drop her a note. He will let me know when they arrive.'

'My grandfather? Why?'

'To observe the proprieties, so to speak. Apparently he isn't keen on another scandal. He agreed to have your things delivered to his house and forward them on. I could hardly have them sent directly here.'

'What else did he say?'

'He agreed to say nothing against our marriage, no matter what his private thoughts might be. And nothing against you.'

She stared up at him. 'Did he say anything else?' *Such as I want to welcome my granddaughters back into the fold.*

Garth shook his head. 'He wasn't pleased to see me.' He looked haughtily down his nose. 'He indicated he rather thought we deserved each other.'

A small smile at the thought of Grandfather and Stanford glaring at each other touched her lips. 'I am glad he won't object.'

'He agreed to the return of the trunk and the desk, too. Glad to be rid of them.'

Well, that was something.

'The Smythes have agreed we can be married at their house by special licence,' he said. 'Later they will hold a dinner party where you will be properly introduced to some members of the *ton*.'

'I know. Lady Smythe left a few moments ago. She wants to know what day you have chosen.'

'I'll send round a note.'

'Oh,' she breathed. 'Then you have a date.'

'Wednesday.' He patted his pocket. 'I have the special licence and a cleric to do the deed.'

Four days hence. 'Are you sure you want to do this?' she asked.

An expression of resolve crossed his face, his shoulders seemed to straighten and he nodded. 'Yes. I am sure.' He glanced at the pile of parcels. 'Aren't you going to open them?' He grinned like a boy caught in mischief. 'I am sure you will like them.'

'These are all for me?'

No one had bought her gifts since her mother died.

'Mmm.' He pushed two of them aside with his foot. 'Those you might want to open in private.'

She eyed him askance. His dark eyes danced and her tummy hopped. 'Personal items.'

'You really should not have spent your money on me,' she said. 'Not when you have the expense of my sisters and—'

He held up his hand. 'Do you think I want my wife walking around in rags?'

'Well, no, but—'

His mouth took on a stubborn line. 'Don't criticise before you see what I have brought.'

By rejecting his gift she'd insulted him, perhaps even hurt his feelings. Though it was hard to tell, for his mocking smile had returned and he sprawled carelessly on the nearby sofa as if he didn't give a damn.

She smiled. 'I'm sorry. Your generosity is appreciated, my lord. I merely didn't want you to get into debt or anything when you have already done so much for me.'

He looked a little mollified. 'A few kickshaws and gewgaws will not put me in the sponging house.'

She was glad to hear it. From what little she knew of the rakehells and bucks who lived in town, they more often than not found themselves in the River Tick.

He must have seen the doubt on her face. 'Don't give me that look. I've been dibs in tune for years. Haven't spent a night in the King's Bench since I gained the title. And besides, now I'm a peer, they can't arrest me.'

But they could lose everything they owned. Wives and children could end up on the street. Many had since the end of the war with France.

Her hand flattened on her waist. Of course, she didn't know yet whether or not she was with child. It could be at least a week or more before she knew.

She knelt on the floor to hide her sudden flush of embarrassment at the thought she might be carrying a child and undid the knots in the string. The paper parted to reveal a silk gown of the most beautiful shade of rose.

'I thought you might wear that at the wedding.'

Her wedding. And his.

She lifted the gown from the paper and held it up. Silk

roses, a deeper shade than the gown, decorated the sleeves and the festoon of silk above the deep hem of embroidered lace. Despite the intricate decoration, the gown was feather-light in her hands. An extraordinary dress. Striking. The deep colours perfect for her complexion. 'It is lovely. Where on earth did you find such a beautiful gown at such short notice?'

He gave a deprecating shrug. 'A seamstress I know. She owes me a favour or two.'

The reason was clear. Whoever this dressmaker was, she would have provided gowns for his women. The pang was painful and raw. Jealousy. How could she be jealous? There was no love between them. At least not on his side. Theirs was a marriage of convenience. As time went on, the more it seemed it was her convenience, for he had nothing to gain from this wedding.

To hide her thoughts she opened the next package and the next, and the one after that. There were morning gowns, and a ball gown, and handkerchiefs and scarves. Even a couple of bonnets and a riding habit.

'Do you ride?' he asked when she pulled the royal-blue velvet out of the tissue paper. It was the most gorgeous habit she had ever seen.

'Yes, I do.'

He looked pleased. 'We can ride out together in the mornings, if you like. I'll purchase a mount for you.'

Expense after expense mounted up. Guilt rolled through her. He hadn't wanted to be married and now he was being forced to spend a fortune.

She looked at the piles of gowns and the lovely fabric lying across her arms. 'It's too much.'

A flicker of pain darkened his eyes. Gone so fast, she could not be sure she had seen it at all. Indeed, now she looked at him, his smile mocked her. 'Only by entering the *ton* yourself can you introduce your sisters to society. Consider this part of our bargain.'

A bargain. That was all this marriage was to him. 'Thank you, my lord. You are generous.'

His mouth tightened, probably at her lack of enthusiasm. But how could she be happy when she came like a beggar to this marriage of theirs? A marriage forced on him because she'd been foolish enough to fall for his charms.

In a bargain both people gained something. What did he have to gain except in his bed? That he could get anywhere.

It must be the child he cared about. A child would bring them together. Happiness curled around her heart.

A hot lump rose in the back of her throat. She swallowed hard and smiled at him. 'Thank you so much. I'll call for a footman to have them taken upstairs.' Oh, dash it all, did her voice have to sound quite so damp? He would think her a watering pot.

'There is one more thing,' he said with a smile. 'The chest and the writing desk will arrive tomorrow as promised.'

'So soon?' Her smile widened. 'How wonderful.'

'You are very welcome.' He looked pleased. 'There is one last thing I must do today. I need the information about this moneylender for my man of business. I will have him take care of the matter right away.' He went to the writing desk and set forth paper, pens and ink. 'Write down his direction, along with that of your sisters.'

She hurried to comply, grateful he was acting so speedily. She quickly wrote down the required information and handed it to him. She stood on tiptoes and kissed his cheek. 'This means everything to me.'

He captured her hand. 'I will be back in time for dinner.'

He kissed her hand and the traitorous warmth rushed up from her belly. The desire for his touch.

She saw the answering warmth in the depth of his dark gaze.

At least they had this in common. It might not be perfect, but it was something they shared.

She would have to be very careful not to let him see her emotions went deeper. She had the sense he preferred to keep everything light and easy. And if she didn't do the same, he would become bored and find other interests; he had as good as said so.

The thought made her feel simply dreadful.

When Garth returned home for dinner, Rosa did not object when he suggested they have dinner in his chamber. No, their chamber.

Hand in hand they left the drawing room, where they had partaken of sherry together, and climbed the stairs. He opened the door and stood back for her to enter.

A small oblong table set for two sat in front of a sofa. Apparently they were to eat side by side. Candles flickered, silver glittered and crystal sparkled. The room looked positively…romantic. There was even a lovely yellow rose gracing a vase in the middle of the table.

Her anxiety of earlier in the day reduced to a faint unease only to be expected in these early days, she supposed. And although she wasn't yet married and she'd already experienced the delights of the marriage bed, she did feel a little like a new bride. Being a wife would be very different to being a mistress. A mistress could walk away.

From what Penelope had said, Rosa guessed that Garth disposed of his mistresses long before they were ready to leave. And he'd made it quite plain he did not intend to change his ways. Then why was he going to all this trouble to woo her?

At the back of her mind, something, some nagging little thing she could not quite grasp, kept making its presence known. A little whisper of disquiet. A feeling there was something she had yet to learn.

Why, when he'd been nothing but brutally honest about his lack of emotion?

He helped her to sit, rang the bell and sat beside her. The butler and two footmen carried in a series of trays, which they proceeded to set before them. The butler filled their wineglasses from a decanter, which he left on the table at Garth's elbow. It was all done with such smoothness, Rosa had the distinct impression this was not the first time they had served dinner this way.

Not something she should be thinking about.

'Will there be anything else, my lord?'

'No, thank you. We will not need you again this evening.'

The man bowed and withdrew, closing the door softly behind him.

Garth lifted his glass. 'To my future bride.'

She picked up hers. 'To my husband-to-be.'

Before she could drink, he held his glass to her lips. And when she had taken a sip, he drank from the same spot on the glass, his dark gaze all the while fixed on her face. Seductive. Tempting.

Not to be outdone, when he had finished drinking from his glass, she held her goblet to his lips. His eyes danced in appreciation as first he took a sip and then she drank.

'Bravo,' he murmured in her ear.

A shiver ran down her spine at the wicked sensation.

'Ready to eat?' he asked.

'I'm famished.'

He lifted the covers from the plates the servants had set

in front of each of them. Oddly, his plate held only cuts of meat and hers only an assortment of vegetables.

He grinned when she gave him a puzzled sideways glance. 'I call this *déjeuner au médiéval*. Watch what I mean.' He carefully cut a portion of chicken breast, then held it up to her mouth.

'Oh,' she said. And he popped it in.

He cut another piece for himself.

She cut up a carrot braised in butter and fed it to him. He dragged it off the fork with strong white teeth. Somehow it seemed sumptuously decadent, to be fed and to feed. There was also laughter when they tried the peas and ended up scattering them all over the floor. He dived for a rescue.

'I'll request no peas next time,' he said, getting up from his knees after chasing one of the recalcitrant vegetables under the table.

'Asparagus works best,' she agreed, holding one of the delicate shoots out to him by a thumb and forefinger.

He bit all the way down it, reaching her fingers, then pretended to take a bite of her thumb.

She laughed.

He popped a mouthful of roast beef in her open mouth.

'Mmm,' she protested. When she finally managed to swallow both her laugh and the meat, she shook her head at him. 'Not so fast. Do you want me to choke?'

A look of mock consternation crossed his face. He placed a hand over his heart. 'Not before our wedding night.' His face turned serious. 'I never want any harm to come to you.'

Her heart gave an odd little bump. It was as if it had stopped for a moment, then started again, but out of rhythm. Her insides felt suddenly loose. Welcoming. Heat rushed to her cheeks. 'I'm glad to know it,' she said with mock severity, hiding her wanton reaction.

He held his glass to her lips once more and she drank

deeply this time. He finished the wine, knocking it back with practised ease. He looked down at their plates. Very little remained. 'Are you ready for dessert?'

'I thought that was me.' Good Lord, was this really her, this bold flirtatious woman? And was that a flush of pride she felt at his sudden boyish laugh and the flare of heat in his gaze?

She liked him so much more when he lost his cynical expression. Affection filled an empty space behind her ribs. She leaned forwards and landed a clumsy kiss on his cheek.

In an instant, he caught her close, turning his head to capture her mouth. His kiss tasted of red wine. His arm around her shoulder felt strong and manly; the touch of his knuckles on her cheek was tender. Something inside her seemed to settle, the way a cat sprawls out in front of a fire. She felt comfortable. Warm. Welcome.

Slowly he let her go, an expression of awe on his face. Or was it simply pleasure? It fled so fast she could not be sure, especially not when he turned away, removed the remains of their feast to the tray side table and lifted the last two covers. Beneath one was a mound of strawberries. The other hid a dish of cream and a bowl of sifted sugar.

'Now how does this work?' she asked.

His eyes were laughing with genuine amusement. 'We could try sipping the cream and then eating a strawberry before we swallowed.'

'A disaster worse than the peas in the offing.'

He grinned. 'You've tried it before.'

Scandalised, she laughed. 'Certainly not. Why don't I dip a strawberry in the cream and sugar for you, and you do the same for me?'

'They look so good, why don't we do it at the same time.'

She smiled and nodded. 'Why not?'

It was harder than it sounded. Trying to bite a strawberry

while aiming for the other person's mouth at the same time. The fruits were particularly large and when she bit into the second one he gave her, the juice ran down her chin.

He licked it away.

His tongue felt delicious on her skin, a sensual sensation low in her core. Her eyelids drooped.

'You taste good,' he murmured, low and enticing.

Pleasure hummed through her veins. A pulse beat low in her abdomen. Excitement stole her breath as desire took hold. But she wanted to give him pleasure, not just receive. Her hand drifted over the strawberries, her eyes selecting the ripest of the fruit in the bowl. She swirled it slowly in the cream.

From a sidelong glance, she watched his gaze follow the movement, his lips already parting, his teeth gleaming white, ready to bite. She scooped up a mountain of cream on the berry and dabbed it on his chin.

His dark eyes twinkled.

And she cleaned it off with several licks of her tongue. The faint graze of his stubble on her tongue had the feel of a cat's lick. She purred.

His eyes creased. 'Oh, my sweet Rosabella,' he breathed. 'There are many more uses for strawberries and cream.' An eyebrow shot up. 'If you dare.'

This was what he was getting from their marriage. This physical enjoyment. And she enjoyed it just as much and saw no reason to be ungenerous. Indeed, after all he had done for her, he deserved far more. 'I dare,' she whispered, flashing him a saucy glance. 'If you do.'

He laughed. Loud and free. A sound full of joy. 'Oh, little nun, do you know how you tempt me? Come.' He took her hand. 'This game needs no barriers between us.'

He pulled her to her feet and twirled her around and made short work of the fastenings on her gown. While he nuzzled her neck, he pushed the gown down her arms and over her hips. It slid to the floor, and she stepped out of it, turning to face him.

'I'm not finished.'

She smiled. 'Your turn.' She undid the buttons on his coat and pushed the tight-fitting garment off his shoulders. She tugged and pulled at the soft wool, dragging it down his muscled arms. Panting, she pulled it off and cast it aside. 'My word, that jacket is tight.'

No response. She glanced up at him and found his gaze fixed on her breasts rising and falling from her exertions. He raised his eyes to her face and she almost drowned in the heat of his desire.

Her insides turned liquid. She flung her arms around his neck, kissed those wonderful sensual smiling lips and leaned in to him. His hands came to her hips, large, warm, gentle. He cupped her buttocks and pulled her hard against his length. His arousal pressed against her belly.

Lovely. Pleasurable. Wildly entrancing. A tilt of her pelvis brought him closer to where she needed him. Urgency flowed through her blood.

Sweeping his mouth with her eager tongue, she tasted strawberries and cream. A hand stroked circles on her back and came around to cup her breast lightly. Too lightly for the powerful waves of longing sweeping through her.

A groan rumbled in his throat. He broke away, his breathing harsh. 'Turn around, sweet. Let us be done with these clothes.'

He stripped her of her stays and chemise and carried her to the bed. Feverishly he untied her garters and ripped off her stockings, all tangled up with her shoes. His hot gaze raked her body as he tore at his cravat, flinging it aside. The shirt quickly followed. He toed off his shoes and peeled off his pantaloons.

She gazed at him. Her almost-husband. So glorious in his nakedness, so lean and finely drawn. His arousal jutted straight up, engorged and dark and magnificent.

An instrument of pleasure.

'Do you like what you see?'

A slow perusal up the flat stomach ridged with muscle, over the wide sleek-as-a-Thoroughbred chest, up a strong column of throat to his face. He was watching her with desire, and something else—pride. Not the pride of arrogance, but a defiant pride, as if he thought she might reject him. Puzzled, she stared at him and saw a vulnerability she had not expected.

'I approve very much.' She licked her lips and his gaze followed the movement.

It seemed to break the spell, for he returned to their table and brought the strawberries and cream to the bed. 'I hope you won't mind if we dispense with the sugar?' His eyes gleamed wickedness, brimming with mischief. 'I am guessing it will be worse than sand for getting in places it is not supposed to be.'

'I will take your advice,' she said, 'for I am sure you have lots of experience.'

He darted a glance from under lowered lashes, then smiled. 'Not at all. Just an assumption.'

So he was going to pretend he had not played this game before. It was rather sweet that he would consider her feelings in such a way. It made her feel special.

He lay down beside her, placing the bowls on her side of the bed. Leaning over her, he picked up a strawberry and dipped it in the cream. 'Let me see,' he said, running his gaze down her body. 'Which part of you do I most want to eat?'

Her inner muscles clenched. She gasped at the wickedly

pleasurable pulse. Her breathing quickened. Her heartbeat went wild.

'Here, I think.' He dabbed the cream on her breasts, right on the peaks, and in her navel. He bit into the strawberry, taking half of it into his mouth, then leaned over to kiss her.

Along with the kiss, she received the ripe fruit in her mouth. 'Don't swallow it yet,' he said.

He swiftly dipped his head and licked her breast, returning with cream on his tongue, which he added to the strawberry already in her mouth.

Wicked. Ridiculous. But very, very sensual. He encouraged her with a nod and she chewed and swallowed as he watched with his devilish smile. He winked. 'What is left is mine.'

He swooped down and suckled her other breast, sending sweet aches all the way to her core. 'Delicious,' he mumbled against her skin as he trailed kisses all the way to her navel, where he swirled his tongue. She sighed with pleasure.

He laughed. Not mocking. Just pure enjoyment.

She loved this side of him. This delightfully boyish, playful rogue. She smiled at him with tenderness, hope blossoming in her heart. Perhaps, in time, there would be more than convenience in their marriage.

She sat up and pushed at his shoulder until he rolled spread-eagled on his back, then she knelt beside him and selected a strawberry, loading it with cream. 'Now what shall I do with this?'

He opened his mouth, his eyes full of laughter.

'Too easy, sirrah.'

There really only was one new place to put the cream. Excitement mixed with trepidation sent trembles running through her body. A drop of cream rolled off the strawberry on to the flat plane of his stomach. It would all run off if she didn't act soon. Taking a swift breath, she dabbed carefully at the head of his shaft.

A groan and his hips came up off the bed, making her recoil. Strawberries scattered across the bed. Somehow the cream didn't spill. He started laughing. Making the bed shake. 'I'm sorry,' he said. 'You caught me unawares. I really didn't expect you to be so bold.'

She frowned. 'Is it wrong?' she asked, looking at her handiwork. If anything his thing, his rod, looked stiffer than ever, where it emerged from the dark nest of hair.

'No. Nothing between a man and a woman is wrong, if both enjoy it. Don't for pity's sake stop now.'

'You must be patient,' she said, seeing his hands grip the sheets, anticipating... Oh, he really liked this idea. She dipped the strawberry again and smeared cream down his rigid shaft, smiling at the hiss of his breath, which set an answering tightness inside her that was altogether too delicious for words. She swirled the berry on the sacs at the base of his shaft, eyeing them with interest, wondering at their soft texture compared to his erection.

A glance at his face showed his eyes closed, his face a mask of calmness, but the tic in his jaw told the truth. She popped the strawberry in her mouth.

He opened one eye. 'Are you done?'

She gave him a saucy smile. 'Not quite. I just want to see how it tastes.' She leaned over him and, after a moment's hesitation, licked at the cream. 'Delicious.'

He muttered something under his breath. The hands flexed into fists and relaxed.

Hmm. She trailed her tongue up his shaft and swirled it around the head, finding the varying textures fascinating. She took the head in her mouth and heard him groan.

Those large hands came down and caught her beneath the shoulders, pulling her upwards. His dark gaze clashed with hers. 'Little nun, we will play this game another time. I find I do not have the patience tonight.'

He tossed her on her back on the bed, roughly moved the bowls to the table, then settled between her thighs. Desperation filled his gaze. He looked stunned. 'I'm sorry, but right now, I want to be inside you.'

Raw power hung over her. The strength to take what he wanted and yet he waited for her assent.

Her limbs melted beneath the heat of that gaze and the gentleness of his hand cupping her cheek. She smiled.

With a deep sigh of satisfaction, he reached down and guided himself into her. He drove hard and fast, with a fierceness she matched in the thrust of her hips. The pleasure was raw. Wild. It drove her to new heights of longing. Harder and faster he pumped his hips, suckling at her breasts, nipping at her ears, while she dug her nails in his back and bit at his shoulder.

She hit the peak fast and hard with a cry that sounded nothing like her voice. Her vision splintered, her body shattered into bliss.

He made sounds low in his throat, sounds of desperation and pain. He withdrew from her, using his hand to spill his seed on her belly. Then he collapsed on her, a dead weight. Delightfully heavy.

Chapter Fourteen

'What do you do to me?' he muttered.

They lay entwined. The fading heat of bliss cradled Garth's body and left his mind soggy. This woman, soon to be his wife, was an unexpected treasure. A mix of cool calm waters and hot springs. God, he'd only just managed to withdraw from her at the last moment. Her passion carried him to heights of desire he'd never encountered with anyone else.

So many times he had played the strawberry game to its conclusion, leaving his partner sated, while he finished the fruit and waited for them to be ready again. He couldn't even get through the game with her.

Never had he wanted a woman so much. With such driving force.

What he had with her was as rare as roses in January. And she was his. For all time.

It felt wondrous, with her nestled against his body, the rise and fall of her chest, the feel of her breath on his shoulder. New. Like a boy, though he hardly remembered that youth.

She deserved a far better man. He would make sure she

had the life she deserved, even if she didn't have the best of husbands.

She shifted. Looked up. 'There is something I need to tell you.'

Something inside him went cold. He had heard those words many times. They signified that, somewhere along the way, he'd been deceived. Normally, he didn't care. Hell, he expected it. This time, with this woman, his future wife, the idea chilled him. 'What is it?'

She rose up on one elbow, her lovely breasts inches from his mouth, like full ripe peaches ready to be consumed. 'At the house. I wasn't looking for a miniature. I was looking for my father's will. He promised to provide for me and my sisters, but no one found a will when he died. I was so sure I would find it there.'

The painful truth. Painful to her—he could hear it in her voice. He tipped her chin and gazed into eyes so sad his chest squeezed all the breath from his lungs. He wanted to comfort her, take away her hurt. 'Perhaps his death happened too fast?'

Her wide forehead wrinkled. 'It wasn't like that. He promised us, me and my sisters, years before, when he married again. He needed an heir. We understood that. Our stepmama hated us and sent us away to school, but Papa promised to provide for us.'

He gave her a small hug. 'So your father left everything to his heir. It is not unusual. Don't worry, I will take care of you and your sisters.'

A brief smile lifted her lips. 'I know.' She pressed a quick kiss to his shoulder. 'And I thank you. But you see, I just find it hard to believe he forgot us. He must have hidden the document away from my stepmother, and now it is lost. I have to believe it. He loved us.'

Love. A false coin. A word mouthed by females to get their

way. Rosabella, however, seemed to believe in its mysterious power, for her eyes had filled with tears even as her expression shone with conviction.

'You think finding a piece of paper will prove he loved you?'

She blinked and he realised his tone had been unnecessarily harsh.

'I know he loved us. But…' She shook her head, her lower lip trembling. 'It isn't right. He promised.'

'People promise many things they don't mean. They speak of love in one breath and in the next they are in bed with someone else. Wives despise their husbands. Fathers abandon their sons. People do whatever is convenient to them. If there is such a thing as love, it is love of self.'

Tears clung to her eyelashes; her almond-shaped eyes were huge and accusing as she stared at him. 'You don't believe in love at all?'

God, what a little innocent she was.

'Don't smile at me like that,' she said fiercely. 'I hate it.'

Startled, he stared down at her. 'Smile like what?'

'Cynical. Mocking. As if I am stupid and only you know the truth.'

Anger sparked hot in his blood. He forced calmness into his voice. 'When you spout about love and promises, I know I am the only one in this room who understands the way of the world.'

'So you are saying I am stupid to believe my father loved my mother or us?'

'I am saying you are putting your hopes in the wrong man.' Damnation, was he jealous of her dead father? 'For whatever reason, he didn't leave you anything in his will. I am sorry he didn't. Clearly it is important to you. But people do what suits them. There is nothing you can do about it.'

She sat up and moved away from him, pinning the sheet

to her chest with her folded arms. There was something in her eyes he didn't understand. Disappointment. Hurt.

He wanted to hit something. He pulled himself up against the pillows, put his hand on her cheek, turning her face towards him. 'So he forgot to leave a will. What difference does it make? I will make sure you and your sisters have everything you need.'

'I made sure we have everything we need.' She jerked her face away. 'It is part of my bargain with you. After all, *we* will not marry for love.'

Inwardly he flinched at the rejection in her voice. It laid bare an emotion he did not want to feel. He replied with cold logic. 'Things will go on a lot better because we both have realistic expectations.'

A flash of a question passed across her face.

'What is it?'

'Why do you?' She bit at the inside of her lip. He wanted to nibble and suck at the outside. He could see from her expression that would not be appreciated. Not right now.

'Why do I what?'

'At the end. You do not stay with me. You pleasure yourself, I think. You did not do it the first time, but since then…'

He huffed out a breath. He had not expected to have this conversation so soon. 'It's a precaution. Nothing to worry about.'

'A precaution against what?' If anything, she looked more concerned.

'You might already be carrying my child.'

'Oh, I see.'

He breathed a sigh of relief. He'd sidestepped that midden.

'And if I'm not?' She frowned. 'You do want children, don't you?'

'I haven't given the matter thought.' Not about having one.

She frowned. 'You need an heir, surely.'

'It isn't of any great concern at the moment. And besides, aren't we having a good time? Wouldn't a child spoil our games?' He waggled his brows suggestively.

She stared at him. 'You prefer to wait?'

'Yes, I prefer to wait.' He smiled and kissed her lips. 'You taste of strawberries.'

'So do you,' she whispered, desire softening her eyes.

He kissed her again until she moaned with pleasure and forgot her questions.

Since Rosa could not go riding with Garth until after they were married, she dressed leisurely in one of her new gowns. She wanted to look her best when he returned. In a few days she would be a married woman. It hardly seemed possible.

She had barely sat down in the drawing room when the butler popped his head through the door.

'I'm to ask where you wish to put the trunk and the desk, my lady,' the butler said. 'The carter is below. His lordship suggested the trunk should go in the attic and the desk in here.'

Of course he thought her mother's chest should be relegated to the attic. In life, her father had hidden her mother away in Sussex.

Oh, now she was allowing her disappointment in her father to flow over into thoughts about Garth. Unfair. Garth had made a suggestion, that was all. 'The desk will do very well in here.' She glanced around and pointed to a low cabinet containing assorted pieces of porcelain. 'It can go there.' The light would be good for writing. 'Perhaps the cabinet can go in the downstairs drawing room. If not, it can go up in the attic. The chest goes in my dressing room.'

At least it could remain there until she had time to go through it properly. Some of the costumes might need wrapping in paper. If she had a child, a girl, she would like her to see her grandmother's things.

She flattened a hand against her stomach. The babe was exceedingly small if she was indeed *enceinte*. It hardly seemed likely. She wished she had someone to ask.

'I'll see to it right away, ma'am.' The butler bowed his way out.

It didn't take long for the butler and a pair of brawny footmen to move the cabinet out and the writing desk in. Rosa stood in front of it when they were finished. It looked good in here. It gave her a warm feeling, a sense of homecoming. She could almost feel her father's cheerful presence in the room. Almost see his sparkling hazel eyes. The deep creases around his mouth when he smiled.

He'd been a happy careless man who cared nothing for society and its mores. And he had loved her mother. He'd given up status and position to be with her.

Rosa smiled at the memories flooding in. He'd also been terribly unorganised, though he had the best of intentions. Without Mother to remind him, perhaps he'd simply forgotten, not his daughters, but the administrative part of making a will. Otherwise why hadn't one been found?

It must be the answer.

Nevertheless, she could not stop herself from looking through the drawers one more time. First the right-hand side, and then the left, pulling them out and turning them over in case something had fallen behind and got caught. Finally her fingers hovered beside the secret compartment.

Breath held, she sprang the latch.

Nothing.

No matter how she peered into the little dark space, or ran her fingers around it, there really was nothing in there.

Heavy steps alerted her to the trunk's passage up the stairs.

She snapped the compartment shut and hurried out to see to its placement. She almost collided with the butler, who was coming in. His face was harried. 'Lady Stanford is here.'

She looked at him blankly.

'His lordship's mother,' the butler explained.

He'd never mentioned his mother, had he? She'd assumed his parents weren't living, if she'd thought about them at all. Why had he never mentioned her? And why was she here? Her heart sank. Was she here to take a look at her future daughter-in-law? Oh, where was Garth?

The butler's grim expression made her heart sink even lower. 'What is wrong?'

'His lordship doesn't usually see her, but she—'

'No need to show me in,' a quavering voice said. 'I can find my own way.'

The butler groaned under his breath.

What on earth? 'It is all right, of course I will see her.'

'Shall I bring tea?' the butler asked.

Rosa smiled. 'Please.'

The butler dodged around the lady who had reached the top of the stairs. Rosa dipped a curtsy. 'Lady Stanford. Please, do come in.'

Her future mother-in-law swept by Rosa and ensconced herself in the chair by the hearth in a rustle of pale blue silk and a flutter of her handkerchief. It was the chair one would usually expect the hostess to occupy. But then Rosa wasn't a hostess. She wasn't anything. Yet.

'Is it true? Are you marrying my son?' the widow said.

Rosa tried a tentative smile. 'Yes. We are betrothed.'

'Hmmph.' The pale blue eyes raked her from head to heel. Her lips pursed. 'Who are you?'

A fair question, if a little rude. 'My name is Rosabella Cavendish.'

'Please tell me there is no truth to the rumour, Miss Cavendish.'

'Rumour?'

She patted her handkerchief to her lips as if the next words might soil them. 'Someone said you were an opera dancer.'

Oh, dear. Someone had let the proverbial cat out of a bag, and from the look on his mother's face she hated cats.

'I did have a part in an opera, yes, but—'

The widow gasped. 'What is Garth thinking? He was probably drunk. Let me give you some money to leave him be.'

Anger blazed like molten metal in Rosa's veins. Her spine grew so stiff it felt like steel. Yet she couldn't blame Garth's mother for feeling this way. 'Didn't he tell you about me?' Surely, it was the first thing he should have done, instead of letting her hear the news by way of gossip?

The handkerchief, a scrap of Mechlin lace, dabbed at her cheeks, though there wasn't a glint of tears in those sharp blue eyes. 'Garth never tells me anything.'

What was going on here? 'I will have him call on you right away.'

'But why are you living here? Who are your parents? This is all very irregular.'

Oh, dear, this really was not a good beginning. 'It is up to Garth to explain.'

The dowager glanced around the room. 'Making changes already, I see,' she said, pointing at the writing desk. 'The cabinet that was there contained very valuable pieces of china all bought by my dear late husband.'

She forced a conciliatory smile. 'And they now hold pride of place in the downstairs drawing room used for guests, instead of up here where they are rarely viewed. Nothing else has changed.'

The frantic waving of the handkerchief ceased as the butler entered with the tea tray. He shot Rosa a wary glance.

What now?

'His lordship is on his way up, ma'am.'

Why look so worried? This was a rescue.

'Thank you.'

Garth sauntered in a moment later, still dressed for riding. 'Mother. That was indeed your broomstick I saw outside the door. What brings you to my den of iniquity?'

Rosa almost choked on her mouthful of tea. Never had she heard such rudeness.

'Riding dress in the drawing room, Garth. I thought I taught you better.' His mother sniffed into her handkerchief as if she could smell dung on his boots.

They were immaculate. He'd cleaned them before coming inside. Or changed into a different pair.

Garth flung himself down on the sofa beside Rosa and propped one heel on the table. 'What does bring you here, Mother dear?'

'I heard ridiculous gossip.' She cast an eye at Rosa. 'About a possible wedding.'

Garth's eyes narrowed dangerously. 'You heard correctly. It's on Wednesday.'

'Am I not invited?'

'Tea, Stanford?' Rosa said, hoping to calm what looked like a coming storm.

'I prefer brandy.' He dropped his heels with a loud thud, lounged to his feet and strolled to the cabinet beside the door.

'Brandy at this hour of the day!' his mother said. The handkerchief danced at the end of her languid fingers. 'It isn't good for you.'

'At this hour or any other hour, should I choose,' he drawled, pouring a drink. 'Would you like some in your tea, darling?' He looked at Rosa.

Was he trying to make his mother think she was some sort of doxy? 'No, thank you.'

What on earth was going on? Hatred writhed through the room like a noxious gas. Rosa wanted to fling open the widow and take a deep breath of smoky London air. Or, better yet, run far away.

They were family. They acted like enemies.

Garth brought his drink back to the sofa with him and sprawled beside her, his legs stretched out, at perfect ease, one arm along the sofa back behind her. He looked rakish and dangerous. Like a wild animal poked with a stick daring someone to put a finger in its mouth.

'Get to the point, Mother dear.' The chill in his voice sent a shiver down Rosa's spine.

Lady Stanford shifted in her seat. Her eyes misted. 'I can't believe you didn't tell me. Nevertheless, I am happy to offer my assistance to your bride. There are things she needs to know about our proud family history. About what it means to be an Evernden.'

'Ah,' Garth murmured. 'The proud family name.' He turned towards Rosa. 'My younger brother married the Duke of Hastings's daughter. I, on the other hand, am the black sheep of the family.' He laughed bitterly.

'Your brother made a brilliant match. I always hoped the same for you.'

'Did you?' Garth said with a feral smile.

The dowager probably didn't put Rosa in her category of a brilliant match. Rosa couldn't blame her. As she handed the cup to the widow, it rattled in the saucer.

He turned his dark gaze on her. 'Don't be alarmed, darling. This is an old conversation, isn't it, Mother?'

The handkerchief waved like a flag in a stiff breeze. 'Please, Garth, don't be…so cruel. I simply came to find out if the rumours were true. That you were marrying an—'

'Opera singer,' he said in a purr.

Rosa had had enough. 'Really, Garth. I must protest. I have no idea why you are taunting your mother this way. Yes, I have performed in an opera, but I am Lord Pelham's legitimate granddaughter.'

'Bravo,' Garth murmured in her ear. His fingers stroked her nape and played with the tendrils of hair that had escaped her pins. Another shiver ripped across her skin. Not cold this time. Desire. Lust flooded her body with heat. As angry as she felt, her body responded instantly to his wicked breath and seductive touch. She fought the urge to snuggle closer.

The handkerchief collapsed on the widow's lap. 'Pelham?' Her reproachful gaze turned on her son. 'The daughter of a man cast out by society? Did you give no thought to Christopher's position?' His mother's voice rose to a wail.

'I think about his position every damned day,' Garth said.

Rosa flinched at the venom in his voice. She wasn't sure which of them was the worst. They seemed to take delight in flinging poisoned darts at each other. No. Garth was worse. He should be trying to reassure his mother, not tear her to shreds.

'What would your father have said?' Lady Stanford quavered.

Garth curled his lip. 'We will never know, will we?' He rose and held out his hand. 'Come, let me escort you to your carriage.' He took the half-full cup from her hand, set it down and bodily pulled her from the chair.

'Garth!' Rosa gasped as he physically pushed his mother from the room and towards the stairs.

Disbelieving, Rosa ran after them. 'Garth, stop it.'

'Stay out of this, Rosa,' Garth flung over his shoulder.

'Why are you being so rude?' his mother asked as he hustled her down the stairs.

'You know why.'

She stopped and turned around. 'You know I only want what is best for you.'

He smiled grimly. 'You only want what is best for you.' He gestured for her to continue down the stairs. Rosa had the feeling if his mother didn't go, he would pick her up and carry her out, he looked so angry.

'Is she expecting a child?' the widow said in a loud whisper while waiting for the front door to be opened.

'I don't know.'

'Oh, Garth. You said you wouldn't have children. You told me after Christopher left—'

'Enough!' he roared, then lowered his voice. 'I will deal with the problem of a child, if it arises. Now go.'

He hadn't wanted children? A dart made of ice pierced Rosa's heart. It seemed to stop beating. Her hands went to her stomach.

Rosa turned tail and ran up the stairs. She ran into the bedroom and closed the door, fumbling at the lock. No key. She darted into the dressing room. This door had a bolt. She drew it across and collapsed to her knees on the rug.

What did that mean, he'd deal with it? The way he'd dealt with his mother was positively cruel. Would he deal with a child the same way? How had she allowed herself to be so misled? His handsome face and charming ways hid a heart of stone.

How long would it be before he treated her equally coldly? And their child? And how would she bear it?

Tears ran down her face as she slowly opened the lid. She pulled out the flimsiest of costumes and held it to her face, inhaling the faint scent of jasmine her mother always wore.

'What have I done?'

Chapter Fifteen

Damn her. Garth watched his mother's carriage draw away. So sweet. So utterly false.

He swung around and went back into the house. Now he'd have to explain his bout of temper to Rosa.

Damnation. And damn whoever had run to his mother with the tale. Surely not Mark? But Penelope might. Women were so predictably malicious.

He took the stairs two at a time. The drawing room was empty. Sighing, he continued up the stairs to their chamber. He'd upset her, he'd seen that from the look on her face. He should have held his tongue between his teeth, but he'd grown so used to fencing verbally with his mother, he hadn't even realised what he was doing until it was too late. Until he saw the shock on Rosabella's face.

At that point he could have bitten out his tongue.

No sign of her in the bedroom. Then where…? Ah, the dressing-room door was closed.

On silent feet, he crossed the room, heard the sound of sobbing. Blast Mother to hell. He turned the knob. The door didn't give.

'Rosabella,' he said softly. 'Open the door.'

A sniff. 'Go away.'

'Open the door. We need to talk.'

'I don't want to talk to you.'

A rustling sound had him frowning. Was she packing? 'Open the door or I'll break it down.'

More sniffles. Damn it to hell, he was never letting his mother across his threshold again. The bolt on the other side of the door slid back.

He opened the door. She was kneeling on the floor, facing him before the chest they'd found in Pelham's house. He hunkered down in front of her.

She looked small and vulnerable crouched before a trunk full of old costumes. A strangely soft feeling invaded his chest. It had fierce edges. As if he could hold her tenderly in his arms, yet fight a dragon if need be.

The only other time he had felt anything like it was when Christopher had been in danger, trying to rescue the woman he later made his wife. And it had been nowhere as strong as this. But then, he'd been drinking hard in those days, so most of it had passed in a blur.

The sensation was unexpected. It made him nervous. Made him clumsy. His usually silver tongue became awkward. He took a deep breath. 'I'm sorry. My mother is such a bitch.'

She raised her gaze. They were swimming in tears. Her nose was red. 'Why didn't you tell me you didn't want children?'

Damn it all. 'You heard.'

'Your conversation was hardly private.'

'I never planned to get married, so naturally I didn't expect to have children.' He scrubbed at his chin. 'There are reasons why I would prefer—'

'Shouldn't you have told me before we made our agreement?' A tear rolled down her face.

'Rosabella. Don't.' He reached over the chest to capture the wayward drop.

She whipped her face to the side, out of his reach. 'Don't touch me.'

The old anger flared at her rejection. Rage mixed with humiliation. 'If you wanted children, you should have put it in writing in that damned settlement of yours.'

She flinched.

He wanted to howl his frustration. 'I didn't mean that.'

Her expression hardened. 'And if I am with child—how will you deal with it? What did you mean?'

He froze. Dear God, had he said that? 'I meant will live with it. Deal with the consequences of losing control. What else would I mean?'

'Control.' She sat back on her heels and wrapped her hands around her waist. 'Live with *it*. Will you, indeed? I'm sorry, the wedding is off.'

The pain of her words knifed through his chest. A new kind of anger flooded his veins. It was hotter than fire. Hotter than molten metal. If he set it free, it would destroy them both. He fought to contain it. 'You don't have a choice. I have kept my part of our bargain. Now you will keep yours. Think of your sisters. Of the child, if there is one.'

'And if there isn't…? There won't be any, will there? Because you'll make sure. You'll do…whatever it is you've been doing.'

He stared at her, almost dumb in the face of her pain. 'You don't understand.'

Her gaze turned cold. 'I understand very well. I made a bargain to marry a degenerate rake who wants to continue his life as if nothing has changed. There really is no point to us being married.'

'You will marry me. Rosabella—'

'I cannot let my child grow up with a father who does not love it.'

'Why not? Plenty do.'

She stared at him, her eyes full of disgust. The look he'd seen on his parents' face growing up. 'I wouldn't let you near a child of mine.'

'I'm not a monster. I would never hurt a child.'

She regarded him for a moment from those velvet-soft eyes. 'Not physically, no. But the way you spoke to your mother, you hurt her, Garth.'

'My mother has no feelings to hurt. Do not speak about what you do not know.'

She shuddered. 'She is your mother. She deserves your love and respect.'

'No. She doesn't.'

Her gaze returned to the trunk. She extracted a small pink satin reticule and stroked the fabric against her cheek.

He watched her warily. Saw the light of joy in her eyes, mingled with a sadness he didn't understand.

'This was my mother's. She let me play with it when I was a child. She told me stories of her life before she met my father. And of how they fell in love. I want the same.' She lifted her gaze. 'I will not marry you.'

He took the blow from her words deep in his chest. Never had he felt such agony of spirit. Not even when he realised why his father hated him had he felt so wounded. He wanted to lash out, to hurt her back.

'I won't let you keep my child.'

Her lovely dark eyes widened. 'You don't want the child.'

He pushed to his feet. 'I won't let a child of mine grow up without its father.'

'A father who doesn't love it? Why would it matter?'

He looked down at her, smiling. 'Make no mistake, Rosabella, we will marry, or you will lose the child.'

The look on her face said she'd fight him to the death.

Sanity eased into his brain. If he said another word right now, there would be no going back.

'We will talk about this later, when we are both in a calmer frame of mind.' He swung around and left, slamming the door behind him. He ran down the stairs and out of the door.

Outside in the street, the bright sunlight seemed almost obscene. There should be thunderclouds, lightning, rain. Where the hell was he going? He needed to get control of his temper, then work out how to woo Rosabella out of her anger. Diamonds should do it. He'd visit Rundell, Bridge and Rundell, then head for White's for a brandy, before heading home.

One thing was certain. She wasn't going to leave him. She needed him. Without him she had nothing. She had nowhere else to go.

The sound of the front door slamming jerked Rosa to her feet. She had to leave before he came back. Before his temper calmed and he used his charm, the pull of the allure she could not deny, and persuaded her to stay. It would be a terrible mistake to remain with a man who had that much coldness in his soul.

Gently she returned the reticule to the trunk and picked up the shoes, their leather cracked and worn, one much heavier than the other. Frowning, she pried the paper stuffing free from the heavy one. Not just paper. A green pear-shaped stone. It tumbled into her lap, glittering as its facets caught the light. She flattened the paper it was wrapped in.

Dear Rosabella, this jewel is your inheritance. It is the only thing I own of your mother's that is not tied to the estate. It was always intended for you and your sisters. It has no sentimental value, bought by another noble admirer for your mother. My beloved Rosabella, sell it and live well. Please care for your sisters. Signed *Andrew Cavendish*, with two scrawling signatures of the servants and dated 18th of June. She stared at an emerald as big as a pigeon's egg.

Elation filled her. Father had kept his promise. He'd hidden his gift among her mother's things where he knew Grandfather would never look. She lifted her gaze from the paper and stared at the dressing-room door. If she understood the value of this stone, she didn't have to marry anyone. She and her sisters were wealthy.

She stuffed the paper and the jewel into the pink reticule and grabbed her cloak from the clothes press. She needed help. And there was only one person she could think of who might know what to do.

Clutching the scrap of pink satin to her chest, Rosa glanced up at the knocker on the modest front door of a town house in Golden Square. Thank goodness Lady Smythe had left her calling card with her address. The hackney driver had no trouble finding the house.

Would she stand by their promise to help? If not, where would she turn next? With more bravery than she felt, she banged on the door.

A rotund cheerful-faced butler opened the door. 'Yes, miss?'

Rosa took a deep breath. 'Is Lady Smythe at home?'

He opened the door wider. 'I'll enquire, shall I, miss? Who shall I say is calling?'

'Lady Rosabella Cavendish,' she said. She could barely remember the last time she'd introduced herself so formally, but she could not risk the butler refusing her admittance.

An eyebrow shot up. He gestured her to come in. 'Please, have a seat, my lady. I'll let my mistress know you are here.'

'Thank you.' Rosa sank down on the hall chair beside the door while he trotted off down the corridor.

She didn't have long to wait before he was back. 'This way, if you please, my lady.'

Rosa let go a sigh of relief and followed him to a small room at the back of the house. When the butler opened the door, she was surprised to find both husband and wife seated at tea in the drawing room. Of course, they would both be home; it was a Saturday.

Lord Smythe rose as she entered. 'Lady Rosabella,' he said. 'Please, sit down. Would you care to partake of some luncheon?'

If she tried to swallow, she would be sick. 'No, thank you. I am so sorry to disturb you. I didn't know where to turn.' She turned to Penelope. 'You did say you would help me if...'

'Please,' Penelope said, 'sit down. Tell us how we can be of service.'

Rosa bit her lip. Would Lord Smythe indeed be willing to help her if it meant going against his friend's wishes? 'I'm sorry. I should not have come here, after all. If you will excuse me.' She turned away.

'Rosabella,' Lady Smythe said. 'Please. Don't go. Mark, tell her she can trust us.'

'By us,' the young husband said, in measured tones, 'I presume my wife means me. I assure you, Lady Rosabella, anything you say to me will be held in confidence, on my honour.'

She turned back, looking at him standing beside his chair. His eyes were a clear grey, his face was open and grave. Something about him engendered her trust. And yet... She looked at his wife, who smiled. 'Mark is employed by the Home Office. His word is his bond.'

Whatever differences lay between these two, it seemed

there was mutual respect. She slipped into the chair offered by Lord Smythe.

'What can we do?' Penelope asked quietly.

'Stanford didn't hurt you, did he?' Lord Smythe asked. 'I've not seen him turn ugly since he'd ceased crooking his elbow.'

She blinked.

'Drinking,' Lady Smythe explained.

Her husband's fair face flushed. 'Canting talk. I beg your pardon.'

'No,' Rosa said softly. 'He hasn't physically harmed me.'

'Lashed you with that damned tongue of his, did he?' the young man said with a snort of indignation. 'He doesn't mean the half of it, you know.'

He didn't know the half of it. 'I need to hire a lawyer.'

He frowned.

'It is a matter of an inheritance. From my father. I found a letter this morning among some things belonging to my mother. I—I'm not sure what to do next.'

For a moment both of them looked at her, mouths agape.

'Oh, good Lord,' Lord Smythe said, his fair brow creasing. 'Is it a legal will? Signed and witnessed.'

'Not a will, but a gift. No will was found when he died. The family lawyer said he didn't make one and probate went ahead on that basis.' She dug into the reticule and handed over the document. 'The letter is signed and witnessed. The signature is his.'

Lord Smythe took the paper and glanced through it. 'Oh, this is a fine kettle of fish. Do you have the stone?'

'Is it legal?' Lady Smythe asked, leaning to look over his shoulder as Rosa put the emerald on the table.

'I have no legal training, but if the signature is genuine, it seems legal enough to stand in a court of law. What we need is at least one of the witnesses to swear to its authenticity.'

'Inchbold,' Rosa said. 'He is caretaker of the property where we lived. He said he remembered signing something for my father, but he wasn't sure what it was. That is his signature.'

'Did you tell Stanford about this?' Lady Smythe asked. 'Can you not use his lawyer?'

Rosa swallowed. 'We had a…a difference of opinion. We are not getting married.'

The hot lump that had been floating somewhere in her chest and her stomach finally lodged high in her throat. The pain of it brought moisture to her eyes.

'Oh, my poor dear,' Lady Smythe said. 'Are you sure?'

Her husband looked grim. 'What the hell did Stanford do?'

Unable to speak, Rosa shook her head. It was hard enough to breathe without letting the tears spill over.

'You can stay here,' Lady Smythe said with a darting glance at her husband.

If anything, her husband looked grimmer.

Rosa breathed hard through her nose and rose to her feet. 'I couldn't. He is your friend. I will go to an hotel.' She would have gone to Bess, because she didn't have any money until the stone was sold, and what little she had she would need to live on, but Bess had left London. Her biggest fear was that Grandfather would try to lay claim to the stone once he heard of it. 'I just hoped you could recommend a lawyer. One who would not want payment in advance.'

'You must stay,' Lord Smythe said. 'Stanford would never forgive me for letting you wander the streets on your own.'

She couldn't help her scornful laugh.

'He wouldn't.' He grinned. 'Besides, I owe him a debt and this is one very good way to repay him. You will stay here.'

'Yes,' his wife said. 'We insist.'

'You won't tell him I am here.' She pressed a protective hand to her stomach. 'You must promise me.'

'Not without your permission. On my honour,' Smythe said.

'On mine, too,' his wife added.

'Then I am glad to accept your help for a few days. I promise I will pay you back.'

'Nonsense,' Lord Smythe said. 'Not when I am in your debt for offering me a way of discharging my obligations.'

It all seemed rather confusing, but in the face of their insistence, Rosa accepted with a sense of relief.

The interior of White's hummed with male conversation and laughter to the accompaniment of rattling dice. Garth ordered a brandy, took a freshly ironed copy of *The Times* from the stand and cloistered himself behind it in an unoccupied corner.

The anger had faded, leaving him confused. Anger he could deal with, but this sense of being wrong left him off balance.

The more he thought about his conversation with Rosabella, the more uncertain he became. All this talk of love made for a very heavy weight on his chest. Why the hell did she put so much store by it? He'd managed perfectly well without it all his life.

How dared she suggest he would harm his own child? Anger refused to flare and obliterate the hurt. She was wrong about him, though. He did care for some people, in his own way. Mark. Kit. Her. These were people he would protect with his life if need be. Just because he didn't get along with his mother didn't make him evil.

He sniffed at the brandy the waiter delivered. The fumes made his stomach roll and he put the glass down on the table.

In a perfect world, he supposed he would have told her

of his intention not to have children. She certainly shouldn't have learned it from his mother. But the world wasn't perfect. It didn't come close to perfect, or he wouldn't be in this position.

Hell, he wouldn't be here at all.

He should not have lost his temper. On the other hand, she could have listened. Who knows, he might even have told her why he was opposed to fatherhood.

Hell. He might be a father. A daughter. He could live with a daughter. A thrill ran through him.

'Stanford.'

Garth pretended not to hear the familiar jocular tones. After all, it was not good *ton* to beat a man to within an inch of his life in a gentleman's club. And right now he was in the mood to hit someone.

The idiot flicked a finger against the newspaper. 'I say, old chap, didn't you hear me?'

Garth lowered his shield. 'I heard you, Fitz. I'm just not in the mood for conversation. I'd advise you to leave unless you want my fist in your face.'

The other man grinned. 'Under the weather, old boy? I had a pleasant chat with your mother yesterday.'

Teeth gritted, Garth put aside the paper and pushed slowly to his feet, forcing the other man to look up at him. He smiled. 'Did you now? What the hell were you doing discussing my business with my mother?'

'Where's your sense of humour, old boy? I met her at a rout.'

'So you thought you'd regale her with my doings, like some gossipy old tart.'

He looked puzzled, then laughed. 'Good God, don't tell me you took the wench home? I saw your face when you ran out of the chop house and followed to see what you were up to. I recognised her in the light of the lantern. I had no trouble guessing your intentions. I simply mentioned to your mother I thought you had a new occupant for the Blackheath town house. She was surprised to hear you were in town. I imagined her putting a flea in your ear, not catching you *in flagrante delicto*. Too funny.'

'Not in the least funny, you idiot.' Garth's cheeks ached from smiling. 'But if you say one more word about meeting Mrs Travenor, anywhere, be prepared to defend yourself.' He took a step forwards.

Fitz backed up. He giggled drunkenly. 'Good Lord, man. Look at yourself. You are completely smitten. You want to be careful or you'll find yourself leg-shackled. You do know she's the daughter of an opera singer? Hapton told me.'

Garth grabbed him by the lapels. 'One more word and I will take you outside and thrash you.'

Something in Garth's eyes must have registered, because Fitz put up a hand. 'On my honour, not another word.' Once released, he reeled away, chortling his fool head off.

Garth would have to talk to him when he was sober. Make sure he remembered the warning.

Smitten? Him? The sot was drunk.

He glared at the curious faces turned in his direction. By thunder, he didn't want to be here. He wanted to soothe Rosabella's ruffled feelings, seduce her into his bed and make her see reason. What the hell was he thinking?

Never before had he walked away and left a woman in possession of the field of battle. They always capitulated. He should have kissed her senseless, not argued with her. Women never listened to reason.

The necklace he'd bought at the jeweller's would help.

In less than fifteen minutes he was striding up the front steps to his town house in the gathering dusk. An odd presentiment caused a prickle at the back of his neck as he entered the front door. Unease rippled through his gut. The house felt empty.

One thing he'd learned over the years was to trust his instincts. It was how he'd discovered the truth of what he was.

'Where is Lady Rosabella?' he asked the butler, handing over his hat.

'I haven't seen her since Lady Stanford's departure.'

Damn. She was either still sitting on the floor crying or... Or she'd done what they all did eventually.

He tore up the stairs and burst through the bedroom door. The dressing-room door lay open, the items from the theatrical chest scattered around it. Of Rosabella there was no sign.

Where the hell could she have gone?

Back to the theatrical troupe? He picked up the discarded breeches she'd worn on stage. Surely she would have taken them with her? He let them fall. Her grandfather? After all she'd done to avoid the old gentleman it hardly seemed likely. Perhaps she'd simply gone for a walk to clear her head. In that case the butler would know, because she would have taken her maid or a footman. Although she might have slipped out alone. She'd done enough of that in Sussex. The thought of her walking the streets of London alone chilled him to the bone. She wouldn't take such a risk.

Doubt tightened his gut, his heart dipped. Rosabella would dare anything.

Think. Where could she go?

Of all the choices, the opera company seemed most likely. She had friends there. He strode into the bedroom, dropping the velvet pouch on the bed, and rang for his valet. He grabbed his riding boots and started pulling them on.

His valet walked in and rushed over to help. 'Leave it,' Garth growled. 'Have a message sent to the stables. I want my phaeton outside the front door in a half-hour. And have

Cook put up some bread and cheese. I'll eat it in the study while I write some letters requiring delivery. Also pack me an overnight valise.'

He stamped his foot into the second boot and stood up. 'Clear?'

'Yes, my lord.' The valet shot off to do his bidding.

Garth ran downstairs and set to work on a letter to Mark, asking for yet another favour, dammit.

A scratch at the door announced the arrival of his supper. He continued writing. 'Put the tray on the table. I'll help myself.'

Metal clicked on wood. The servant didn't leave.

A reprimand ready on his tongue, Garth raised his head. 'You.' He leaned back in his chair. 'I might have guessed.'

Mark sat down and crossed one leg over the other, his face sombre. 'I'm surprised you didn't.'

'This document is valid, you say?' Garth rubbed the back of his neck. Rolled his shoulders. Tried to get his mind around this new development.

'As far as I can tell. I will get a lawyer to have a look. If it is, she is independently wealthy and is quite adamant that she no longer needs to marry you and will pay back every penny you spent on her behalf.'

'I need to talk to her.'

Mark shook his head. 'I'm sorry. She is also adamant about not seeing you.'

The words were a knife between his ribs. 'She could be carrying my child.'

'You damned fool. Don't you know better than to seduce an earl's granddaughter?'

'Devil take you, Mark. She lied. About everything. Hell.' He got up and paced the floor. 'Not one scrap of truth has she told me. First she was a widow. Then I discover she's an innocent. Then she's searching for a portrait. Like an idiot, I help her. Next she runs off to be an opera singer like her mother, but her mother, it turns out, was married to a nobleman.' He swung around and glared at his friend quietly nursing a brandy. 'Everything was a complete fabrication from beginning to end. And still I've offered marriage.'

'Noble of you.'

'I had no intention of ever getting married.'

'Did you tell her that?'

'More or less. I wasn't going to lie to her. She wouldn't believe it if I did.'

'What did you do to make her run off?'

The note of accusation in Mark's voice brought his simmering temper to a boil. 'What did you do to make Penelope run off the moment you stepped out of the house?'

Mark glared at him, then his shoulders slumped. He stared morosely into the fire. 'She didn't want me to go north without her. We argued and then I left. I didn't have a choice. My income depends on me doing my job. There is trouble brewing in the north. We have to find out what is going on before it gets out of hand. I can't take her with me. It's far too dangerous. Penelope knows she was wrong and that is the end to it.'

The glow he'd seen in his friend when he first married had not returned. Apparently love was as fleeting as it was elusive. The idea of it made him feel cold. 'Seems as if we are both caught between a wall and cartwheel.'

'I know. Who knows why they do what they do?' He shook his head.

'And yet here you are, offering me advice.'

Mark looked up at him. 'I'm trying to help. Yesterday your marriage was all set, today she's at my house refusing to see you. It isn't about money. Something must have happened.'

Bitterness rose up in his throat. 'Mother happened.'

Mark straightened. 'Your mother?'

'She arrived while I was out. Fitz saw me and Rosabella together and blabbed on about it, I gather. Mother dropped some pretty strong hints that she didn't think Rosabella was good enough for our family. She is such a damnable hypocrite. I threw her out.'

'So you defended Rosabella?'

'Oh, you know how it is between me and Mother.'

Mark gave a little grimace, which said he understood very well.

'We were still sparring at the front door and Rosabella must have overheard me say that while I didn't particularly want a child, I'd tolerate one if it came along. By the time I returned from seeing Mother off, Rosabella was up in the boughs and not listening to reason. I said some pretty harsh things, if I recall, and thought it better to leave before I said more. By the time I cooled off and returned, she was gone. I suppose finding that damned letter and the stone was all the excuse she needed to slough me off. Rosabella has pretty strange notions about family members loving each other.'

Mark nodded. 'I see.'

His temper flared 'What in hell's name do you see? I ruined the girl. Now we have to be married.'

'You muffed it. In my experience, women are a bit odd about marriage and such. They don't care about logic. They want to be courted. Wooed.'

'I wooed her exceedingly well, right into my bed.' He squeezed his eyes shut. 'I thought she was a widow.'

'You seduced her. It is not the same. Not in their eyes. Women today expect a man to be romantic.'

'Damn it, what are you suggesting?'

'You must like her or you wouldn't have—'

Garth put up a warning hand. 'I find her attractive, yes. It might not be my first choice, but I am not as unhappy about this marriage as I might have expected.'

'You could be a little more enthused. Tell her you care for her.'

The very idea of talking about feelings tied his stomach in a knot. 'Why is she being so idiotic about this? She could be carrying my child. There is no choice but marriage, no matter how much money her father left.'

Another wince from his friend. 'You—'

'All right. I'll talk to her. Tell her I care. It is all nonsense, but if it makes her happy, I'll do it.'

The doubt in Mark's face offered little hope of success.

'Don't worry, I know how to charm a woman.'

'That's what she's afraid of.'

'What?'

'It is why she doesn't want to see you. She is afraid you will charm her into wedding you. That's what she told Penelope.'

Garth glowered at him. 'Why the hell did she come to your house in the first place?'

'Penelope. She told her yesterday that if she ever needed help she could come to us.'

'Nice of her,' Garth snarled.

'You didn't want me to turn her away, did you?'

No. His blood turned to ice at the thought of Rosabella with no one to turn to. Alone in London. Vulnerable. He shook his head. 'No. If it had to be anyone, I'm glad she came to you and Penelope.'

Glad for her. He just wished she hadn't left.

Her departure had created an empty place in his chest. He felt as if a piece of him was missing. A piece he hadn't realised was part of him until he lost it.

No. Rosabella was his responsibility and he wasn't going to let her go. 'Convince her to let me talk to her.'

Mark pushed to his feet. 'I'll try, but you know I have never seen a woman as determined as Lady Rosabella.'

Chapter Sixteen

For the first time in three days, Rosa felt as if she had time to think. Penelope handed her a cup of tea. 'Everything is arranged, then?'

Rosa nodded. The solicitor had just left. Earlier a jeweller had valued the stone at ten thousand pounds. A fortune. Such a sum carefully invested in the Funds after the debts were paid would mean that she and her sisters would lack for nothing.

The best part was knowing Father had not forgotten them. Knowing his love had remained strong and true, even if the form of it had been a complete surprise. Everything had finally worked out just as it should. She should feel happy. Carefree.

She didn't. She felt as if her heart had been torn in two and might never feel whole again. She'd let herself fall for a man without any heart at all.

She took a sip of tea. 'Yes, that is everything.' She managed a smile, even if it was a bit wobbly. 'I can't thank you and Mark enough for all your help. If there is anything I can ever do for you, please do not hesitate to ask.'

A sad little smile crossed her friend's face. She straightened her spine. 'I don't think there is anything anyone can do.'

They both knew she referred to the strained relations between her and her husband.

The same fate awaited her if she married Garth. A pang of loss stopped her breath. For all that she knew the kind of man he was, she missed him. She missed his touch, and his laughter, when he wasn't playing the cynical nobleman. She'd thought the face he showed to the world was a mask, but she'd been wrong. The charming honest man he played when he was alone with her was a front. The face he used to seduce women. The true man was the one she'd seen with his mother.

The choice was to shut him out of her life or let him break her heart over and over again. Once was enough.

Penelope put down her tea cup. 'He came again this morning.'

Garth. No, she really must think of him as Stanford now. 'I heard.'

'He says he will come every day until you see him.'

'He will be spending a great deal of time at your front door.'

'Mark said he has something he needs to say.'

She'd heard that, too. Instinctively, her hand flattened on her stomach. She put down her cup with a sigh. 'I suppose I should tell him myself.' It would stop him from bothering her. It was the only reason he had for persisting in his suit and with that reason gone he could continue on his merry dissipated way.

'It would be the kind thing to do.'

But scary. Garth was very persuasive when he had her alone. Charming and seductive. It had been that way from the first. Just hearing his voice from a distance made her insides clench and her hands tremble with longing.

Surely not? She'd had time away from him, enough distance to recognise her weakness and to come to terms with what was, rather than what she dreamed could be. He would never love her. It was not what he wanted. She was not what he wanted. Not really.

'Next time he calls, I will see him, if you will stay with me.'

Penelope winced. 'He won't like it, but I will, if that is what you want.'

'I do.'

'When did you want to look at houses?'

Several possible properties had been brought to her attention by the lawyer Mark had retained.

'Tomorrow. After I have seen Garth.'

'Are you sure you do not wish to come out to dinner with us tonight?'

'No, thank you. Your advice is wise. I should wait until next Season before going out in society. Get established. Make some morning calls with you, if you are still of a mind, and then seek a sponsor for the presentation of my sisters at court.'

'Then you won't mind if I leave you now to dress for dinner?'

'Not at all. I think I will just take supper in my room and seek an early night. It has been a long and tiring few days.'

Penelope stood and leaned over her, giving her a kiss on the cheek. 'I am so happy everything worked out so well for you. I just wish…' She shook her head. 'Never mind.'

She left the room in a rustle of silks.

With the owners out and supper over, the house was quiet and still. Rosa still hadn't written to her grandfather. He deserved to know she had changed her mind about marrying Garth and the sooner the better.

She sat down at the desk and sharpened her quill. The words didn't come easily. She didn't know if it was the heat of the evening making her hot and sticky, or the difficulty phrasing the letter. She wiped her hands on her handkerchief and tossed a crumpled attempt into the waste basket beside the hearth.

She pulled another sheet out of her desk drawer, her father's desk, which Garth had sent over on her second day here, and began anew.

Dear Grandfather, I hope your health is as good as ever.

She tapped the feather against her lip. *While we have not always been in accord...*

The sound of a bump came from beyond the window that looked out over the small walled garden at the back of the house. Someone outside? One of the servants going to the privy? Oh, she was so easily distracted from her task. Not this time. She would finish it.

A large figure hurtled through her open window and landed with a thump on one knee. A scream rushed from her throat. She leapt to her feet, the chair falling backwards with a clatter.

'Hush,' the figure said, rising. 'It is only me.'

Garth? Here? In her chamber. 'What on earth are you doing? Are you drunk?'

A sardonic smile crossed his lips. 'Drunk doesn't seem to help.'

She ran for the bell pull. He stepped in front of her, large and intimidating, sullen. 'Hear me out.'

'I will hear you tomorrow. I already told Penelope I would.'

'I know,' he said grimly. 'She told me when we met at

dinner. I wouldn't have gone, but I thought you would be there.'

'Come back tomorrow.'

'I don't need an audience.'

Rosabella tried not to look at the bed. 'There is nothing we need say to each other that would possibly cause us embarrassment in the presence of another. Indeed, should we meet at any time in future, it will never be alone.'

His shoulders stiffened. His eyes narrowed. 'I didn't think you'd be so cowardly. If you can hear me tomorrow, you can hear me now.'

The proud arrogant bearing told her he wouldn't leave, no matter what she said. She folded her arms over her chest. 'Very well. Have your say, but stay on your side of the room.'

He flashed a grin of triumph and she had the strong desire to bash him over the head with a fire-iron.

He crossed the room to the door, turned the key and put it in his pocket. 'In case you decide to run away before I'm finished.'

'Perhaps you should also remove the ladder in case I go through the window. It was a ladder you used, I assume?'

'Taking a leaf out of our honoured Lord Chancellor's book,' he said cheerfully.

Years before, Lord Eldon had run off to Gretna Green with an heiress by escaping with her down a ladder. In the end, it had been one of the most successful and happy of marriages. If Garth thought she would elope with him, he had porridge for brains.

'Hurry up and tell me what you want. I am tired and in need of a good night's sleep.'

His eyes slid to the bed and a smile curved his lips.

Heat warmed her belly as she remembered their last night together. Dash it, he only had to smile and she lost all reason.

Why had she reminded him they were in her bedroom? She tapped her foot. 'Well?'

He cleared his throat as if it had suddenly gone tight.

A nervous Garth? Now that was something new.

He dropped to one knee in front of her. She backed away, putting her hands behind her when he reached for them. It didn't stop his flow of words. He fixed his dark eyes on her face with no vestige of a smile. 'Rosabella Cavendish, I am asking you to be my wife.' He held her gaze for a long moment. 'I love you.'

The words lacked conviction and still the air rushed from her lungs. The three words she'd most longed to hear on his lips scored a path through her heart, leaving it bloody and torn. Why did he have to say them now, when she didn't need him? When she couldn't pretend they were real, because she knew the truth? Her heart urged her to run to him, to let him fold her in his arms, to tell him what was in her heart, but she didn't believe him. She couldn't. When he grew tired of her, he'd take her heart and flail it with his tongue. The pride, the arrogance, his presence here, was all about winning. He just wanted his own way.

In the end, neither of them would be happy.

No matter the pain in her heart, the longing to give in, she shook her head, knowing she was right. 'You don't have any idea about love. You said so yourself.' She took a deep breath, knowing what she would say next would sever the tie between them forever. 'And besides, it is not necessary—I am not carrying your child.'

If she had known better, she would have thought the fleeting expression on his face was disappointment. As it was, she could only assume it was chagrin at being forced to bend his knee, tell her what he thought she wanted to hear, only to be refused.

'Not with child,' he said slowly. His eyes were unfathomable, his expression carefully blank.

Though he showed no emotion, she was sure he must be pleased at the reprieve. 'No. So there is no need for your sacrifice.'

His eyes blazed. 'Damnation, Rosabella, it was not and is not a sacrifice.'

'When you never wanted to be married in the first place?'

'I've changed my mind. Didn't you hear me say I love you?' He held out his hand to her. 'I ruined you. You have to marry me. I'm not entirely devoid of honour.' He smiled at her, encouraging her to relent.

Honour. The real reason for this display. His honour was at stake. His declaration of love was nothing but words.

'You don't believe in love.'

'I'm pretty sure I love my brother.' He looked as if he'd said something painful.

'But not your mother or your father.'

'No.'

'It is your duty to love them.'

Bleak eyes stared back at her. 'Why, when they both wished I had never been born.'

'Why would you say such a thing?'

His expression tightened. He shook his head slightly as if to clear his thoughts. 'Let us just say I was not the son they wanted.'

'No one can choose their children.'

His smile was grim. 'So my father discovered.'

'The way you spoke to your mother…' Just thinking about it made her feel sick. Who was to say how long it would be before she was the target of his cruelty? Before he was throwing up the fact that she'd trapped him into a marriage he didn't want. She'd have no defence. A man who did not love his mother had no concept of love. 'I'm sorry, I really do not think we would suit.'

'I care for you, Rosabella.'

He sounded so sincere, she wanted to believe him, she really did. Her whole body vibrated with the longing to go to him. But what they shared was not love. It was attraction. A physical thing. Having seen the love between her mother and father, she would not settle for less. Not when she didn't have to. 'Love is much bigger than a word. It is deed and thought. You destroy people with wicked words and think nothing of it. You threatened to take my child from me if I did not do as you wanted. That is not love.'

His hands opened and closed. 'I was angry. I didn't mean it.'

'Love isn't a weapon.'

He stared at her, his face draining of colour. 'Then you will not accept my offer?'

'I'm sorry,' she said, crippled by the pain in her chest and trying not to show it.

'I'm sorry, too.' He closed the distance between them, took her mouth in a kiss of passion. Hard and fast and full of anger. It softened to something else: regret, loss. Or were those emotions all in her own mind?

Only by force of will could she remain stiff, unyielding, cold to his touch. And even then her heart reached out, beating hard and fast in her chest with longing. She felt herself weakening and stiffened her spine.

He pulled away, breathing hard.

She touched a finger to her lips. 'Goodbye, Garth.'

He spun around and unlocked the door. He opened it, stood for a moment with his back to her. 'I'm sorry.' He strode out.

Tears running down her face, she closed the door to the sound of his running footsteps on the stairs. The pain inside her chest felt worse than anything she'd ever imagined. This time he would not come back.

They would never make a child together, or play cricket on the beach with their children. She would never marry.

She couldn't. He would always take up too much room in her heart.

Love isn't a weapon. But what the hell was it? Garth stared into his burgundy, hoping the answer might emerge from its ruby depths. It didn't.

He pushed his untouched dinner aside with an impatient hand and took his glass to the window, looking down into the street. It was like one of those childhood riddles where the answer, once known, was obvious, but took ages to tease out. A half-smile touched his lips. Kit had been good at those riddles. Garth had preferred action.

Action hadn't worked so well with Rosabella. Now he was floundering around in quicksand with no handy branch in sight to pull him out of the mire. He'd been so sure she'd relent once he said the words. Once he'd kissed her, reminded her of the pleasure they had together.

The love she wanted was beyond him.

Love. Such a stupid word.

For some reason his facial muscles refused to form their customary expression of scorn. They wanted to do something stupid like form a smile as he pictured her face, her courage in her convictions as she faced him, her perseverance in seeking what she knew should be found. The soppy sort of smile that went along with baskets of puppies or sunrise over the ocean. Or the sight of a baby.

He would never have a baby. He'd sworn it to himself when Kit left for America. It seemed like a way of making up for being born. What an idiot to be disappointed when she said it hadn't come to pass.

He should have guessed she wouldn't have him. He'd been unwanted since the day he was born.

He downed the wine.

She was right. She was better off without him. He was broken. Missing an important part everyone else took for granted. Or at least the good people.

Kit had it. Mark had it, though it didn't seem to be making him happy.

Perhaps he was better off without it.

He just wished he felt better off.

Love isn't a weapon. She'd looked so sad when she said that. Every time he thought about the hurt in her eyes, he couldn't breathe for the pain in his chest.

If this was love, he'd prefer a quick death. He slammed his fist on the nearest piece of furniture. A spindly-legged table. A vase toppled to the floor with a satisfying crash. Shards of china scattered. He crunched through the debris, intending to ring for a maid. A habit. Make a mess, have it cleaned up.

His hand stilled on the cord.

He'd certainly made a mess of things with Rosabella. No one could clean that up.

Love isn't a weapon. Was she right about that? It damned well felt as if she'd pierced him with a sword and twisted it.

Was that love?

A groan rose in his throat. If it was, then it was only one-sided.

Alone in the house for the afternoon, Penelope having gone off to make her calls, Rosabella reviewed the advertisements in *The Times*, carefully looking on the map to ensure each address fell within the circle drawn by Mark. Outside of that circle the *ton* would turn up its nose.

'Lady Stanford,' the butler announced.

Garth's mother? Her heart stopped beating. She drew a quick painful breath and felt it falter to life louder than before.

She rose and dipped a curtsy as the lady swept in. Once more she was startled by the widow's fair beauty. If she was this lovely now, she must have been a diamond of the first water as a young woman. 'Lady Stanford.'

'Lady Rosabella.'

Rosa forced a stiff smile. 'The butler should have informed you of Lady Smythe's absence.'

The lacy handkerchief appeared as if by magic in her gloved hand. Drooping from her fingertips, it looked a bit sad. 'I'm glad we are alone. I just had to see you before the wedding.'

'There is no wedding. I'm sorry Garth didn't tell you and you have had a wasted journey.'

Lady Stanford's blue eyes widened with childish innocence no doubt many men found appealing. 'No wedding.' Her expression brightened. 'Well, let me offer you my congratulations. It seems you have had a lucky escape. I am sorry I was a little concerned about your...er...profession, but you really are better off without him.'

Rosa's scalp tightened. Prickles ran across her shoulders. Wasn't that what she'd been telling herself? Then why did she feel so annoyed to hear it from this woman's lips? Shouldn't a mother defend her son? She eyed the widow's innocent blue eyes and saw a hardness she hadn't noticed before. 'Perhaps you would care to explain?' She gestured to a chair. 'Pray be seated.'

With much twitching of skirts to achieve just the right drape, the lady proceeded to settle herself.

Warily, Rosa watched her. 'May I offer you some refreshment? Tea, perhaps?'

'Thank you, no. My carriage is waiting.'

She frowned. 'Are you here on Lord Stanford's behalf?'

The widow patted the blond ringlets touching her cheek and glanced around the room. 'Certainly not. Garth is nothing but trouble. His father was the same. A rake and a seducer.'

Rosa gasped. 'Lord Stanford?'

She fluttered a dismissive handkerchief. 'Silly girl. Garth isn't an Evernden. You have only to look at my younger son to see it. He married a Duke's daughter, you know.'

Rosa furrowed her brow. 'What are you talking about?'

'He will try to cozen and charm you like his dreadful father did to me. He ruined my life.'

'Garth's father?'

'No, Garth. The child of a man who was not my betrothed. What was I to do? I was set for a brilliant match and quickening with child. All my hopes were about to be shattered.' She dabbed at her eyes. 'My father wouldn't hear of calling off the marriage. The settlements had been signed. He got Evernden so drunk on our wedding night, he never knew a thing.'

'You passed off another man's child on your husband?'

'What else was I to do? My father would have cast me off. If only he'd been a girl. My husband realised the moment Garth was born he was no son of his. In time, he forgave me, knew I had been taken advantage of, but he could never bear the sight of Garth. Thank God for Christopher. It broke my dear husband's heart that his true son would never inherit.'

How cold she sounded. How uncaring. Rosa couldn't believe a mother could be so lacking in warmth for her own child. 'Why are you telling me this?'

The widow pursed her lips. 'I just wanted you to know what sort of man he is, that is all. Nature will out, they say. He ran wild as a boy. We sent him away to school. It did no good. I half expected him to kill himself before he came of age.'

A chill breeze ran through the room. Did she mean she hoped Garth wouldn't survive his boyhood?

'Be warned, Lady Rosabella. Garth is just like his father. Do not be taken in by his charm. He will ruin your life as he ruins everything he touches. Even his brother left the country to get away from him.'

The woman despised her own son. What kind of childhood would Garth have had with parents who hated him? Was it any wonder he knew nothing of love?

Anger like nothing Rosa had ever felt before coursed through her veins. Anger for a child left out in the cold, unloved and unwanted. Mixed in with the anger was the terrible knowledge of how much she'd wronged Garth. The bleakness she'd seen in his gaze was not born of cynicism, it was born of this woman's cruelty, her selfishness.

How could he know how to love when he clearly had never been loved? It was a miracle he could express any kind of affection. And she'd scorned him when he told her he loved her.

Anger as cold as ice and sharp as steel took control of her tongue. She rose to her feet with all the dignity of an earl's daughter. 'Please leave.'

'I beg your pardon.'

'Go. Now. You are not welcome here. Garth is right. You are a cruel unfeeling woman.'

'You go too far, young lady.'

Not nearly far enough.

Lady Stanford got up with a huff. 'Take heed, Lady Rosabella. Don't make my mistakes.' Head high, she left the room.

The warning came too late. Rosabella had made exactly the same mistake when she'd judged Garth and found him wanting.

She wasn't sure she could put it right.

* * *

Armed with a taper, the butler entered Garth's study to light the candles. Garth raised his chin from his chest and studied the window. Nightfall. Where had the day gone?

The man finished with the candles on the mantel and proceeded to the wall sconces.

'That'll do.' He didn't need any more light. The images in his head were perfectly clear without candles.

The butler crept away. All the servants had been creeping around since Rosabella left.

He chuckled grimly.

Poets spoke of love as if it was something to be desired. In his experience, it was a knife in the back. A blow to the kidneys. A flogging with fishhooks would be easier to bear.

Thank God, Kit was coming home. He'd missed his brother like the devil. More than he'd ever expected. He could take some small satisfaction in knowing that one day his brother would take his rightful place as Lord Stanford. That he would right his mother's wrong.

Small comfort.

His father—he shook his head—Christopher's father, would be have been pleased. Hell, it would even make his mother happy.

It was bloody ironic really.

It had nothing to do with his parents. He cared nothing for what they thought. It was Christopher who mattered.

Yes, he really did love his brother. And he did love Rosabella, though it was better that she didn't believe him. Better for her.

The candles blurred. His throat burned. He blinked to clear his vision, swallowed the stupid lump in his throat. Pointless emotion. The kind he'd learned to suppress as a lad.

A scratch at the door. 'My lord?'

'Not now.'

'You have a visitor, my lord.'

He rested his forearms on his thighs and stared at the carpet, a twisted mess of greens and blues. Did he really want company? Friends to drag him into St James's where they'd drink and wench and laugh until they couldn't stand and finish the night in some whore's bed.

He shuddered. 'Not tonight,' he called out. He forced himself to his feet. Tomorrow. He'd go out tomorrow. Or later in the week. He didn't have the heart for it tonight.

Loss was best suffered in private.

Yet he couldn't just sit here staring at the walls. The papers on his desk caught his eye. Work. There was always lots of work in the management of an estate. He wanted it in tiptop shape for Christopher. Or Christopher's son.

A pang shot through his chest. Regret. For the child he might have had? Not possible, surely?

He'd always known he wouldn't have a child.

And yet he couldn't help wondering what kind of babe he and Rosabella would have made together.

He sat down in front of the pile of papers and read his steward's note about the tenant who couldn't pay his rent.

The door opened.

He cursed. 'I'm busy.'

It closed again.

The tenant wasn't lazy, he'd had bad luck.

Whoever had entered hadn't left. He could hear them breathing. With a sigh he lifted his head.

He shot to his feet. 'Rosabella?'

She stood in the gloom and for a moment he thought he was seeing things. She looked pale and drawn and exceedingly nervous.

His heart ached for the pain he saw on her face.

'Why are you here?' Now there was a welcome. He came around the desk. 'Please, sit down.'

She clasped her reticule in front of her like a shield. 'I'm sorry for interrupting your work.'

She looked ready to flee.

'Not at all. I am glad of the break. Can I offer you some wine?'

She shook her head and perched on the edge of a sofa. Clearly whatever it was she had come to say, she didn't plan to stay long. He blinked again, just to make sure the wine hadn't caused her apparition.

He sat beside her. Not touching her, though he wanted to, but near enough to smell the scent of jasmine, to see the rapid beat of the pulse at her temple. She swallowed as if she was afraid. Perhaps she thought he'd ravish her. Again. Hell, he really had treated her badly.

'How can I be of service?'

'Your mother came to see me this afternoon.'

Cold filled his veins. He tried hard not to care, but his little nun had burrowed deep into his heart, and knowing what his mother would have told her made him feel sick. Ashamed.

'So you know I'm a bastard.' He slapped the words down in front of her to prove he didn't care.

'Oh, Garth, I'm so sorry.'

'You are sorry? The accident of my birth has nothing to do with you.'

'No, I mean I'm so sorry about what I said.' Her low voice trembled, her words were jerky.

He must be misunderstanding her meaning. He frowned. 'You said nothing that wasn't true.'

Tears welled in her beautiful eyes, the gold and the brown melding together. She struggled to speak.

His chest ached at the sight of her sadness. 'Please, Rosabella, don't cry. It was wrong of me not to tell you. It is good that you know. You were right about me. I cannot give you the love you deserve.'

The tears welled over, running down her cheeks. She gasped for breath. 'Oh, Garth, no.'

He took her hands. 'I am so sorry, Rosabella. I did you a terrible wrong. I should never have laid a finger on you. I knew right from the beginning you were different. Too good for me. I am an evil rotten bastard.' He gave a short painful laugh, an attempt to lighten the moment. 'In every way.'

Her fingers curled around his. 'No. You are not evil. I was cruel to say what I did.'

He still didn't understand. 'You were right. I don't have a heart. Never have had.'

But the longer she stayed, the more aware he was of her perfume and her delectable body, and the memories of strawberries by the fire. Next he'd be throwing her on the floor and kissing her until she forgot who he was.

'You are not listening.'

Listening. He was barely breathing. He got up and moved to the hearth. He forced a smile. 'You shouldn't have come, but I thank you. You have a kind heart and deserve a good man.'

Her chin wobbled. 'How can you say I am kind when I said such awful things? All your life you have lived without love and yet you said you loved me. I was so busy thinking about myself, I didn't hear you.'

Something in his chest ached. The heart he denied having, he presumed. An oddly sweet feeling he recalled from his boyhood, when his grandmother was kind. Was that also love?

If so, he wasn't sure what to do with this version of it either. He came back and took both of her hands in his, looking down into her lovely face, wishing he could make her feel better. 'Please, Rosabella, you have no reason to blame yourself. You found the will and have rescued your sisters. I am sure you will soon find the right man, too. Please, love, no more tears.'

Love. God, had he said it again? Hopefully she wouldn't notice.

She sniffled. 'I have something I need to say.'

'No more tonight.' He really couldn't stand to see her so anguished. Over him. Over his heartlessness.

'You need to go home. We can't have you ruining your reputation, now can we?'

She pulled her hand free of his. He felt the loss keenly. Her face turned serious. Once more she looked like a Madonna, cool and calm and untouchable. A smile tugged at his lips at the memory. It was the face he'd adored the moment he saw her. Something too big swelled up in his chest, making it difficult to breathe, a tenderness so vast he couldn't contain it. So this was love, too.

If only he'd discovered it earlier.

But no. He was the wrong man for her. He'd never be able to get it right. Love her as she deserved.

'May I escort you home?'

'I have something I want to say.' She went down on one knee, like a supplicant at an altar.

Shocked, he stared at her. 'What are you doing? Get up.' He reached out to bring her to her feet.

She grabbed one of his hands in both of hers.

The touch jolted through him.

Rosabella stared up at him. So darkly handsome. So lean and tall. His eyes were shadowed with concern, his frown deepening by the moment.

He had no idea why she'd come here tonight or what she was trying to tell him. It might even be too late. All his life he'd been denied love. And she, who professed she loved him in her heart, who thought she knew all about love, had thrown his words in his face.

He'd accepted her rejection, because he really hadn't expected her to love him back.

She prayed she wasn't too late.

'Garth Evernden, I love you. Will you marry me?'

His expression turned wary and puzzled. 'Rosabella, no,' he said softly. 'You do not need to do this.'

'I do,' she said, her voice catching. 'You see, I was too cowardly to take the risk of believing you when you said it. I feared you didn't mean it.'

His head came up, comprehension slowly dawning on his face.

'And when you gave up so easily,' she whispered, 'I believed it confirmed my suspicions that you were saying it to get your own way. Only I was wrong. You gave up, because you didn't believe anyone could love you. And, Garth, I do, I really do.' She gripped his hand hard. 'You must believe me.'

His mouth kicked up at one corner. Devils danced in his eyes. He pulled her up to her feet. 'This poor fool has been believing you every time you opened your lovely mouth.'

'Then you'll have me back?'

'Will I?' He swooped in to kiss her. A dizzying warm loving kiss that came to an end all too soon. He raised his head. 'But, Rosabella, are you sure? I couldn't bear it if you changed your mind.'

'Love doesn't change its mind. For better or worse, I love you, Garth.'

His eyes glittered with moisture and then he laughed, albeit a little thickly. 'I love you, too, little nun.'

'I'm hardly little. And definitely not a nun.'

'Ah, but you are my kind of nun.' He covered her mouth with his and swept her up in a tide of desire.

This was right. This was true. She could feel the love when he held her.

This was where she belonged. In his arms.

'I need to sit down,' he said with a rueful smile after a while. 'My knees feel a little weak.'

'Mine, too. With relief. I wasn't sure you would take me back.'

'Oh, Rosabella. How could you doubt it?'

He sat on the sofa and settled her on his lap, cradling her head against his chest as if she was more precious than jewels. They sat quietly for a moment, their hearts beating in unison. It felt so comfortable, as if she'd come home. But before she could settle, she had one more thing to say. 'Garth, about children.' She felt his body shift, his mouth open. She touched a finger to his lips. 'I can understand now why you might not wish for children of your own. As long as we are together, it will be enough.'

He kissed her fingertip and captured her hand in his. 'Your generosity unmans me. I know how much store you set by a child.'

'My sisters are sure to have children. I will be a wonderful aunt.'

He huffed out a breath. 'I have to tell you, I had grave doubts about my suitability for fatherhood, but it is not the only reason for not wanting them.'

'Tell me.'

'You know my situation. You know I have a younger brother. Lord Evernden's true son. I made a promise that my brother or his son would one day inherit the title that should have been his.'

The man had depths of generosity she'd never realised. 'I should have known your intentions were honourable.'

He gave a short laugh. 'It is not something I like bruited abroad.'

'You are a good man, Garth. Don't let anyone tell you otherwise.'

'If we had made a child...' His voice cracked a little and he took a quick breath. 'If it had come to pass, I'm sure I would have loved it.'

'I know,' she whispered. 'And I love you for that, too.'

A soft sadness filled the room. A bittersweet regret tempered by their love. The mist of tears filled her vision. He kissed her cheek softly.

She sighed and nestled into his neck, content to sit quietly and hold him.

A door crashed open behind them. Garth put her aside and rose to his feet.

A tall fair-haired gentlemen stood grinning on the threshold. 'Garth, you dog. I might have guessed why your man didn't want to let me in.'

Garth pulled Rosabella to her feet and held her close in a move that was all about protection. 'Kit, this is Lady Rosabella, my future wife.'

The young man's open face looked comically shocked. 'Not you, too, and after all you said about me and Mark?'

'Rosabella, this is my younger brother, Christopher Evernden.' He peered over his brother's shoulder. 'And out in the hallway, pretending not to see us, is his wife, Sylvia.'

A lovely blonde with a babe in her arms squeezed past his brother's wide shoulders.

The Duke's daughter. Rosabella dipped a deep curtsy. 'My lady.'

'Ah, I see you have been fully educated by my mama-in-law,' the young woman said quietly. 'I suppose she failed to tell you that my mother was a courtesan.'

Rosa's jaw dropped. She glanced at Garth, who grinned and nodded. Then his face turned sombre. 'What brought you home, little brother? Not trouble, I hope?'

'No trouble,' the young man said, hugging his wife and tickling the baby's chin with the other hand. 'I made a fortune over there. Lots of opportunity for a man who has a mind to work. But Sylvia's father left her an estate in Hampshire. A nice-sized piece of ground. With this young fellow coming along so well and Sylvia missing her brother, the Duke, you know—' his hazel eyes twinkled '—we thought we'd come home to live.'

Garth clasped his brother's hand. 'Welcome home.'

'It is good to be here. May I greet my future sister-in-law with a brotherly kiss?'

'On the hand,' Garth said, half laughing, half serious.

The love between these two brothers was clear and bright as they grinned at each other.

Garth peered down at his nephew, fair and with blue eyes like his parents. 'A true Evernden.'

'Hold him,' Sylvia said, placing the child in his arms.

His expression went from comical dismay as he took the bundle to one of adoration. 'He's a fine little man.'

'Isn't he, though?' Christopher said with smug satisfaction. He smiled at Rosa. 'No doubt you'll be equally blessed in time.'

Rosabella flinched. Garth looked at her face and thrust the child back at his brother. 'Damn,' he said softly.

Christopher frowned. 'What have I said?'

Garth shrugged. 'Rosabella has agreed—the title is to come back to you, or to your son.'

'Oh,' Lady Sylvia said, with concern in her eyes as she looked at her husband.

Christopher's lips thinned. 'Mother told me about your decision.'

'I knew she would,' Garth said.

His brother raised a brow at his wife and she nodded. Clearly they'd talked about this, and Rosa, seeing the pain in Garth's eyes, wondered if this was the right time to discuss such a sensitive matter.

Christopher must have sensed it, too, because there was compassion in his eyes when he spoke. 'When Mother wrote to me, I can't deny I was pleased. It felt just. Fair. I admired you for it. Not that I ever envied you the title, you know. I never realised you were…'

'A bastard.' Garth's voice was harsh, his face like granite, but Rosa could feel the rawness of the wound he was desperately trying to hide. She wanted to hold him, but knew his pride would rebel at any sign of sympathy.

Christopher gave a quick shake of his head. 'Garth, I hated the way they treated you, but I didn't much care for the way you acted with Mother either.' He shrugged. 'I thought, given your chosen style of life, it might be for the best.' He gazed down into the face of his sleeping son. 'I can't do it, Garth. I can't deny you the joy I felt when this little fellow was placed in my arms. Really, I can't.' He leaned over and kissed his wife's cheek. 'The title. The land. They mean nothing by comparison. You made a great older brother. You'll be a good father. Don't deny yourself something as wonderful as this, because of what our parents did.'

Garth swallowed hard. 'Kit, no.' He swallowed again.

'It would be a greater wrong than anything Mother did, my dear fellow. You deserve this as much as anyone. If not more.'

Rosa's heart contracted at the sight of the sadness leaving her beloved's face. It was as if she could see the weight of guilt leave his shoulders. She squeezed his hand, because she couldn't speak a word.

'I made a promise,' Garth said, still hesitating. 'I'd be going back on my word.'

'You'll be relieving me of a burden. One estate to manage along with my business interests are all that I need. Provide my son here with a cousin. Remember the fun we had as lads. You and me. I want that for my son and yours.'